A Day After Forever 2

The Payback

By: Willie Dutch

STREET KNOWLEDGE
PUBLISHING

Website: www.streetknowledgepublishing.com

A DAY AFTER FOREVER 2: THE PAYBACK ®

A DAY AFTER FOREVER 2: THE PAYBACK

Is a work of fiction. Any resemblances to real people, living or dead, actual events, establishments, organizations, or locales are intended to give the fiction a sense of reality and authenticity. Other names, characters, places and incidents are either products of the author"s imagination or are used fictitiously. Those fictionalized events & incidents that involve real persons did not occur and/or may be set in the future.

Published by: Street Knowledge Publishing
Written by: Willie Dutch
Edited by: Dolly Lopez
Cover design by: Marion Designs/ www.mariondesigns.com
Photos by: Marion Designs

For information contact:
Street Knowledge Publishing
P.O. Box 345
Wilmington, DE 19801
Email: jj@streetknowledgepublishing.com
Website: www.streetknowledgepublishing.com

ISBN 10: 0-9822515-3-X
ISBN 13: 978-0-9822515-3-9

Dedication

I dedicate this book to the woman that"s responsible for my career, Ms. Linda Williams. If it wasn"t for you, I would probably still be receiving rejection letters in the mail. (Smile) I can"t thank you enough for the support you have given me, both personally and professionally. I love you and I promise that I will not let you down.

Table Of Contents

Acknowledgements

Okay! I'm reloaded! I'm back with another hot joint for da streets. But I can't start this off without shouting out all of my peeps first. So here it goes...

First, I wanna thank everybody that showed me love by copping "A Day After Forever." All of the distributors, retailers, book clubs, barber/beauty shops, and most importantly, the readers. I am nothing without y'all.

Joseph "JoeJoe" Jones, C.E.O of Street Knowledge Publishing, I appreciate everything you're doing for myself and my fellow brothers in da struggle. I told you I gotcha, fam. It's our time now!

To my family and friends... the Fisher family, the Watkins family, the Gilmore family, the Stewart family, the Green family, the Ross family, the Lewis family, the Chase family, Slick (R.I.P), Kev-O (R.I.P), K.G. (R.I.P), J.T. (R.I.P), Sherman, Gino and all of my homies on lock. Much love. And to anyone that I left out, please don't take it personal, because it wasn't intentional. (Smile)

I gotta also give props to the *Five Percenter Newspaper, Street Elements, Street Literature Review,* Leon Jean Publications, Thug-N-Lawz Ent., Freeway Enterprise.com, Dolly Lopez and to the gods of this street lit shit, Donald Goines, Iceberg Slim, and Chester Himes.

On that note, I'm not going to hold y'all up any longer. I'll holla at ya on da next one. And there will be a next one, 'cause I ain't going nowhere. So get used to it haters! (Ha-ha)

But seriously, I hope y'all enjoy my latest joint. And don't forget to hit me up and let me know what you think at myspace.com/williedutchbooks or williedutchbooks@yahoo.com

One!..

PROLOGUE

(The Recap)

Miko Harris sat alone on the chaise lounge in her living room with her face buried in the palms of her hands, sobbing and crying uncontrollably. She had been sitting in that same spot for two hours straight, praying silently to herself and trying to figure out a way to get out of the trouble she was in. Her thoughts switched to Seven, her deceased lover and friend, as she wondered what he would do if he were in her situation.

"Seven, I wish you were here. I need you so much right now," she said out loud, not realizing what she was saying. After all, if he were there, she would not be in the predicament she was in, in the first place.

Miko suddenly began to feel claustrophobic, like the walls were closing in around her. She decided to take a walk in her backyard patio to get some fresh air and clear her head. The breeze felt good as she paced back and forth on the wooden deck, and her thoughts began to race in her mind as she played back the events that had led up to that point.

The previous two years had been filled with both highs and lows for Miko. The high point would have to have been when she met Seven, a handsome and street savvy hustler who had managed to literally sweep the sometimes siddity-acting Miko off of her feet. Her life was like a real Cinderella story, as she went from living in a government run housing project to a high-rise condominium almost overnight, thanks to her newfound Prince Charming.

Miko's problems started when her best friend of nearly eight years, Jahzay, became jealous of Miko and Seven's relationship. After trying to sleep with Seven behind Miko's back, Jahzay and Miko's friendship came to a quick end. During that time, Jahzay went through some problems of her own. From dealing with a terrible cocaine addiction to becoming a prostitute, her life had quickly spiraled out of control.

Meanwhile, Miko and Seven's whirlwind love affair couldn't have been better, but unfortunately, their happiness would not last "forever" like they once said it would. Eventually, Miko ended up pregnant, but Seven would not live to see the birth of his unborn seed. Instead, he would die a gruesome and brutal death at the hands of a vicious killer who went by the alias "King Tut." What made Seven's death even harder for Miko to handle was when she found out that he was set up by one of his closest friends and business partners, named Binky.

Miko refused to just sit around and do nothing, so she made up her mind that she would seek justice for herself, especially after she learned that the same man who murdered her lover had murdered her father ten years prior. That surprising revelation gave her even more of a reason to want revenge. So along with the help of Smokey, one of Seven's other crewmembers, she set out to avenge the deaths of the only two men she had ever loved in her entire life.

But Miko's vengeance didn't bring them back, nor did it do anything to help her financial situation, which at the time was slowly getting worse and worse. She eventually was forced to move back into the very same projects she had fought so desperately to get out of. Ironically, it was during her moving process that she came across a manila legal envelope addressed to her from Seven. After searching through the envelope's contents, she nearly fainted when she discovered that Seven had left her a financial nest egg totaling over one million dollars.

Miko's life would instantly change for the better. She moved into a new home in an affluent Sugarland subdivision, bought her a new BMW X5 Jeep, and most importantly, paid for her college tuition. She also set up a trust fund for her and Seven's son, Elijah Jr. She even patched things up with Jahzay, who had gotten her life back on the right track, and was now engaged to Smokey. But, as fate would have it, Miko's luck would again take a turn for the worse, not even a year after receiving the blessing from Seven.

During a recent visit to Seven's gravesite with their son, Miko was approached by a strange Asian man who called himself Jimmy Chan. The unfamiliar man was the leader of the Red Dragons, a ruthless Asian crime syndicate known for their far-reaching drug enterprises and their penchant for violence. Miko had to pick her jaw up from off of the ground after Jimmy Chan told her that Seven owed him two million dollars at the time of his death, for a shipment of XTC pills Jimmy Chan had given him on consignment. But the real shocker came when Jimmy Chan said that he expected her to pay back the debt, and gave her only six months to do so. He made it very clear that she and her family would be in a lot of danger if she didn't repay the debt. And he didn't seem like the type to make empty threats.

It had been over a week since that less than friendly encounter, and Miko still didn't have a clue how she was going to come up with the two million dollars Jimmy Chan was demanding, especially in such a short amount of time. Something inside her said that Jimmy Chan was not one to play with, so going to the police was out of the question. After all, he had managed to find her and her family once. He could surely do it again. Miko was left with just two options: either pay him what he wanted, or pay the consequences.

Part One

Chapter One

Forevermore

"What do you mean, I can't touch it? I'm the one who opened the damn thing!" Miko screamed into her cell phone.

She was growing more and more irritated as she argued back and forth with the manager of the local branch of her bank. They were discussing the trust fund she had opened for her son, Elijah Jr. She'd used a huge portion of the money Seven had left for her. She wanted to make sure her son would have a good education. Under the terms of the agreement, the money in the trust could not be touched until Elijah Jr. turned eighteen years of age.

Miko knew that, but she was hoping there was some way to get around that "small detail", as she put it. She needed money, and she needed it fast. Her desperation was starting to show outwardly, and everyone around her noticed it. After a few more less-than-friendly exchanges with the bank manager she hung up the phone in his ear. But not before telling him, "And fuck you very much!"

Miko sheepishly looked over at her little brother, Tai, who was sitting in the passenger seat of her gray BMW X5. Tai was staring in shock. He wasn't used to hearing his sister talk like that. Around him Miko, was usually calm and almost never lost her temper. That was a conscious decision on her part. She wanted to set a good example for him. Since a severe stroke put their mother in a nursing home, Miko had been more of a mother figure to Tai than a sister. Plus, he was just an infant when their father was savagely murdered. So, as Tai saw it, it was just him and her against the world. And he wouldn't have it any other way.

"So, what are we gonna do now, Sis?" Tai asked over the music on the radio. He made sure to emphasize the word *we*. That was his way of letting Miko know that he had her back.

But Miko didn't even hear his question. She had drifted back down memory lane. Her eyes were fixed upon her little brother's face. He reminded her so much of their father, from his slim build and height, to his slanted green eyes, high cheekbones and high yellow complexion. Tai was just twelve years old, but Miko could already tell that he was going to be something else when it came to females.

"Miko, watch out!"

Miko broke out of her trance and looked up just in time to swerve out of the path of an oncoming eighteen-wheeler, and narrowly avoid a head-on collision. "Damn, I'm trippin! I have so much on my mind I can't even focus," she explained. "I'm sorry. Were you saying something?"

"Yeah, I was asking you what are we going to do now that we can't pay the Asian dude?"

"Oh, I guess now we should just go home, pack our things, and find us a hotel until I can figure out something."

Home for Miko was a stylish two-story stucco home in the affluent subdivision of Sugarland. It was literally her dream home, built using blueprints Seven had drawn up before his death. It had five bedrooms, three baths, and a hand laid tile pool built with lava rocks in the backyard. But as much as she had grown to love her home, she knew that she would soon have to part with it. After she was given the ultimatum by Jimmy Chan, she immediately put her house up for sale. The problem was that home sales didn't happen overnight. It was usually a time-consuming process, and time was not on her side.

Miko shared the home with her brother, her son, and her son's grandmother, Ms. Jacobs. Ms. Ernestine Jacobs was Seven's mom, and to Miko's knowledge, his only surviving family. Ms. Jacobs still thought she was young, even though she was approaching fifty years old. She wore her hair in a short crop style, and kept up with all the latest slang and fashion trends. She had average facial features to go along with a statuesque figure, which she loved to show off. She and Miko shared a very close relationship, unlike most in-laws. In fact, they often acted more like sisters. However, that hadn't always been the case.

Miko and Ms. Jacobs' relationship began with a mutual dislike for one another. Ms. Jacobs hated Miko from the moment they met after Miko mistook her for one of Seven's jump-offs. That mistake led to Miko cursing her out, and from then on it was war. For the most part, Miko didn't exactly hate Ms. Jacobs, she just didn't like her a whole lot. She felt like Ms. Jacobs was never a real mother to Seven, and that she just used him for money to support her drug habit. And, because Ms. Jacobs was partly to blame for Seven's death, Miko still had yet to completely forgive her.

Ms. Jacobs had been a lifelong drug addict. She took her first hit of crack in 1984, when Seven was just four years old, and continued getting high right up until his passing 22 years later. Ironically, the end of her son's life would signal a new beginning for her own. The guilt associated with his murder became too much for her to shoulder. She checked herself into a recovery center shortly after his burial, and eventually cleaned herself up. She even got a job and found herself a man after turning her life around.

When Miko walked into her house with Tai, she nearly had a fit. From her doorway she could see directly into the kitchen. Elijah Jr. was lying on the floor crying and hollering when Miko ran over to him. He had apparently fallen from the countertop while climbing up to reach the snack cabinet. His shirt, hands and face were completely covered in what appeared to be grape jelly, and his lip was busted. Miko picked him up, and in her best baby voice said, "Shhh! Wha's da matter wit' mama baby?"

Elijah Jr. just sniffled and kept right on crying.

Miko was fuming! In her mind she was thinking, *Where in the hell is his damn grandmother at?* She passed her son to his uncle and stormed up the stairs two at a time. She screamed out her mother-in-law's name, but there was no answer. It pissed her off knowing that she couldn't depend on Ms. Jacobs to watch her own grandson, especially since she had been gone only a few hours. Normally, he would have been gone to daycare, but under the circumstances, Miko had to take him out due to the costs.

Reaching the top of the stairs, Miko followed the sounds of an old Sam Cooke tune to Ms. Jacobs' room. She again yelled out her mother-in-law's name, but was drowned out by the loud music. Miko pounded on the door like she was the police until she heard the music suddenly stop. There was a lot of movement on the other side of the door. Then it swung open to reveal a wide-eyed Ms. Jacobs, standing there. She had on a bathrobe with a head full of rollers. She looked at Miko nonchalantly and asked, "What's all the commotion about?"

"I'm trying to find out why in the hell you're up here doing God knows what, while my baby is downstairs unsupervised!"

"I must've dozed off after my bath."

"Well, you sure don't look like someone that has just woke up, to me!"

Ms. Jacobs knew what Miko was hinting at, so she changed the subject in a hurry. "What do you mean he's downstairs? I put him to bed hours ago."

"He's a little kid! Don't you know you can't just -- You know what...? Never mind. I see I'm just wasting my breath and my energy."

"So what, you think I can't take care of a child now? raised one of my own, or have you forgot?"

"Oh, trust me, I haven't forgot. But I don't exactly call what you did 'raising' a child!"

Ms. Jacobs was hurt by Miko's last comment, and Miko knew that she had gone too far. She tried to apologize by saying, "Look, I'm just a little frustrated because I'm under a lot of stress right now. I'm sorry if--"

"You don't have to be sorry," Ms. Jacobs cut in. "You're right. I wasn't much of a mother to my son, but that doesn't mean I can't be a good grandmother to Junior!"

"You're right. I'm wrong. Now, can we just forget about this, because I have something important to tell you?"

"What is it?"

"I couldn't get the money, so I was planning on getting a room until I can come up with a plan. I don't think it's safe for us to stay here anymore."

"Is that all?"

"Yeah, I guess."

"Well, if you would excuse me, I have to finish gettin' ready for work."

Ms. Jacobs slammed the door in Miko's face, leaving her standing in the hallway feeling guilty.

She proceeded to pack up her things and get Elijah Jr. cleaned up. She and Tai just grabbed the things they needed. They decided that they would return for the rest of their possessions once they found a stable place to live.

Miko was turning her bedroom upside down and throwing things everywhere when Tai walked in and said, "Are you ready?"

"Not quite. I'm looking for my Cartier watch. I planned on selling it if I had to, but now I can't even find it!"

"Where'd you leave it?"

"That's just it. I always keep it in my jewelry box, but it's not there. I don't know, maybe I'm trippin'."

"Did you ask Ms. Jacobs if she's seen it?"

Miko looked up at Tai, and a light bulb went off in her head. She ran like an Olympic sprinter straight to Ms. Jacobs's room. She turned the knob and was surprised to find the door unlocked. Ms. Jacobs was sitting on her bed, applying makeup to her face when Miko entered. Miko asked her, "Hey, have you seen my watch laying around anywhere? The one with the pink diamonds in it."

Ms. Jacobs' eyes darted to the floor, then she said, "No. You sure it's not with the rest of your stuff?"

Miko followed Ms. Jacobs' eyes from the floor to the nightstand, and back down to the floor again. She did a double take after glancing at the nightstand, and noticed what looked like a crumpled up store receipt. The yellow slip of paper aroused Miko's curiosity. She took a step towards the nightstand, but was cut off by a teary-eyed Ms. Jacobs. She looked at her daughter-in-law with a sorrowful expression and pleaded, "Please, let me explain."

Miko ignored her plea, pushed past her, and picked up the slip of paper. She had to see if her instincts were right. And right they were. Staring at the Val-U-Pawn receipt Miko shook her head in disbelief. Ms. Jacobs had pawned the most expensive piece of jewelry she owned for a measly $1,500.

"Where's the money? Where's the fucking money you got for my damn watch?" Miko demanded.

"It's all gone, Miko. It's been gone for days now."

"I can't believe you! You know how hard I've been trying to come up with some money, and you go and steal from me!"

Silence.

Miko was more hurt than she was angry. Her trust had been betrayed, and her heart was broken.

Ms. Jacobs expected her to yell and curse, but Miko did neither. Instead, she just stared at Ms. Jacobs then turned and walked away. Her silence and the look she gave hurt Ms. Jacobs more than any cuss word ever could.

Miko promised herself that she wasn't going to shed one tear. She was through crying for good. She gathered up her already filled suitcases, and she, Tai, and Elijah Jr. prepared to leave the place they had called home for the past year.

Their first stop was at Miko's godmother's house. Ms. Nadine was already expecting them. Miko had phoned earlier and asked her to watch Elijah Jr. until she could get settled. She didn't want to drag him along with her from hotel to hotel, and Miko knew she could trust her godmother with her son.

Miko knocked on the door of the old Victorian style house located on the outskirts of Third Ward. A moment later, the door swung open and Ms. Nadine appeared, wearing a warm and inviting smile. She had aged considerably since Miko had last seen her. She was beginning to look every day of her sixty years. Her seashell-filled, shoulder-length dreadlocks were totally gray, and deep wrinkles lined her face. Miko's nose picked up the familiar smell of burning incense that was always present in Ms. Nadine's home. Ms. Nadine said that they "kept the evil spirits away".

Ms. Nadine St. Clair wasn't superstitious. At least, not in her opinion. On the contrary, her beliefs were the direct result of her strong Jamaican roots. Born in a shantytown in Kingston, she grew up around hoodoo, and even practiced it herself as an adult. After marrying Francis St. Clair, the two of them migrated to North America and settled in Houston, Texas. They started an African-American bookstore, which Ms. Nadine continued to run long after her husband's death.

It was at that same bookstore where she met and befriended a young college freshman named Miko Harris. With no kids of her own, Ms. Nadine soon would view Miko as the daughter she never had. She even hired her on as a manager of the store.

For Miko, Ms. Nadine was like a surrogate mother. With her real mother in a vegetate state, Ms. Nadine was the only person she could talk to about her womanly concerns. And she was always there when Miko needed her. This time would be no different.

"C'mon in out thee cold, why don't cha," Ms. Nadine said in her thick Jamaican accent.

Miko did as she was told, and entered inside with Elijah Jr. asleep in her arms. She took a seat in the living room on one of the plastic covered sofas while Ms. Nadine went into the kitchen. She returned with two steaming coffee mugs in her hands, and said, "Here, have some green tea, eh. Mi finna put thee baby to bed, si." She grabbed Elijah Jr. and the bag Miko had packed for him, and left out of the room.

After a few sips of the herbal tea, Miko felt relaxed, and the faint stirrings of a headache she felt were gone. She was finished with her cup by the time Ms. Nadine made it back to the living room.

Ms. Nadine gave her a funny look and said, "Mi chile was t'irsty, no?"

"I guess I was. I would love to have another one, but I really gotta run. Tai is outside waiting in the truck."

"Okay, but you make sure to call me as soon as you get settled in, eh. And tell dat big head buoy thee next time him come over and don't speak, mi g'won ring him neck!"

"I'll make sure he gets your message."

The two of them said their good-byes, and hugged one another like it was the last time they would see each other. Miko couldn't help but think that it probably was.

●●●●●●

The next day, Miko was lying back on one of the double beds in her suite at the Luxury Inn. She chose to stay in that hotel because it was located all the way across town on the north side, and more importantly, it was affordable. She had over ten thousand dollars in cash in her purse. She had withdrawn it from her savings account, but she knew that it wouldn't last long when she was living from pillar to post. She hadn't been to work in weeks, and was sure that her employers at the Family Law Center had replaced her already.

She was scrolling through the phonebook of her Nextel cell phone when an entry suddenly jumped out at her. The name and number belonged to a hustler she'd met over a year earlier when she had briefly tried her hand at selling weed. "That's it!" she screamed out, nearly waking up her brother, who was asleep in the other bed. "Why didn't I think of that before?"

She pressed the speed dial button and crossed her fingers in hopes that his number hadn't changed. Two rings later, a deep voice came on the line saying, "What it do?"

"Yes, may I speak to... Clupe?" Miko hesitated.

"Yeah, who dis?"

"This is Miko."

"Miko?" he repeated, trying to see if the name sounded familiar. It didn't. "Baby girl, you must have the wrong number, because I don't know anybody named Miko."

Miko immediately remembered that she had given him a fake name and said, "Did I say Miko? I meant this is Myisha."

"Sweetheart, I know several Myishas, so you will have to be more specific."

"I don't know if you remember, because it's been so long ago. But we met at the cleaners off Tidwell and did a little business together."

"Exactly what type of 'business' are we talking about? Let me guess. We fucked, and now you're calling to tell me you wanna go on the Maury Show to see if I'm the father of your crumb snatcher!"

"No! You obviously have me mixed up with someone else. The business I'm talking about concerns money, and something that I bought from you. Now, do I have to spell it out for you?"

Silence.

"Ohh! Now I remember you! You're the chick that made me... never mind. But anyway, wha's good, ma?"

"I was calling because I was trying to hook up with you again for the same thing."

"Damn! For a minute I thought you was calling to take me up on the offer I gave you."

"Haven't you heard to never mix business with pleasure?"

"I feel ya. So, what was you looking for?"

"I need to buy about twenty pounds."

Click!

"Hello! Hello!"

Miko stared at her phone with an expression that said, *I know this nigga ain't just hang up in my face!* She tried calling him back a few times, but she kept getting his voicemail.

Ten minutes later, she received a call from an "anonymous" number. When she answered it, a female voice directed her to "Be at Taco Cabana off Tidwell and I-45 in an hour."

Miko was there in half that time. She wasn't sure exactly what type of games Clupe was playing, but she was willing to play along, as long as she got what she wanted in the end.

She parked her SUV in a secluded parking space near the rear of the restaurant and waited for his arrival. After about an hour had passed, she decided that enough was enough, and started to leave. Just as she was about to turn the key in the ignition, she noticed a car with tinted windows slowly circling the parking lot. She knew that it had to be him, and began to feel anxious for some reason.

The car pulled into an empty space beside her truck, and Miko noticed that there was a woman driving. She recognized Clupe immediately, as he hopped out the passenger side of the car and walked up to her SUV. He tapped on her window and said, "Get out the truck!"

When Miko got out of her truck, she caught Clupe staring at her body and nodding in approval. She gave him a once over and was equally impressed. From his crisp retro Air Jordan's, to his matching Michael Jordan collegiate jersey, he was clean. He had cut his braids since the last time she saw him, and now rocked a fresh bald fade. His thick eyebrows and straight white teeth added to his overall sex appeal.

Clupe removed his dark sunglasses so he could get a better look at Miko. Examining her closely, he concluded that she wasn't as sexy as he had remembered --she was even sexier! Even in the loose-fitting warm-ups she was wearing, he could see the curves of her 5'7", 125-pound frame. She was petite, yet thick in all the right places. Her Black and Korean heritage gave her an exotic look that was accented by her green, cat-like eyes. He broke the awkward silence between them by saying, "You must never have been told not to talk like that on the phone."

Miko figured that was why he had hung up on her, and apologized for her mistake. He then stepped closer to her. She could smell the scent of his Unforgivable cologne as he grabbed her around her torso and moved his hands along her back. Miko pushed him off and said, "I don't know what type of party you think this is, but I don't get down like that!"

"Chill out, baby girl! I ain't tryin' to feel on you or nothing," Clupe told her. "I just had to make sure you ain't have no bugs crawling on you. If you know what I mean."

"Whatever! So, do you have the weed or what?"

"Whoa! Slow your roll, lil' mama! Do you got da money with you?"

"I wouldn't have drove out here in the middle of the night if I didn't. How much is it?"

"Eight-thousand."

Miko opened the door of her SUV and retrieved her purse. After counting out the $8,000, she gave the money to him and said, "Now, where's my shit?"

"We have to go pick it up. I'll ride with you so you won't think--"

"Then what are we waiting for?"

They took a twenty-minute drive and ended up at Settegast Village Apartments, off of North Wayside Drive. Clupe directed Miko to pull into the Section 8 apartments, and she did so, with his lady friend following closely behind them. They parked in front of building #1307, where Clupe jumped out saying he would be back in a minute.

That minute turned into thirty before Miko started to get a funny feeling about the whole deal. Clupe's lady friend had left five minutes ago, which prompted Miko to call his cellular number. His phone was obviously turned off, because the voicemail kept picking up on the first ring.

She finally said, "Fuck it!" and went to knock on the door she had seen Clupe go into. A light-skinned, heavyset black woman opened the door with a puzzled look on her face and said, "Can I help you?"

"Yes, I hope so. I was looking for Clupe. I watched him come in here about thirty minutes ago, and he had me waiting in the parking lot."

The middle-aged woman seemed to be even more confused then. She looked at Miko and said, "Clupe been gone nearly a half an hour, now."

"What do you mean, he's been gone? I have been sitting outside in front of your apartment door, and I didn't see him leave!"

"Baby, dat's becuz he ain't go out da front. He went out da back," the lady explained as she pointed to a door behind her.

Miko's heart dropped as she stood there on the porch in disbelief. The walk back to her car was like the "Green Mile". She couldn't afford to lose eight dollars, let alone eight thousand! She felt played, and that made her furious. She broke down crying during the short trip back to her hotel room. She found herself in a hole that she didn't think she could climb out of.

Miko had run out of ideas and would ultimately have to face Jimmy Chan's wrath. She needed help, and needed it badly. There was only one person she knew who could possibly give her the help she sought. And that was Jahzay.

Chapter Two

"Oh, hell to tha naw! Nigga, I know you didn't just say what I think you said!" Jahzay fumed. With one hand on her hip and the other waving about wildly, she continued her tirade. "First, you tell me you don't have the rest of my man's money you owe him. Then you have the nerve to ask me can you hit it?! Puhleeze! Nigga, you couldn't even afford this pussy!"

Jahzay left her latest tongue lashing victim standing on the corner speechless, as she burned off in her car. She was out trying to collect the money that was owed to her man, Smokey, while he sat in jail for murder. But it was easier said than done. It seemed like everyone who owed him either had a sudden case of amnesia, or was conveniently nowhere to be found. The few dudes she was able to track down would always promise to get with her later, but later never came. She was growing tired of getting the runaround, so she decided to take matters into her own hands.

Smokey had told her to take the remaining XTC pills out of his stash and give them to an associate of his. Of course she told him she would, but she had no intentions on doing what he said. Instead, she took the pills, which totaled into the tens of thousands, and started selling them herself. Using Smokey's cell phone and his already established clientele, getting rid of the pills proved to be easy. After all, Jahzay wasn't new to the game --she was true to it.

She was used to being a hustler's chick. Every nigga she had ever been with was somehow involved in the streets, including her baby daddy. Over the years, she picked up on the tricks of the trade, and eventually dabbled in it herself. She lived by the motto: "A bitch gotta do, what a bitch gotta do!"

So, in her eyes, she'd made the best decision for the both of them. Her man needed money for his attorney fees and commissary. Plus, she still had bills to pay and a child to take care of...not to mention another one on the way. She couldn't depend on his "associates" or any of his so-called homeboys to do for her what she could do for herself.

Smokey could get mad, but the reality was that people only respected your gangsta when they knew you could touch them. But when you were locked up, you were out of sight and out of mind. Almost everyone on the streets knew that Smokey was in jail, and probably would be for a very long time. If he was convicted of the two murder charges, he was facing a minimum sentence of life without parole. Jahzay didn't like to think about that possibility. Call it denial, but she honestly felt like Smokey would be returning home to her at any minute. She held on to that hope, because hope was all she had.

Jahzay "Jazzy" Merchand, at 23, was the oldest of four siblings born to West Indian parents. She was from Buckingham Projects, where she and Miko grew up together as teens. After graduating from high school, she became pregnant with her first child, a little girl whom she named Alize, in honor of her favorite alcoholic beverage.

Yes, Jahzay was "ghetto fabulous" and proud of it, but her ghetto ways soon caught up with her. She ended up strung out on cocaine, and selling her body for money and drugs. Her life was in shambles until she met the man she considered to be her "guardian angel", Smokey played a major part in helping her get back on her feet. That's why she felt so obligated to him, and loved him the way she did.

The rapper Chamillionaire's "Ridin' Dirty" ring tone began playing, signaling yet another call on Smokey's cell phone. It had been ringing off the hook the entire day. Without hesitation, Jahzay answered it and spoke a few words into the receiver. When she hung up, she did a U-turn in the middle of the street and mashed the gas on the Acura Sports Coupe Smokey had bought for her before his arrest.

The caller needed a thousand pills delivered to him in the neighborhood of Scenic Woods. At the rate she was going, Smokey's stash wasn't going to last long. Pretty soon she would have to come clean and fill him in on what she was doing. She was hoping that he would introduce her to his connect, whom she had yet to meet. She made her drop-off and started contemplating how she would break the news.

Jahzay looked at the diamond-faced Chopard on her wrist and realized that it was almost time for her to go see Smokey. She usually went on the weekends, but decided to go that day since she wouldn't be able to make it on Saturday or Sunday. Since Smokey's arrest, she had missed only one promised visit to see him, and that was because of a doctor's appointment. But even then, Smokey was tripping. He demanded to see the bill from the doctor, because of his lack of trust. Jahzay figured that he was just insecure because he was out there being a dog when he was out.

Jahzay wasn't stupid by far. She just chose to overlook certain things in hopes that Smokey would one day change. She didn't even bother to confront him about all of the whores that continued to call his phone long after his arrest. And she didn't even trip on them either. When they called, she would politely tell them that her husband was in jail, and unless they had some money to send him, not to bother calling back. They never did. She knew they were just doing what boppers do, so she couldn't fault them. However, she could fault Smokey, but she came to the conclusion that it wouldn't do her any good. She believed it was a fact of life that all men cheated. Period. But he had run out of second chances.

Whether Smokey believed it or not (he didn't), Jahzay had not slept with another man since their relationship first started. That in itself was an amazing feat for her, as much as she loved sex. It had gotten even harder since he had been gone, especially with her hormones going out of control with her pregnancy. Sure, they had phone sex on an almost daily basis, and there was always her reliable eight-inch dildo, but none of that compared to having the real thing. As bad as she needed some, she still couldn't see herself betraying the one man who had been there for her.

With Alize over to her grandparent's home, Jahzay had the house all to herself. She enjoyed the peace and quiet, but the loneliness she felt was killing her. She took a hot bath, then quickly got dressed in a sexy, yet conservative sundress. She observed her figure in the bathroom mirror as she applied her makeup and brushed her hair, which was cut in a bob. Before she picked up the added pounds that came with being pregnant, she was a brick house. She had pert breasts, a wasp-like waist, and an ass you could sit a drink on! Her facial features were appealing as well, thanks to her doe-like eyes and dimpled smile. She wasn't conceited, but even with a protruding belly, you couldn't tell her that she wasn't a bad bitch.

After grabbing the "package" Smokey had asked for, she set out to see her man.

The line inside the Harris County Jail, at 701 San Jacinto, was literally out the door. Everyone and their mama were trying to get in before visitation hours ended. The sad part was, that the visitors were mostly comprised of young Black and Latino females. They were all trying to see their loved ones, some with their kids in tow.

Jahzay waited patiently as the line slowly inched forward, until it was her turn at the processing window.

She went through the usual routine of showing her driver's license, signing forms, and emptying the contents of her purse. It seemed like there was always a jailer who brought their problems from home to work with them. That time was no different. The old lady at the window tried to give her a hard time, but Jahzay just ignored her snide remarks. She wasn't about to let some miserable old bitch steal her joy. It was all worth it to her as long as she got to see her man. When she was cleared, she passed through the metal detector and took the short elevator ride four stories up to the trustee floor.

Jahzay exited the elevator, and was happy to see that her favorite corner seat had not been taken. It was the perfect spot for both business and pleasure, because it was out of the view of the mirrors the guards used to watch the inmates and their visitors. Plus, there was a loose screw in the glass, which allowed her to sneak cigarettes and "handlebars" in to her man. She took a seat and started humming the melody to Lyfe's "It Must Be Nice" as she prepared to see the love of her life.

●●●●●●

For James Terrell Roberts, or Smokey as he was known, life in jail was miserable, to say the least. Most Black men were career criminals by the time they reached his age of 29 years old. But that was Smokey's first time being locked up, and it was getting the best of him. As much as he tried to adjust to his new surroundings, he just couldn't get used to it.

There wasn't much to like about the place. Twenty-four inmates were forced to share one shower, one shitter, one TV, and three telephones, one of which didn't even work. The guards treated you like shit, and the food tasted like shit. In Smokey's case, the conditions were made worse by the fact that they weren't just temporary. Watching dudes get released every day and knowing he wouldn't be, weighed heavily on him.

The only thing that kept him from going insane was Jahzay's love and support. She held him down every step of the way. His books stayed fat, and he received a letter or card on a week-to-week basis. She was always home at night when he called, but that didn't stop him from stressing over whether or not she was creeping on him. That was mainly because of the guilt he was feeling behind his past acts of infidelity.

Smokey had just finished working out and taking a shower when he heard his name called over the intercom for a visit. He knew how easy it was to lose your figure in jail by lying around eating pastries and potato chips all day. That's why he made it a habit to exercise twice a day, every day. He maintained his ripped up form by lifting two trash bags filled with fifty pounds of water, each. A broken broom handle served as a bar, and his bunk served as his bench. Aside from that, he did 1,000 pushups and sit-ups every morning.

Most of the other inmates in his pod were intimidated by his size, but they would never admit to it. Smokey towered at 6'4", weighed 270 pounds and had no more than ten percent body fat. His muscular frame was covered in tattoos, but they were barely visible on his charcoal-black skin. It was no wonder that quarterbacks feared him when he was a high school football star.

Smokey put on his county issue orange jumpsuit and walked out of his dorm, smiling ear to ear. He loved getting visits from his girl. It was the only time he could escape from his reality --at least mentally. He just hated being strip searched afterwards. It was the most degrading thing he had ever been through in his life, but not because he was naked in a room full of men. Being a former jock, he was used to that. But it was something very unsettling about having another man tell you to, "Lift your nuts, and spread your cheeks!"

When he was buzzed into the visitation area, Smokey went straight to his usual spot, with his back facing the guard booth. His eyes filled with lust as they locked on the sexy chocolate specimen seated on the other side of the two-inch thick glass. He started with her face, then slowly eased downward before stopping at her exposed cleavage.

Jahzay had a wicked smile on her face when she saw the huge bulge growing in Smokey's pants. She licked her lips seductively and teased, "I see somebody is happy to see me!"

"You don't know the half of it!" Smokey replied. "Say, my man's in the picket, so we might get a few extra minutes. Did you bring that issue?"

Jahzay smacked her lips and spat, "Have I ever let you down?"

"Naw, baby. And I know you never will."

Jahzay reached into her purse and pulled out the pack of Newports and Zanaxes she'd brought along with her. She removed the screw and slid the items through one at a time. Smokey placed them all in a plastic bag and taped it underneath his stool. Another trustee would retrieve it and bring it to him later.

After replacing the screw, Jahzay said, "Now that we got that out the way, there's something important that I wanna talk to you about."

Smokey raised a suspicious eyebrow and said, "It's not what I think it is, is it?"

"No, I'm not fucking nobody! Damn! Is that all y'all niggas in jail think about?" Jahzay snapped.

"Then what else could it be?" Smokey asked nonchalantly.

"I, um... I don't know how to say this, but... I mean... I don't want you to start trippin'. I --"

"Will you just say what the hell you gotta say!"

Silence.

"Well, remember when you told me to give the rest of those pills to Greedy Mack?"

"Yeah, what about 'em?"

"I kind of sold'em myself, because I didn't really trust him. Baby, please don't be mad at me!"

Smokey just smiled and said, "I was wondering when your lil' slick ass was gon' finally get around to telling me."

"You mean you already knew? Don't let me find out that you been in here talkin' to one of your lil' boppers! I'ma whup her ass, then break this glass and whup yo's!"

"I don't need no ho's to tell me shit! The streets talk, and niggas in here find out shit faster than niggas out there do!"

"Whatever!"

"I mean, did you actually think you was just gon' sell all them pills and not have it get back to me? Be for real!"

"Well, since it's out in the open now, and the whole fuckin' jail knows, what do you want me to do? I'm going to need the hook-up, because I'm almost out."

"I have to think about that. Selling the pills I had left was one thing, but I don't know if I want you getting too deep in da game and making a career out of it. Besides, you pregnant with my lil' shawty."

"But, Smoke --"

"But, nothing! I said I'll think about it. Now that's the end of that."

"Alright, alright! You ain't gotta get an attitude about it."

Seeing that Jahzay was upset, Smokey decided to change the subject. "What color panties you got on?"

Jahzay grinned and said, "I'm not wearing any. I took 'em off before I got out of the car."

That made Smokey rub his hand across the hump in the front of his pants.

Jahzay thought he looked good enough to eat. She found it amazing how he kept himself groomed, and his hair cut using just a comb and a razor. She exposed the nipple of one of her breasts as a tease. Then she raised up her dress, opened her legs, and leaned back to give Smokey a clear view of what he had been missing.

Smokey commanded her to finger herself, and like a good girl, she did what she was told. Starting with one finger, then two, she slid in and out of her slippery canal. In between moans, she whispered, "Let me see my dick, daddy!"

Smokey wasted no time in honoring her request. Jahzay was talking dirty to him as she pleasured herself. Smokey began stroking the length of his penis feverishly, while staring at Jahzay's juicy love nest. "Ooh, yeah, baby!" he called out after a couple of minutes of masturbating. When he erupted, he shot his load all over the floor of the small booth.

Smokey was wiping himself off with toilet tissue when his name was called over the intercom, telling him that his visit was over.

Jahzay didn't get a chance to get off, which left her frustrated. But as long as her man was satisfied, she was good. She had just bought a new toy she was dying to break in anyway.

They exchanged "I love you's" and blew each other kisses before Smokey was again ordered to wrap it up. He gave Jahzay the "I'll call you" signal by making a telephone with his hand and placing it next to his ear. She responded with a nod, and turned to leave.

Back inside his tank, Smokey was feeling good. He couldn't imagine doing his time without Jahzay. He had to admit that she was everything he needed. But that still didn't stop him from keeping in touch with some of his old jump-offs. As a matter of fact, it was one of them who told him that Jahzay had been hustling. He justified his actions by making himself believe that he needed some security in case Jahzay ever decided to leave him. He didn't know what he was going to do about hooking her up with his connect. But his reluctance wasn't just caused by him not wanting her to hustle. Even more so, it was because he didn't want another hustler with more money and more clout getting next to his girl. He thought that would be just too much temptation for Jahzay to handle.

When Jahzay stepped off of the elevator in the main lobby of the jail, she saw something that made her do a double take. One of Smokey's ex-girlfriends named Karen was standing in line, waiting to be processed. Jahzay put her hands on her hips and said to herself, "After everything I've done for this nigga, I know he ain't got another bitch coming to see him!"

Karen's turn had come to be processed, and she stepped up to the window with her nose in the air. She filled out a slip and handed it to the Black female jailer behind the counter. After typing in the name of the inmate Karen had written down, the jailer said, "I'm sorry, but James Terrell Roberts has already had his one visit for today."

"What do you mean he's already had a visit?" Karen asked incredulously. "There must be some mistake. You see, today is *my* day!"

"She meant exactly what she said, bitch! He's already had his visit --with his wife!" Jahzay said loudly over Karen's shoulder.

Karen turned around in shock as a wave of fear hit her. Jahzay looked like a madwoman. She grabbed

Smokey's prissy mistress by her hair and scratched her across the face. Before anymore damage could be done, two deputies pulled the two females apart. Jahzay continued to hurl slurs at her foe, even after being warned to stop. It was only after the officers threatened to throw them both in jail that Jahzay regained her composure. She was told to leave the premises, and did so without incident, but not before telling Karen, "I'll see you on the streets, bitch!"

Speeding up the highway, Jahzay's vision was so blurred by her tears that she could barely drive. She didn't understand how Smokey could do that to her. She knew that she was a damn good woman to him, and she didn't deserve to be hurt. That was the last time she would allow it. She would always love Smokey, but she would never be able to forgive him. She made up her mind that she would no longer sit around and be faithful to a man that wasn't faithful to her. She looked at herself in the rearview mirror and said, "I don't need no nigga! It's time for me to do me!"

Chapter Three

Jimmy Chan sat alone inside his leased penthouse near downtown Houston. He was watching his all-time favorite movie, "Heat," starring Al Pacino and Robert Deniro. He absolutely loved Deniro's character, because he felt that they shared the same values. Here he was, with a chance to escape the authorities with the love of his life and his cut of a multi-million dollar heist. And what does he do? He turns around to settle an old score and ends up getting caught. It was the "principle" Jimmy Chan reasoned as he analyzed the scene over and over again on his DVD player.

Ironically, it was those same so-called principles that were behind his most recent trip down South. Yes, he was the leader of a drug empire that raked in approximately one hundred million dollars in annual profits. However, Jimmy Chan was not one to take losses in stride. He would lose sleep over one hundred dollars, let alone one million! It was because of this vicious tenacity that no one dared come up short of whatever amount of money that was owed to him. And whenever someone did, they became another one of the many stories that made up Jimmy Chan's legend.

One such story involved the husband of one of Jimmy Chan's younger sisters. As the story went, his brother-in-law had lost his job as a butcher at a Brooklyn meat processing plant. After falling on hard times, Jimmy Chan's sister asked that he give her husband a chance to make some money to take care of their family. He agreed to help him out as a favor to her, but would soon find out that his brother-in-law was not cut out for his line of work. He botched the very first deal Jimmy Chan sent him on when he accepted some counterfeit money in exchange for the drugs he was supposed to deliver.

Jimmy Chan was furious when he got the news of how his brother-in-law had been made a fool of. To Jimmy Chan, that made the entire organization look bad, and he couldn't afford to have his reputation damaged. His henchmen quickly found the guy who'd run off with their product, and brought him to their leader. Jimmy Chan and his brother-in-law met them at an abandoned warehouse. When they arrived, he gave his brother-in-law a gun and ordered him to kill the man who had crossed them.

Jimmy Chan's brother-in-law hesitated, so he pulled out his own gun and shot the man himself. Afterwards, Jimmy Chan lived up to his nickname of "The Blade". He tucked his handgun into the waistband of his trousers, and pulled out a switchblade knife. Before his brother-in-law caught on to what was happening, Jimmy Chan was already stabbing him repeatedly. In Jimmy Chan's words, his brother-in-law was a "disloyal coward", and therefore, deserved death for his dishonor. In all, Jimmy Chan stabbed him thirty-six times for a loss that totaled just $10,000. And that was his sister's husband.

He was even more deadly and unforgiving when dealing with people outside of his circle, especially Blacks. That's why he would have no problem killing Miko if he had to. In fact, it would be his pleasure.

However, she would be a lot more valuable to him alive than she would be dead. The fact was, he knew that there was no way that Miko could produce the one million dollars Seven owed him, nor the one million dollars in interest. But that was the whole idea. He needed her to fail so he could then enact his real plan, which was to flood the Houston area with his product, and eventually take over the whole market down South. Things had gotten hot up in New York, and he needed a new home. The only problem was that he didn't have any way to open doors for himself. That's where he hoped Miko could help him.

Ever since Seven's untimely death, Jimmy Chan had been missing the action down in the "Bayou City". Seven had brought in enormous profits for the Red Dragon organization, and they were just about to increase their shipments to him when he was murdered. Jimmy Chan knew that there was a lot of money to be made in Houston, and endless possibilities. Who better to exploit those possibilities than the wife of one of his most loyal and profitable associates?

Jimmy Chan felt that Miko knew a lot more about Seven's business dealings than she was willing to admit. He figured he would use her until he found someone whom he could trust. Then she would become expendable. Maybe she could even introduce him to one of Seven's old business partners who was capable of moving a million or more XTC pills in a matter of weeks. He would soon find out.

He hadn't thought of what he would do if she somehow managed to come up with the money. He reasoned that it would be a nearly impossible feat. It would also validate his claim that she still had ties to the streets long after Seven's absence. And if so, then he would demand that she work for him... or else.

The clock was steadily ticking, and Jimmy Chan's patience was wearing thin. He took a sip from his glass of whiskey and lit up his fourth Marlboro cigarette in an hour. He didn't indulge in any of the hard narcotics. Nicotine had been his drug of choice ever since he was nine years old. He had come a long way from that shy little boy who would steal cigarettes from his father's pack when he wasn't looking.

Jimmy Chan was the third of five children. This included two older brothers and two younger sisters. His father and oldest brother were soldiers who died fighting in the Vietnam War. His other brother was displaced after their small village was raided, and the family never saw or heard from him again. When that occurred, Jimmy Chan's mother smuggled him and his two younger sisters out of their war torn country. They eventually found themselves in the "Land of the Free", where they settled in with relatives in New York.

Growing up as a Vietnamese immigrant during those times was hard. All of the abuse and mistreatment Jimmy Chan received as a youngster turned him into a monster as he grew older. The anger and rage he held inside, coupled with a severe "little man" complex, made him a force to be reckoned with. He soon developed a reputation as a cold-blooded killer who sliced his victims up with his favorite weapon --a switchblade.

Jimmy Chan was always smart and very meticulous. It was inevitable that he would use those gifts in the world of crime. But, even he couldn't have imagined the heights he would ascend to in such a brief span of time.

As a teen, he started running with one of the many small Asian gangs that existed at that time. He quickly moved up in the ranks, and soon became their appointed leader. He soon became impressed with the business acumen of another Vietnamese teenager by the name of John Woo, who was the leader of a rival gang. When the two of them first met, their mutual respect for each other was obvious, and they became close friends. Realizing that two heads were better than one, they formed a formidable alliance. Their two gangs morphed into one super gang that became known as the Red Dragons.

With Jimmy Chan's muscle and John Woo's hustle, the Red Dragons were destined to become a respected and elite organization. And that it did. They started off extorting local businessmen for a share of their profits, and offering protection to those who could afford it. That, along with other small hustles, kept the money rolling in steadily, but it was nothing compared to what the drug game would bring. It was John Woo who suggested that they should expand their operations. After a trip overseas, he came back with an idea to increase their profits by way of the heroin trade. Once he got his partner's approval, he secured a connect, and they were off to the races.

For years heroin was their biggest investment, and brought in their biggest returns. The only drawback was that there was too much competition from the Chinese and Afghans, and demand was slowly decreasing. So when John Woo heard that the popularity of a drug called "XTC" was rising, he decided to get in on it early. His hunch paid off tremendously. The small pills were easier to traffic, and they could manufacture them themselves, thereby eliminating the middleman. That meant more profits for them in the end. Their organization's net worth doubled in no time as they became the primary suppliers of the drug in New York. And the more money they made, the more feared they became.

Standing on his balcony overlooking the city, Jimmy Chan took in the sights and sounds of his newly adopted hometown. It wasn't New York, but he viewed that as a good thing. There was less smog, less traffic and a lot more peaceful. He had a love/hate relationship with the South. He loved what they called their "Southern Hospitality", and the enormous amounts of money that could be made below the Mason-Dixon. But he hated the laws and how tough they were on people trying to earn a living, albeit illegally.

That attitude was shaped by his past experiences. The last time he "messed with Texas", it led to a three year stint in a state prison for a gun possession charge. That was the longest and toughest three years of his life. But, it proved to be fruitful, because that is where he met and befriended Seven. Their relationship began when Seven stopped another inmate from stabbing Jimmy Chan with a shank. He literally owed Seven his life. But that alone would not stop him from killing Miko if he had to. Nothing would. After all, business was business.

Jimmy Chan walked back inside of his penthouse and entered the bathroom. While running himself a hot bath, he observed his naked body in the mirror. His fingers traced the huge red dragon that covered the entire right side of his torso. He was so skinny his ribs were showing. No matter how much he ate, his weight never rose above 115 pounds. His face looked worn and tired, and his hair was graying more and more each day. The alcohol, cigarettes, and stress of running a multimillion dollar criminal empire was wearing on him, and he looked much older than his 39 years.

Jimmy Chan was a very lonely and miserable man. His short 5'4" frame and the fact that he was impotent made him despise the opposite sex. The spoils of his success no longer made him happy. The money, the cars, and the homes meant nothing to him. The only thing that gave him satisfaction, though only briefly, was making someone else as miserable as he was; By making others feel his pain; The moment right when they ceded their power to him as they took their last breath. That's what gave him strength. That's what he lived for. And that is what Miko would die for.

Chapter Four

The sound of money machines filled the small living room of the one bedroom apartment. They simultaneously rattled and beeped as they were fed stack after stack of large bills. The apartment served as a stash house for the four men inside. It was leased through a dummy corporation based in Nevada. But the real owner was a man whose name was synonymous with power and respect in the Houston underworld... the leader of the "Get Money Clique", Koran Yusuf.

Along with his younger brother, Tariq, Koran started the G.M.C. with the idea to create a Black La Cosa Nostra. What began as just an alliance of local neighborhood D-boys soon turned into a multimillion dollar drug organization, with over twenty members. Their empire stretched from Houston to Miami, and all parts in between. They were on a mission to get rich or die trying, and anyone who dared to get in their way was dealt with swiftly.

Of course, their meteoric rise to the top did not go unnoticed by the feds. The D.E.A. and A.T.F. had labeled them "public enemy #1", and they were hell bent on bringing them down. However, Koran's generous political contributions earned him some friends in high places. His connections and solid leadership made the G.M.C. and elusive target for the authorities. But even he knew that his luck would not last forever. So, to escape his foreseen downfall, Koran decided to fall back behind the scenes while his brother handled the day to day duties.

Koran went on to put the bachelor's degree he earned in business at Prairie View A & M to good use. He turned his share of the dirty money profits into clean money by investing in legitimate businesses. He opened up two urban clothing stores, started an online retail site, and bought into an existing luxury car lot called Hot Wheelz. They leased exotic whips to celebrities and businessmen who wanted to ride around in something fly when they came into town.

Koran was a smart hustler, and his conviction-free criminal history was proof of that. At thirty-one, he had yet to receive even a traffic ticket. Everyone knew of him, but not too many people really knew him. That was intentional on his part. He wasn't flashy at all, and he didn't let many people inside of his immediate circle, especially women. Only one woman could say that she'd gotten close to him, though many had tried.

As if his money and status wasn't enough, Koran's handsome looks made it hard for him to keep the females from throwing themselves at him. He could easily pass for a professional basketball player with his tall and lanky frame. He rocked a clean shaved bald head that the ladies loved to rub, and a neatly trimmed goatee. But his real strength was his baby-faced smile. His pearly whites were a perfect contrast to his rich chocolate skin tone.

Tariq was the exact opposite of his brother. They were like night and day. He was only two years younger than his brother, but he acted much younger. Where Koran was reserved and calculated, Tariq was outgoing and impulsive. In school, Koran was into his studies, while Tariq was more into sports. And when it came to the game, Koran was looking for a way out, and Tariq was looking for a way to advance. The only thing the brothers really had in common was their looks.

Tariq shared the same dark chocolate skin tone and baby-faced smile as his older brother. Only he rocked a full head of shoulder-length dreadlocks and long thick sideburns. He was a couple of inches shorter too, at only 5' 11". His stocky build was evidence of his days as a teenage Golden Gloves boxer. When it came to the ladies, he considered himself a bona fide player. *Ménages a trois* were a common occurrence in his world, and like Snoop Dogg, Tariq "didn't love them ho's!"

The two brothers both came up from humble beginnings. Their parents were devout Muslims from the island of Guyana. They raised their only two sons in a strict religious household before a fatal car accident took both of their lives. Koran and Tariq were in their late teens when it happened, and from that day forward, things would never be the same.

As youngsters, Koran and Tariq bounced around all over Houston, depending on what job their father had at the time. They finally settled in the southeast neighborhood of Hiram Clarke. It was there where they were introduced to the world of hustling. Their illegal endeavors took them from that small, three bedroom house, to levels they thought they would never reach.

Koran lived in a sprawling 4,500 square foot mini-mansion. The Italian styling, tile roof, and palm trees on the lawn gave the home a tropical feel. It had six baths, a large kitchen, and five bedrooms with a fireplace in the master. His fleet of automobiles included both new whips and old school classics like his '69 Cutlass Supreme.

Tariq boasted two homes where he divided his time. But his favorite was the quarter million dollar beach house he owned on Galveston Island. The view from his balcony overlooked the Gulf of Mexico. The entire home was done in white, with marble floors throughout. Tariq loved the high ceilings and the peacefulness he felt when he was there. On any given day, he could be spotted rolling down Seawall Boulevard in his drop top Mercedes-Benz or his customized slab.

Inside the apartment, the brothers continued counting the money they planned to use to cop their next shipment of kilos. They were accompanied by one of their G.M.C. capos, Clupe, and their chief of security, D-Bo. Making D-Bo their C.O.S. was a no-brainer. He was as big as his namesake, and a straight up killer.

Lying on the floor in between them were the last 90-g's of their re-up money. That would give them a total of one million dollars. When they were finished, the money would then be wrapped and prepared to be shipped to their coke connect down in Miami. The work would then be distributed amongst their crew once it arrived. Just as Tariq was about to place another stack into the money machine, his cell phone started buzzing on his belt clip.

"Talk to me," he answered coolly on the third ring.

Silence.

"A'ight. I'll see you tonight."

When he hung up his cell phone, the other three men were staring at him with smirks on their faces. Koran was the first to speak. "It's just like you to be on the phone talkin' 'bout some pussy while we're up here counting a million dollars in drug money!"

"I can't help it. I'm a pimp, big bruh," Tariq replied, putting on his best pimp voice.

"That's funny," Koran responded. "I ain't never heard of a pimp fuckin' his ho's!"

"Yeah, man," Clupe added. "It looks like you pimpin' from da waist down, playa!"

The entire room erupted in laughter. Even Tariq had to crack a smile himself. Then out of the blue. he asked Clupe, "What happened to that lil' yella bone you was tellin' me about the other day? Since we're on the subject of ho's."

"Man, I told you she called and told me she needed twenty pounds of weed, right?" Clupe answered him.

"Yeah, yeah, you already told me that part. But what I wanna know is, did you hit it?"

"Let me finish. So anyway, I started feeling a little funny about the situation. To make a long story short, I got the eight g's from her and left her waiting in the parking lot of the Village, while I slipped out the back of dopefiend Shirley's spot."

"You did what?" Koran spoke up heatedly.

"I came up on a free eight grand, that's what!" Clupe defended himself.

"What? You pressed for money or something? Cuz if so, I'll let you hold something. That way you won't have to dirty up yo' name by pullin' some bullshit like that again!"

"It wasn't even about the money, my nigga. What'chu would've done if a broad called you out of nowhere asking for twenty pounds of weed after you hadn't heard from her in over a year? And keep in mind, the last time she hollered at me, it was for one fucking pound! Shiiit, I thought she was workin' with dem people or somethin'!"

"He gotta a point right there," D-Bo said while lifting his enormous frame from off of the floor to stretch his legs.

"So, now that you know she's not a C.I., what you gon' do?" Koran asked Clupe.

"What the hell you mean, 'what I 'ma do?'" Clupe fired back.

"You know how my brother is, dawg," Tariq said. "All self-righteous and shit."

"It's not that. I just believe in keeping da game one hun'ed," Koran told him.

"Look," Clupe started. "If you just feel like you gotta save da world, go ahead. You can pay her back yourself!"

"Give me her number and I will."

●●●●●●

Jahzay and Miko were driving along Highway 6 in Jahzay's Acura, bumping the latest Keisha Cole CD. They had just come from visiting Miko's mom, Yoko Harris, at the nursing home for stroke victims. The plan was to leave there and go straight back to Jahzay's house, but they ran into a detour in the form of a handsome young guy in a candy-painted slab. The driver of the old school Buick honked his horn several times while signaling for Jahzay to pull over. Before Miko could object, she felt the car veering over to the side of the road.

Jahzay came to a stop in the parking lot of a dollar store, and both the driver and passenger of the slab got out and walked up to Jahzay's car.

"Aw, shit! Here we go!" Miko said, as the ugliest of the two tapped on her window. Not wanting to be rude, Miko reluctantly rolled down her window. She instantly regretted it when she got a better look at him. She thought he looked like a skinnier version of the rapper, Bone Crusher, lazy eye and all. It didn't help his cause that he was riding with a cutie like the guy that was leaning in Jahzay's window. Miko barely heard "Bone Crusher" speak, because his killer breath met her before the words "What's hap'nin'" did. She looked to her left and saw Jahzay grinning from ear to ear, so she decided to simply hold her breath and put up with gingivitis-man for her friend's sake.

"So, how did you get a name like Lil' Rome?" Jahzay asked the Allen Iverson look-alike with the blinged out smile.

"It's short for Romeo, which just happens to be my government name," Lil' Rome replied.

"Romeo?" Jahzay repeated. "Don't tell me you're one of those wannabe playas!"

"The only thing I 'wanna be' is your man," Lil' Rome answered back with confidence.

"Boy, you pro'lly not even old enough to drink, yet. Talkin' 'bout you wanna be somebody's man!" Jahzay teased him.

"I may not be old enough to drink, but I'm old enough to eat, ya dig!" Lil' Rome responded with a smirk. Then he added, "So, where ya baby daddy?"

"He pro'lly wit' ya baby mama!" Jahzay shot back.

"In that case, it's only right that me and you hook up," he responded.

Jahzay didn't know it then, but Lil' Rome knew exactly who she was. That's why he wasn't tripping on the fact that she was pregnant. He figured that he would come up quick if he had a bitch on his team like Jazzy. Plus, he'd heard that she had some bomb ass pussy, and he couldn't wait to find out if the rumors were true. They exchanged cell phone numbers and ended their conversation, which made Miko smile to herself.

When they pulled off, Jahzay looked over at Miko and said, "Bitch, you can't even front. Dat nigga was fiiine!"

"Yeah, but his homeboy was jacked the hell up!" Miko said, as she threw the number dude had written down out the window.

"It's not all about looks all the time. Shiiit, look at Flava Flav!"

"Well, this ain't 'The Flava of Love', and I damn sho' ain't no Deelishus!"

"Bitch, that's what's wrong with you. You too damn picky. Any dick beats that damn showerhead you're so in love with."

"Whatever! At least I don't have to worry about my showerhead cheating on me with another bitch," Miko said.

Jahzay cut her eyes at Miko. She wished she hadn't even told Miko about the episode with Smokey. Miko didn't mean to hurt her friend's feelings, it just slipped out. She was already frustrated and irritable because of her money problems. Miko was just about to apologize when her phone started ringing on her lap. She didn't recognize the number, but answered it anyway. "Hello."

"Is this, ah... Myisha?" the caller asked hesitantly. "I'm a friend of Clupe's and --"

"Did you just say 'Clupe'?"

"Yeah, I just--"

"Since you're such good friends with that bitch-ass nigga, make sure you tell him that I got somethin' for his ass when I see him!"

Click!

Koran called Miko back several times before she got tired of hearing her phone ring. She pressed the call button and shouted, "Look, maybe you didn't get the fucking message! I don't--"

"Will you shut the hell up, and let me say what I gotta say!" Koran barked.

His tone of voice shocked Miko, and for a full minute, she was all ears.

Koran cleared his throat and said, "My name is Koran, and like I said, I'm Clupe's potna. I just wanted to apologize and repay the money he owes you."

"You got my money?" Miko said excitedly.

"Yeah. So you need to tell me where and when you wanna meet so I can give it to you."

They made arrangements to hook up later that night at Joe's Crabshack. Although Miko was still mad at Clupe for making a fool of her, she was happy that the mystery man was returning her money.

Koran was starting to second-guess his decision. He knew that he was doing the right thing, but Miko was making it difficult with her attitude. He just wanted to get it over with so he could focus on more important issues. But, if he didn't make things right, his conscience would kill him. He believed in the old adage, "What goes around, comes around". Besides, the actions of one could reflect negatively on the whole organization, and the "thief" label was one Koran tried to avoid at all costs.

The time rolled around for them to meet up. Miko was so anxious to get her money back, she showed up forty-five minutes early. She was sitting on the patio of the restaurant drinking a martini when a snow-white G-Wagon pulled up. She assumed it was Koran, and she was right.

He climbed out of his SUV looking like he'd just stepped out of the pages of *GQ Magazine*. He had on a cashmere blazer over his button up, a pair of crisp blue jeans, and Kenneth Cole loafers that matched his jacket. The fitted cap he wore cocked to the side completed his outfit and gave him a sophisticated thug look.

Miko was left speechless by Koran's stunning good looks, but she refused to let her admiration show. She had to remain focused on the business at hand, which was getting back her $8,000.

Koran disappeared from sight and reappeared at the entrance to the patio. He was looking around the small crowd of patrons for someone who fit Miko's description.

She got his attention and waved him over to her table. He had barely taken his seat when Miko said, "So, did you bring it with you, or do we have to go for a ride, too? That is how your *friends* operate, isn't it?"

"Damn! No 'hello' first?" Koran asked, taking off his hat and rimless D&G glasses. "And for the record, I'm not my *friends*."

"Humph! Well anyway, this is not a social meeting, so we can skip the formalities. Let's just get this out of the way as quick as possible."

"Waiter!" Koran called out, ignoring Miko's request.

Miko sighed loudly. She was annoyed, and it was written all over her face. The young pimple-faced restaurant employee took Koran's order, and asked if Miko wanted anything. All he got for an answer was a roll of her beautiful green eyes. The waiter knew not to mess with a pissed off Black woman, so he turned and left to fill Koran's drink order. He came back a couple of minutes later with a glass of Courvoisier, and was off again.

Sitting across from Miko, Koran couldn't help but notice how sexy she was, even though she was dressed down in a pair of plain jeans, a T-shirt, and crosstrainers. Her hair was wrapped in a bun, and her face was makeup free, but she didn't need the help of cosmetics to look good. She was one of the prettiest chicks he'd ever had the privilege of meeting. There was something mysterious about her that made him want to get to know her better. He didn't believe in love at first sight, but he was definitely feeling something inside of him that he couldn't explain.

He tried to make small talk, but Miko just ignored him. They sat there in silence until Koran finished his drink and asked, "So, Myisha, you ready?"

"I thought you'd never ask! And, it's *Miko*, not Myisha," she snapped.

"Miko, huh?" Koran said, as they got up to leave. He hit his alarm and reached for a small leather case that was lying on the floor of his truck. He handed Miko the case, and she immediately checked the contents to make sure all her money was there. After counting it, she realized that not only was it all there, but there was an extra $2,000 as well. She grabbed the two stacks and said, "You must've miscounted. It was $8,000, not $10,000."

"Damn, you really are green!" Koran said. "I didn't miscount it. The extra two stacks is just a lil' sumptin' for ya troubles."

"I can't take your money!"

"Listen, woman! Just take the damn money before I change my mind. You don't even have to thank me."

"*Thank* you? Thank you for what? If your boy wouldn't have beat me outta my shit in the first place, we wouldn't be going through this!"

"I didn't mean it like that."

"I hope not. I'm going to accept your little gift, but I don't want you thinking that I owe you anything in return."

"You gotta deal. And by the way, I'm sorry we had to meet like this, but I'm not sorry we met."

A smile appeared on Miko's face, and it gave Koran hope that maybe he would get to see her again after all. But he was in for a reality check. Miko quickly killed any thoughts he may have had on hooking up with her. When he asked if he could call her under different circumstances, she flashed the huge rock on her ring finger and said, "I'm sorry, but I'm married."

During the trip back to her hotel, Miko could not stop thinking about her meeting with Koran. The brother had it going on as far as she could see. She wondered why it had been so easy for her to lie about being married. Would Seven really want her to put her life on hold and be single forever? She didn't think so, but she had yet to open up to another man since his death. At that moment, she realized that she didn't want to grow old alone. She slid her engagement ring off of her finger and allowed images of Koran to fill her mind.

Call it instinct, but something inside of Koran's gut told him that Miko was lying about being married. But then again, he wasn't sure. The only thing he knew for certain was that he was attracted to the woman named Myisha --or Miko --or whatever her name was. And, he had a feeling that she was digging him too, regardless of the mad role she was playing. He was set on finding out more about "Ms. Mysterious", and he was ready for the challenge of making her his own.

Chapter Five

"Roberts, legal visit!" the guard in the picket called out over the loudspeaker.

"'Bout muthafuckin' time!" Smokey exclaimed as he jumped up from the game of chess he was playing with another inmate. He hurriedly tossed on a white T-shirt and pressed the button to be let out of his pod. He made the short walk down to the private booths that were used for attorney visits.

Smokey looked forward to his weekly visits from his lawyer, but not just to get the latest updates on his case. The visits served as a way to smuggle all types of contraband in and out of the jail. Plus, he got to eat the free-world food that his lawyer would bring him. There was a wide slot at the bottom of the glass divider that was used to pass things through to one another, and inmates were almost never searched after a legal visit like they were after a personal visit. All one needed was a down-ass lawyer on his team. And Smokey had just that.

Waiting inside the crammed booth was Jerry Goldstein, Esquire. Goldstein had over a dozen clients just like Smokey. As a matter of fact, he made a living by keeping dope dealers out of jail... as long as they could afford his enormous fees, of course. He didn't care about moral issues or the character of the guys he defended. He would represent Osama Bin Laden if the price was right. The way he saw it, his conscience wasn't going to pay his monthly alimony to his two ex-wives, so he didn't pay it any mind.

Goldstein was a fifty-four year old, Jewish defense attorney who ran his own private practice. He'd cut his teeth as a relentless Assistant D.A., prosecuting the same criminals he would later defend. A balding, overweight man of 5'3" tall, Goldstein resembled Archie Bunker from the television sitcom "All in the Family". He maintained a comfortable lifestyle, which was a hard thing to do for a man as impulsive as he was.

The lawyer loved to bet on the horses, and favored trips to the local brothel more than trips to the local synagogue. After being diagnosed with bronchitis, Goldstein had to give up his lifelong tobacco habit. As a reminder of what he was missing, he kept an unlit cigar clamped in his mouth, which he chewed on whenever he was nervous or in deep thought. But while bronchitis kept the attorney from smoking, it did nothing to slow down his five hundred dollar a day cocaine habit. His ride on the "white horse" was a never-ending merry-go-round that he could never seem to get off of. He'd even started accepting cocaine as payment in some cases.

When Smokey walked into the booth, Goldstein stood and greeted him. "How's my favorite client?"

"I bet you say that to all the guys," Smokey joked. When he was seated he added, "On da real, I'll be a whole lot better when you get me up outta here."

"That's what I've come to talk to you about. But first, you have to try some of this," Goldstein ordered, sliding a container of food through the slot.

"What the hell is this?" Smokey asked, examining the food closely.

"A dish my wife makes. Try it, it's delicious," Goldstein urged him. "I tell ya, she isn't much in the sack, but boy, this woman knows her way around a kitchen!"

Smokey sampled some of the food, then he said, "So, did you bring that other thing for me?"

"Jesus fuckin' Christ! You're busting my balls here! Look, now you got me cursing. Father, forgive me!"

"Check this out, you slimy muthafucka! I pay you a lot of money to do what I say, when I say do it. Do you understand?"

"Yeah, yeah."

"Good. 'Cause the last thing we need to have is a failure to communicate. You never know when you may have a *little accident*, ya dig?"

Goldstein picked up on the threat, and decided not to test Smokey's patience or call his bluff. He slid a small package to Smokey, who then stashed it in his Fruit of the Loom underwear. Goldstein placed his gold rim spectacles on his nose and pulled a manila folder from his briefcase. "Now, about your case. I got some good news, and I got some not so good news."

"Give me the good news first," Smokey told him.

"Well, I've finally talked the powers-that-be into giving you a bond."

"That's what I'm talkin' 'bout right there! I wish I could kiss you right now!"

"Save your saliva for your cellmates. And before you get all excited, let me tell you the not so good news."

"Shoot."

"You're going to have to grease a few palms in return. And I'm not talking about chump change here."

"Exactly how much *greasing* are we talking about?"

"Well, as it stands, you'll be looking at $75,000 for each count. And, that's assuming they don't put the third body on you."

"That's cool. I got a bail bondsman at A-Better that'll get me out for ten percent of that."

"But wait. That's not all."

"Somehow I figured that."

"It's going to cost you another fifty big ones under the table.

"Fifty g's! You must have been snorting drain cleaner if you think I'm gonna let them muthafuckas extort me!"

"Look, I know it's a lot, but--"

"But, my ass! You're damn right it's a lot! Who da fuck I look like? O.J. Simpson or somebody?"

"No, and I damn sure can't pass for Johnny Cochran either. In other words, I can't do magic. I mean, jeez, they found DNA evidence that puts you at the scene of the crime."

"My trial date is in a couple o' months, so I think I'll sit it out until then. As far as I know, I might need that money to fight with. You said yourself, I got a lot of things going in my favor."

"Yeah, that's true. They've admitted that there was another gun used to kill the Bernard Holmes fellow. But that doesn't necessarily guarantee an acquittal. Your story about being the victim of an attempted robbery has too many holes in it to stand under the scrutiny of the prosecutor's cross-examination."

"I think I'll take my chances. But, I do want you to see if they'll come down to, say... $25,000."

"I'll try, but I can't promise you anything. They can be some stubborn old bastards at times. If they don't budge, then what?"

"We'll cross that bridge when we get to it."

"If you say so. But I'm going to give you a week to think it over before I meet wit'em."

"I gotcha."

●●●●●●

A few days passed after Goldstein's visit, and Smokey still hadn't made up his mind. He wanted to get out badly, but he was playing hardball in hopes that the crackers pulling the strings would drop their fee.

It was mail call, and every one of the 24 inmates in his pod were standing in line, listening for their names. It was the county jail version of "The Price Is Right".

Smokey was hoping to get a letter from Jahzay. He hadn't heard from her since the day of the incident with Karen. He was filled with regret, and the emptiness he felt was killing him inside. Every time he tried to call Jahzay, the phone just rang and rang. Then when he'd call her on three-way, she would answer the phone, only to hang up in his face as soon as he said anything. When he didn't hear his name called, he trudged back to his bunk with his head hung low.

The guy that slept directly across from Smokey's bunk was sitting on his bed reading a letter he'd just received. He pulled out an envelope filled with pictures, and within seconds, half the pod was standing around his bunk. They passed the photos around to each other while commenting on what they saw. The pictures found their way into the hands of Smokey's homeboy named Reece. As soon as Reece looked at the first photo, his eyes darted towards Smokey. His face held an expression of shock.

Smokey caught the look and asked his homie what the deal was. Reece told him that he didn't want to know, which only made Smokey more curious. He jumped out of bed and snatched the pictures away from his homeboy. When he looked at them he became teary-eyed, and his lungs seemed to instantly collapse.

Reece saw that his homie was mad as hell, and could only guess what was about to happen next.

"Who sent you these flicks, playa?" Smokey asked his bunkmate.

"My lil' kinfolk, Rome just shot 'em to me. In the letter, he says it's some bopper named Jazzy," the dude replied.

"Rome, huh?" Smokey said as he crumpled the photos up in his balled fist.

The guy jumped up and said, "Say, playa, what da fuck's wrong with you?"

Smokey's answer came in the form of a left hook to dude's jaw, and a right uppercut to his midsection. He folded up under the pressure of Smokey's might, as blow after blow landed to his face and body. The only thing that stopped Smokey from killing him were the deputies on duty. The officers rushed into the pod and broke up the one-sided fight. Smokey was taken to the hole, and the other guy was taken to the infirmary.

The other inmates sided with Smokey and lied on his behalf. They gave statements saying that the fight was started by the other guy, and that Smokey was only defending himself. That was mainly because Smokey was the one bringing in the cigarettes and the drugs. Plus, no one wanted to get on his bad side and become his next victim. As a result, Smokey was allowed to return to his same pod when he was let out of the hole. His victim was moved to another cell.

Bright and early the next morning, Smokey was on the phone tapping the pound button like he was playing a video game. He was trying to break through the call block that Jahzay had placed on her home phone. He finally gave up and slammed down the receiver in frustration. He needed to talk to her, and fast. His only option was to have someone call her and hook him up on three-way. Even then, there was no guarantee that she would talk to him, but it was worth a try. He picked up the phone and dialed his sister's number.

When his sister clicked the line back over after calling Jahzay, Smokey felt a lump in his throat. He was filled with so many emotions: Fear, anger, and jealousy, not to mention his wounded pride.

On what seemed like the thirtieth ring, Jahzay finally answered with an agitated, "What?"

"Jazzy, this is Smoke. Just listen for one minute!" he rattled off like an auctioneer. He expected to hear a dial tone, but he was surprised when she said, "Oh, so now you wanna talk, huh? What could you possibly have to say to me?"

"I just want you to know that I already know about you and ole dude, Rome, or whatever the bitch ass nigga's name is. How you gon--"

"Oh, you mean this dude right here!" Jahzay cut him off and passed the phone to Lil' Rome.

"Hey, what it do, playboy? I would appreciate it if you didn't call my gal no mo'. This is *my* pussy now! And by the way, I guess it's true what they say: pregnant pussy *is* the best you can get!" Rome said before he burst out laughing.

"Say, ole ho ass nigga, you gon' get your issue for fucking with my woman!" Smokey said.

Jahzay broke in saying, "Naw, nigga, I *was* your woman! It ain't no fun when the rabbit got the gun, is it? Respect the game, *pimp!* And if you need something done, tell that ho you had coming to see you to do it!"

Click!

Smokey was ready to explode when he hung up the phone. He paced the floor back and forth, contemplating ways to kill Jahzay and her new boy toy. The fact that he had cheated on her first didn't change the way he felt. He never thought she would take things that far. Yet, there he was, hurting inside, but too prideful to let his cellmates see him cry.

He'd had all he could take. He picked up the phone and called Goldstein's office. The secretary placed him on hold after accepting his collect call. After a few minutes of listening to the sound of elevator music in his ear, Goldstein came on the line saying, "Heeey, James! What can I do for you?"

"I changed my mind," Smokey said. "I need to get out of here like yesterday! I don't give a damn what it costs!"

● ● ● ● ● ●

Jahzay was curled up in her bed, reminiscing about the day that Smokey proposed to her. It was the most romantic and loving gesture she'd ever experienced. They were eating dinner at one of their favorite restaurants when he popped the question, and produced the sparkling engagement ring that still adorned her left hand. Sadly, they never got the chance to have the actual wedding. Smokey was arrested before they could even set a date.

A single tear rolled down her cheek. She was in her second trimester of her pregnancy, and filled with doubt and uncertainty. She still loved Smokey and wanted to have his child. But she didn't want to be hurt again, by him or anyone else. It was just too much to deal with. And because of that, she figured that it would just be easier to remain single.

Jahzay wondered to herself how things had gone so wrong, so quickly. She felt bad for the way she'd been treating Smokey, but she reasoned that he had brought that on himself. She could forgive, but she couldn't forget. Their lives would never be the same, but he was still the father of the baby she carried, and she planned to make sure that he was part of their child's life, whether he was locked up behind bars or not.

Jahzay's thoughts were interrupted by the touch of Lil' Rome's lips on her skin as he kissed her on her shoulder blade. Easing into bed behind her, he used his tongue to trace from the back of her neck to her right ear lobe, while his hand probed around her silky mound. He noticed that she was unresponsive to his movements and asked her, "What's wrong, boo?"

"I just got a lot on my mind, that's all. And I'm really not in the mood," Jahzay answered.

"Well, I got sumptin' that'll take ya mind off of things and make you feel all better," Li1' Rome whispered softly into her ear. He raised her right leg up slightly to give him access to her awaiting kitty. He reached around her and stimulated her clitoris with his fingers. When he felt her getting wet, he pushed his engorged dick all the way inside her with one long thrust.

Jahzay let out a shriek as Lil' Rome filled her up with his throbbing rod. He slowly grinded up against her from the back in the spoon position. As his strokes intensified, Jahzay got more into it. She was panting and clutching the sheets on her bed. Before she knew it, her legs locked up and her juices were gushing out of her being. And just like that, she had totally forgot about every thing that had been troubling her.

Chapter Six

Ms. Jacobs and her boyfriend of the past year, Carl Sr., were the modern day version of Ike and Tina Turner. To Ms. Jacobs, it seemed like they were always arguing and fighting. Most of the time, she didn't even know what for. They'd met while Ms. Jacobs was in drug rehab getting help for her terrible crack cocaine addiction. Her habit had gotten so bad, that she had even sold out her own son for a piece of the white rock. The guilt caused by her actions, along with the revelation that she would soon become a grandmother, finally made her seek out treatment after more than twenty years of drug abuse.

Like Ms. Jacob, Carl Sr. had also been admitted into the drug treatment center after being forced to do so by a concerned loved one. A certified auto mechanic by trade, he lived a comfortable family life before he succumbed to the addictive force of crack cocaine. In less than a year after taking his first hit, provided by one of his co-workers, Carl Sr. had lost his job and his family, and had turned into a true dope fiend. Since then, he had spent his life going in and out of numerous rehabs, only to relapse and repeat the cycle weeks later.

While in the Serenity Center Drug Abuse Program, Ms. Jacobs and Carl Sr. hit it off immediately and quickly became close friends. Their friendship soon became courtship, and they were both instrumental in each other's subsequent recovery.

After graduating out of rehab, Ms. Jacobs moved in with Carl Sr., who had already found employment and gotten back on his feet. He rented a small one-bedroom apartment for the two of them to stay in until they could save up enough money to get a house. During the first four months of their relationship, Ms. Jacobs was happier than she'd been in a very long time. But, unbeknownst to her, the happiness she felt would soon turn to pain and grief almost overnight.

●●●●●●

One day, Ms. Jacobs came home early from her job at a local fast food burger joint after becoming very ill. When she arrived home after the short bus ride, she was pleasantly surprised to see Carl Sr.'s work truck parked in its usual spot. She instantly began to feel better and couldn't wait to get inside the apartment so she could make love to her man. He would usually still be at the paint and body shop he worked at when she returned home, so she wanted to take full advantage of the rare opportunity to spend some much needed quality time with him.

She climbed the flight of stairs up to their second floor apartment and fumbled with her house keys as she proceeded to let herself in. She opened the front door wide, expecting to see Carl Sr. sitting on his favorite loveseat, watching television, but he was nowhere to be found. She called out his name, and when she didn't receive an answer, she went into the back of the small apartment and checked the bedroom they slept in. With no sign of him anywhere, she turned around and started walking down the narrow hallway that led back into the living room area. All of the sudden, she was startled when Carl Sr. quickly stepped out of the bathroom and hurriedly slammed the door behind him.

Ms. Jacobs got very suspicious when she didn't hear the toilet flush, and decided to investigate the situation. "I know this nigga ain't got no tramp up in *my* house!" she muttered under her breath as she looked closely at Carl Sr. "Hell naw! I'ma cut his ass if he do!"

Carl Sr. was standing in front of the bathroom door, looking nervous. He was drenched in his own sweat, and his eyes were bulging out of their sockets. He gave Ms. Jacobs a guilty look and asked her, "What are you doing home so early?"

"I should be asking you the exact same thing!" Ms. Jacobs fired back while looking him upside the head with her hands on her hips. She noted how pathetic he looked standing there with his ungroomed beard, looking like Anthony Hamilton on crack.

"There wasn't much work to do at the shop, so the boss-man let me take the rest of the day off," he explained unconvincingly.

Ms. Jacobs would later find out that the truth was that he'd been fired from his job for over a week by then, after his supervisor learned that he had been stealing tools from the shop and trading them for crack cocaine. She wanted to believe him so badly that she shrugged it off and tried to walk past him to use the bathroom. He stepped in front of her and blocked her path. With his body between her and the bathroom and his arms outstretched, Carl Sr. defiantly held his ground.

"What the hell are you hiding? I have to use the damn restroom, so get out of my way!" Ms. Jacobs protested.

"I can't let you go in there! Now, gone, woman!" Carl Sr. barked with a stern look on his face.

"You got me all the way bent, nigga! I pay rent here, too, just in case you forgot, muthafucka!" she retorted.

With that said, Ms. Jacobs pushed him to the side and swung open the bathroom door, half expecting to see another woman inside. What she saw was much worse. When she entered the tiny bathroom, she was so shocked she was speechless. Sitting on top of the counter was a plate filled with a pile of white rocks of crack cocaine, a razor blade, and a homemade plastic pipe used for smoking the addictive substance. The whole room smelled like stale smoke and sweat. She turned to face Carl Sr. with a look of disbelief on her face and tears in her eyes.

He tried to explain, but it was useless to even try to make excuses. He knew he had messed up big time, and Ms. Jacobs' expression said it all. She stormed out of the apartment without saying another word, and went to stay with a co-worker of hers temporarily.

Over the next couple of weeks, Carl Sr. repeatedly begged Ms. Jacobs to forgive him and take him back. His efforts eventually paid off. She'd been missing him dearly, so she went back home in hopes that he would get his act together. He promised her that he would leave the drugs alone for good, and initially, he did. But, after a while, he went back to his old dope fiend ways again. She still tried to stick by his side, even after his second relapse. She was determined to help bring her man up, but the weight of his addiction would only help to bring her down.

One day while Carl Sr. was sitting at the kitchen table getting high, Ms. Jacobs walked in with a bag of groceries and a frustrated look on her face. Her stress was caused by the daily trials of her job. Carl offered her a hit of his white medicine to help her "relax". He'd tried unsuccessfully to get her to get high with him on numerous occasions, but on that day, the temptation was just too much for her to resist. She gave in to his advances. All it took was that one hit for her to get hooked back on the lethal drug. And just like that, she was strung out.

●●●●●●

Ms. Jacobs and Carl Sr. were sitting on the bed in her room at Miko's home in Sugarland. Miko warned her that it was dangerous for them to be there, but Ms. Jacobs wrote it off as just Miko being paranoid. Besides, they didn't have anywhere else to stay after they were kicked out of their apartment for not paying rent.

Ms. Jacobs was taking her turn smoking the twenty dollar rock they had bought from one of their dealers, courtesy of Miko's toaster-oven that they'd stolen and pawned. Carl Sr. was watching her intently as she inhaled the thick white cloud of smoke into her lungs and held it in.

"Got-damn! You gon' smoke up the whole muthafucka by yourself, I guess!" Carl Sr. complained.

"I just got it a second ago, so why you trippin'?" Ms. Jacobs replied.

"Bitch!" Carl Sr. shouted at her, snatching the glass pipe from out of her hands and slapping her across the face. "Who you think you talkin' to, huh?"

Ms. Jacobs just sat there without responding. She'd gotten used to the verbal and physical abuse, along with the sudden outbursts of violence, so she just stared at the floor in silence while Carl Sr. smoked the last of what was left on the glass stem. He looked at her pitifully before saying, "It's your fault we could only afford to get a lousy ass twenty, anyway. I told you we should have pawned the DVD player before she came and took it! "

"I'm not taking anything else away from this house for you, or nobody else!" Ms. Jacobs stated with conviction. "My daughter-in-law still hasn't forgiven me for stealing her watch that time. And I haven't forgiven myself!"

"Oh, so it's like that, huh? Well, I'm about to blow this joint. You know where to find me whenever you get your mind right!" Carl Sr. told her.

He got up from his seat and grabbed the dirty jacket he'd tossed over one of the chairs inside the room. Ms. Jacobs begged and pleaded with him to stay there with her, but her pleas fell on deaf ears as he walked out the door.

It was pitch black outside when he stepped out onto the front porch and into the cool night air. He lit the GPC cigarette he had tucked behind his ear with a match, and took a long drag before proceeding up the driveway.

He jumped inside of his beat up Ford pick-up truck and backed out into the street. He started up the road before noticing a stalled black sedan with its hazard lights flashing about three or four houses up the quiet residential block. A large man dressed in all black was waving his arms wildly, trying to flag him down. Carl Sr. pulled up to the stranded motorist and rolled down his window to see what the problem was.

The strange figure told him he would pay him fifty dollars for a boost, and Carl Sr.'s greed immediately got the best of him. He wondered why such a late model car would need a boost, but he quickly dismissed the thought. Instead, he chose to focus on how much crack he would be able to buy with the fifty dollars he was about to receive.

He pulled his pick-up truck over to the side of the road and parked in front of the broke down vehicle. Carl Sr. reached behind his seat to grab his jumper cables, and was startled when the stranger suddenly appeared in his driver's side window. Before Carl Sr. could react, the large man raised a gloved hand that held a black semi-automatic handgun with a long silencer screwed onto the barrel. In the blink of an eye, the Asian-looking gunman squeezed the trigger of the nine-millimeter, sending one hollow-tipped bullet into Carl Sr.'s neck, and another right between his eyes. Blood covered the pick-up truck's passenger side window as Carl Sr.'s lifeless body slumped over sideways in the seat.

Inside Miko's house, Ms. Jacobs had just finished crying and asking God to get her out of the messed up situation she was in. She loved her man with all of her heart, but she knew that the only way for her to kick her worsening crack habit would be for her to leave him alone. She missed Miko and her grandson dearly. She hadn't seen or spoken to them since the fight she had with Miko over the stolen watch. But, she promised herself that she would call her daughter-in-law as soon as morning came to tell her how sorry she was for betraying her trust.

With nothing to do and no more drugs to smoke, Ms. Jacobs started cleaning up the house to pass time until Carl Sr. decided to return. She walked down the stairs of the two-story home, making a conscious effort not to look at the pictures of Miko and Seven that lined the walls. It had been over a year since Seven's death, but Ms. Jacobs still could not bring herself to look at her son's face, knowing that she was partly to blame for his murder.

While sweeping up the kitchen floor, she heard a barely audible knock coming from the front door. Her spirits were instantly lifted as she welcomed her man's speedy return. She quickly dropped the broom onto the floor and ran full-speed towards the front door yelling out, "Hold on, baby! I'm comin'!"

To Ms. Jacobs surprise, it wasn't Carl Sr. who was standing on the other side of the doorway, but a short Asian guy with dark sunglasses over his eyes. She knew that it couldn't have been anyone other than the Asian man Miko had told her about. She instinctively began to inch backwards away from the door, as she trembled from the fear she felt.

Jimmy Chan took a puff of his Marlboro 100 and tossed the cigarette butt to the ground. He then removed his sunglasses, and with a sinister grin on his face asked, "Aren't you going to invite me in?"

Those were the last words Ms. Jacobs heard before she fainted to the floor.

Chapter Seven

Miko answered her cell phone on the first ring without looking at the caller I.D. She knew who would be on the line and had been expecting his call the entire day.

"I thought we agreed that you would call me yesterday," Jimmy Chan stated. "I am very disappointed with you, Mrs. Harris."

"I-I-It must've slipped my mind," Miko stammered.

"You know, in my homeland it is very disrespectful to lie," Jimmy Chan admonished her.

"I just need a little more time, that's all."

"I'm sorry, but that's something that I just don't have to give you. Maybe if you had a little... how do you say, *incentive*. Yes, that's it. Maybe then you would be more anxious to help me."

"No, it's not that. Believe me, I'm trying. It's just--"

"Save your worthless excuses! I see that I'm going to have to set an example for you. Say hello to Tai for me."

Click!

"Wait!" The line went dead before Miko could try to explain herself. She wondered what Jimmy Chan meant by his last state-ment. All of the sudden, something clicked inside of her head. She recalled her first encounter with Jimmy Chan and the threat he'd made to her. A wave of panic swept over her. She frantically dialed Ms. Jacobs' cell phone number. After repeated tries, she decided to just leave a message on her voice mail. She then checked her watch. It was almost three o'clock and there wasn't a minute to spare. She grabbed her purse and car keys and ran out the door.

Miko sped up the highway, switching from lane to lane as she darted through the afternoon traffic. About thirty minutes later, she was pulling up in front of the entrance to Our Mother of Mercy Intermediate School. Tai was enrolled there as an eighth grader. Cars were lined up on both sides of the street, filled with anxious parents waiting for their children to be let out of school.

A loud bell sounded, signaling the end of another school day. A sea of kids of all shapes and sizes came flowing from out of the doors. Miko didn't waste time finding a place to park. She turned on her hazard lights and jumped out in the middle of the street. Of course, that pissed off the motorists behind her, and they let their feelings be known by blowing their horns repeatedly and shouting obscenities.

Miko paid them no attention as she scanned the faces of the hundreds of kids rushing toward her. She began to worry when she didn't see any signs of her brother. The students were all required to wear maroon colored uniforms, which made it even harder for her to spot him. She was starting to think the worst when she saw him walking her way with a backpack slung over his shoulder. She ran up to him and nearly burst into tears as she gave him a tight hug. Tai was confused by his sister's show of affection, but he returned it anyway.

"C'mon, let's get out of here," Miko told him. When she raised her head up, she noticed two Asian men in black suits standing by the exit. They looked out of place among the crowd of parents and teachers. Their heads swiveled back and forth as they surveyed the scene from behind their dark sunglasses. One of the men tapped the other one on the shoulder and pointed towards Miko and Tai. His partner looked at a picture he held in his hand and nodded. They started in Miko's direction, so she grabbed Tai by the arm and led him away. He stayed close by her side as they moved hastily towards her jeep.

Looking over her shoulder, Miko noticed that the men had quickened their pace. They were gaining ground on her fast. Tai was getting frightened, but Miko encouraged him to stay calm and keep walking. They bobbed and weaved through the crowd on the sidewalk until they reached the front gate of the school.

Miko spotted a crossing guard standing beside her jeep, preparing to write her a ticket. She'd never been so happy to see a police officer in her entire life. The two Asian men who were following her must have seen him, too, because when Miko looked back, they were nowhere in sight. She thought of a quick lie to explain why her Jeep was parked illegally. It was convincing enough to avoid being issued a ticket.

Once inside the X5 Tai asked, "Who were those dudes we were running from?"

"I think they work for Jimmy Chan," Miko replied.

She inched up in the slow moving traffic and made a right turn at the corner. She was just beginning to calm down and regain her composure when something caused her jeep to lunge forward violently. The impact nearly caused Tai to fly into the dashboard. Miko looked into her rearview mirror, and a black BMW sedan with tinted windows and a smashed bumper came into view.

"Shit!" Miko shouted. "Put on your seatbelt!"

Tai did as he was told, and Miko buckled hers as well. The sedan rammed into them again, causing Miko to swerve out of control. She straightened her wheel and pressed down on the gas pedal as far as it would go. She entered the on-ramp of Highway 290 with the BMW right on her tail. She veered to the left, narrowly avoiding a collision with another vehicle.

The driver of the 760 increased his speed and pulled side by side with Miko's jeep. Miko knew that they'd been sent to kidnap her little brother. Jimmy Chan was obviously trying to make good on his promise, but Miko wasn't giving up without a fight. She was willing to die in order to save her brother.

The sedan accelerated and hit the passenger side of the jeep, sending sparks flying into the air. Miko tried to swerve out of the way, but she was too slow. The force of the collision knocked her jeep sideways and shattered the glass in the passenger window. The other cars on the highway began to slow down to avoid an accident.

Tai was crying uncontrollably. Miko commanded him to cover his head and place it between his legs. She then reached into her purse and pulled out her small .380 handgun. While steering with her left hand, she used her right to aim the gun out of the jeep's window. When Jimmy Chan's men pulled even with her, she emptied all eight shots out of the pistol. The bullets pierced the metal frame of the sedan and busted all the windows out.

Miko glanced into the vehicle and saw the slumped form of the passenger leaning forward awkwardly. She figured that she'd at least hit one of them. At that moment, the driver raised his right arm across his body and pointed a pistol at her. She ducked quickly as he squeezed the trigger, sending a stream of bullets into her jeep. Luckily, neither she nor Tai was hit.

With no bullets to return fire and no escape in sight, Miko was stuck. She switched lanes until she was in the far right lane of the highway. She had an idea. It was a long shot, but she prayed it would work. She had the advantage of being familiar with the area, so she decided to use that in her favor.

She pushed her wrecked jeep to the limit and created a space of about two car lengths between her and the sedan. They raced on for another quarter of a mile before they reached the point where three highways intersected in a maze of ramps and overpasses.

Miko approached the Loop 610 exit. She waited until the very last second before she slowed down and jerked the wheel to the right to make the sharp turn. The BMW's driver was unable to react quickly enough, and his car hit the guard rail head-on at over one-hundred miles per hour. The driver was ejected from the car. He flew about thirty feet into the air before hitting the concrete. He was killed instantly. The car exploded and burst into flames.

Miko saw the thick, dark smoke coming from the burning BMW in her rearview mirror. She sighed in relief as she fled the scene.

Tai stayed bent over with his head buried between his knees for the next several miles. Miko needed to find a safe place for him to stay until she could take care of the situation with Jimmy Chan, and she had a good idea who would be willing to help them.

●●●●●●

Miko drove through her old neighborhood with Tai asleep in the seat beside her. She nervously stared in her rearview mirror, expecting a police officer to pull her banged up jeep over at any minute. She made a left into the entrance of Buckingham Projects and pulled up to the building of her old friend, Mrs. Brousard.

Mrs. Annie Mae Brousard had lived in Buckingham Projects for as long as Miko could remember. She was a middle-aged widow, having lost her husband several years earlier to prostate cancer. She'd bore two children: A twenty-one year old daughter named Joanna, and a twelve year old son named Timothy. Timothy was Tai's best friend and former classmate.

Miko knocked on Mrs. Brousard's front door after climbing up three flights of stairs, with Tai right behind her. Mrs. Brousard lived in the so-called "nice" section of B.H.P. She answered the door with a welcoming smile. Her face was radiant and void of the crow's feet and blemishes that most women her age had. The terrycloth housecoat she wore seemed to swallow her tiny frame. As usual, her apartment smelled like the inside of a soul food restaurant.

When Mrs. Brousard saw the way Miko and Tai looked standing there on her porch, she immediately grew concerned. The first words out of her mouth were, "My Lord, what happened to the two of you?"

"Mrs. Brousard, I really need your help," Miko replied with tears in her eyes.

Mrs. Brousard ushered them inside and offered them both a plate of food. Tai and Timmy were excited to see each other, and Tai couldn't wait to tell his friend about everything that had happened. They ran off to the back room after dinner, leaving Miko and Mrs. Brousard alone to talk.

Miko explained the whole story to her as she listened closely without saying a word. When she finished, she asked Mrs. Brousard to do her the favor of keeping Tai until it was safe for them to go home.

Mrs. Brousard replied, "Of course! I would do anything to help y'all out."

Miko told her that she'd return later on that night with Tai's clothes and other belongings. She then kissed her brother on the forehead and left in a hurry. She raced home to gather their things. She hoped Ms. Jacobs would be there so they could talk. There was so much left unsaid between them. Miko felt it was time for them to resolve things and move on.

Her nerves were shot by the time she made it to her home. She looked around for any suspicious vehicles before easing into her driveway. After she saw that the coast was clear, she jumped out of her jeep with the engine still running. Within seconds, she was running through her front door and inside her home. The first room she entered was her kitchen, where she grabbed a box of bullets from a drawer. Next, she took a large trash bag from the cabinet and started filling it with any and everything she and Tai might need. She walked into her little brother's room and packed his remaining clothes into a suitcase before heading to her own room. When the suitcase was filled to capacity, she decided to pick up the rest of their stuff later.

On her way back downstairs, she heard the sound of a television set coming from Ms. Jacobs' bedroom, and stopped to turn it off before she left. She opened the door and was surprised to see the back of Ms. Jacobs' head as she sat in a chair facing the television. Miko put her hands on her hips and said, "Here I am, worried sick about you, and you're in here watching a damn talk show!"

When Ms. Jacobs didn't respond, Miko assumed that she'd fallen asleep in front of the television. She walked over to awaken her mother-in-law, but what Miko saw caused her to recoil in shock.

Ms. Jacobs had a crazed expression on her face, and her skin had turned bluish. Her eyes were rolled back into her head so far that only the whites showed. A needle was sticking out of her outstretched forearm.

Miko fell to her knees and sobbed loudly. She called out to her mother-in-law, but her cries went unanswered. Ms. Jacobs was dead.

Chapter Eight

Miko was almost in a hysterical state as the police detectives on the scene questioned her about Ms. Jacobs' death. She was flinging her arms wildly and cussing at the top of her lungs to whoever was in earshot. Her sudden outburst came after she overhead one of the police detectives tell his partner that Ms. Jacobs' death was an "apparent suicide". Miko knew that that was hardly the case. There was no doubt in her mind that her mother-in-law's death was the handiwork of no one other than Jimmy Chan himself.

The detectives were attempting to calm her down so they could proceed with their investigation, when Jahzay pulled up. She was driving Smokey's black 2006 Yukon Denali. When Miko saw Jahzay get out of the SUV, she ducked her head under the yellow crime scene tape and ran straight towards her friend. Jahzay hugged her tightly and said, "I got here as fast as I could. I'm sorry, Mi-Mi."

"Me, too. I was starting to think you didn't get my message."

"Shit, you look like you could use a drink right now."

"I could use more than just one!"

"So, what are they saying happened?"

"She overdosed on heroin, and these muthafuckas talkin' 'bout it's an 'apparent suicide'! Can you believe that shit!"

"Miko, you can't rule that out as an option. I mean--"

"I can't believe you just said that! I thought you was on my side, but you sound just like the rest of these crazy ass people!"

"This is not about sides. I'm just sayin', what makes you so sure that it wasn't a suicide? You said yourself that she hasn't been acting the same since you found out that she was stealing from you to support her crack habit. "

"First of all, for as long as I've known Ms. Jacobs, I've never known her to use heroin. Period! Let alone shoot the shit up her arm with a fucking needle!"

"So, maybe she couldn't find any crack and decided to try it."

"There's one thing you're forgetting about. Ms. Jacobs was left handed, and the needle was sticking out of her left fucking arm! Now how do you explain that, since you're playing detective?"

Jahzay was speechless. For a while she was starting to think that Miko was just blowing the whole Jimmy Chan thing out of proportion. But, she began to sense that the situation was more serious than she may have thought.

After the investigators and coroner were finished, the two detectives gave Miko their cards and told her that they would be in touch. Hours had passed since they'd first arrived, and both Miko and Jahzay were extremely tired.

Jahzay looked at her visibly shaken friend and said, "You know, on second thought, I think we both may need that drink now!"

● ● ● ● ● ●

The next few days were very stressful for Miko. An official autopsy revealed that Ms. Jacobs' death was indeed caused by an overdose, which caused the detectives to rule out any foul play and close the case for good. That angered Miko even more, and she went down to the police station to give them a piece of her mind.

When the coroner finally released Ms. Jacobs' body, Miko was left with the task of taking care of her burial arrangements. Because she was the closest thing to a family Ms. Jacobs had, Miko had to make all the decisions. She chose to have her remains cremated, and her ashes sprinkled over Seven's gravesite. She had a small memorial for the spreading of the ashes that included herself, Elijah Jr., Tai, Ms. Nadine, Jahzay and Alize.

Not even a day after the service, Miko caught a glimpse of a familiar looking, old model pick-up truck while driving home. The Ford truck was being pulled out of a ravine near her neighborhood by a tow truck. Later that night while watching the news, she was shocked to hear that an unidentified man was found inside the vehicle, with multiple gunshot wounds to the neck and head. She knew that Ms. Jacobs' boyfriend had a red truck, but she hoped that it was just a coincidence. However, she decided to make sure that the man that was murdered wasn't him.

She waited around for the next broadcast of the murder. When the midnight news broadcast came on, Miko's worst fears were realized.

The female newswoman on the scene stood in front of the beat up red pick-up that Miko recognized as belonging to Carl Sr. She reported that the victim had been positively identified by his driver's license as Carl David Jones Sr. Miko buried her face in her palms and sighed deeply. Tears began to stream down her cheeks as she thought about her deceased mother-in-law. She wondered if she would share the same fate.

In the middle of her breakdown, her cell phone began to ring on the bed beside her. She grabbed the phone and checked the caller I.D. screen. The call was coming from an anonymous line, so she decided to let it go through to her voicemail. When her answering machine picked up, the caller hung up without leaving a message. The same thing happened three more times before Miko answered it out of curiosity. She pressed the send button and spoke into the receiver, "Wassup?"

"I take it you have gotten my little message by now," Jimmy Chan said in the annoying accent Miko had grown to hate.

"Fuck you, you bastard!" Miko yelled into the phone.

"Those are some very ugly words for a woman as pretty as yourself to be using, Mrs. Harris. Besides, I'm calling to offer you an olive branch of sorts."

"The only thing I want from you is for you to leave me and my family alone and get the hell out of my life!"

"On the contrary, I think you will like what I have to tell you once you've heard me out. Or you can test my patience and end up just like..."

"Go ahead and say it, you heartless muthafucka!" Miko spat.

"Now that I have your undivided attention, allow me to get straight to the point."

Jimmy Chan started off by telling Miko how much he missed Seven as a "friend" and also as a business partner. Miko immediately knew that she wasn't going to like what she was about to hear. He went on to say how much he wanted to reestablish his operation in Houston. He stressed to her that he felt like she could really help him do just that. He'd come up with a plan to front Miko with as many XTC pills as she could handle, and once she sold an "acceptable" amount, he would be willing to consider cancelling her debt. He made it sound real simple, but Miko still felt funny about the idea. She made her concerns known.

"Are you crazy?" she snapped. "I don't know anything about selling no fucking ecstasy!"

"I find that hard to believe, being as though you were married to one of my most loyal clients."

"I told you once already, Seven never involved me in any of his business dealings. There has to be another way I can repay you."

"You're a very resourceful and brave young woman, Mrs. Harris. More so than you give yourself credit for. You showed me that during that little... *episode* on the highway the other day, so I'm sure you will be more than able to handle our arrangement, and help an old friend out."

"I'm sorry, but I can't."

"I'm afraid you don't have a choice in the matter, Mrs. Harris. I must advise you that the Luxury Inn is not known for its security."

Jimmy Chan's implied threat rattled Miko so badly that she jumped up from her bed and ran to check the locks on her room door. She screamed into the phone, "Why are you doing this to meee?"

"Because, I have reason to believe that Seven left you my money, and I want it! You have twenty-four hours to make up your mind."

Click!

Miko just sat there crying on the edge of the hotel bed. She had to make one of the most important decisions of her life, and she didn't have a lot of time to think about it. After spending over an hour weighing out her options, she came to the conclusion that it would be in her and her loved ones' best interests to take Jimmy Chan's offer... anything to get him out of her life for good. At the very least she could buy her some time to come up with a better idea.

It was five o'clock the next evening when the word "anonymous" popped into her caller I.D. again. Miko was in the middle of having her jeep placed in the shop and picking up a rental car her insurer had paid for. She answered the call on the second ring and listened intently to the voice on the other end.

"So, Mrs. Harris, what have you decided to do?" Jimmy Chan asked her.

Miko reluctantly said, "I'll do it."

"That's a very smart decision," he said before giving her the directions to the place that they were to meet. He instructed her on what to do once she got there.

Miko grabbed a pencil and paper, and wrote down the information he gave her and read it back to him to make sure she had it right. Jimmy Chan warned her that if she even thought about involving the police, he would personally see to it that she died a slow and painful death. Then he would kill her son as well. She got the point loud and clear, and decided not to tell anyone what she was planning to do.

At nightfall, Miko headed out Highway 59 to meet her new employer. The meeting spot was an old industrial building on the eastside of Houston near the Ship Channel. It didn't take long for her to reach her destination in the speedy Grand Prix. She turned into the gravel covered parking lot of an abandoned shipping yard and parked like she was told. To her right, she saw a line of metal-framed warehouses. The parking lot was completely deserted, which made her a little nervous.

She was about to pick up her cell phone and call Jimmy Chan, when all of the sudden she was blinded by a bright light shining directly in her eyes. She lifted her hand to her face to block the glare so she could see. Suddenly, the driver's side door of her car swung open and a pair of strong hands grabbed her by her arms. The unknown man dragged a kicking and screaming Miko out of her car and across the parking lot.

The gravel rocks peeled the skin from off of Miko's forearms, and tore small holes in her jeans. When they came to a stop, she found herself laying on the ground next to a dark colored automobile. The rear door to the vehicle swung open, and the huge hands grabbed her again and tossed her into the backseat.

Miko looked over to her right, and was staring Jimmy Chan directly in the eyes. His eyes were dark and lifeless and seemed to be staring into her soul. He was dressed immaculately in a black long sleeved turtleneck, black linen slacks, and a pair of black Feragamo loafers. Miko spat in his face and said, "What kinda bullshit is this!"

Jimmy Chan pulled out a handkerchief and calmly wiped his cheek off. He then fired up a Marlboro 100 and said, "In certain parts of Asia, your name means 'sorceress'. Maybe that can explain the effect you have on men."

"Well, in that case, I should be able to cast a spell to get you the hell out of my life!" Miko fired back.

Jimmy Chan laughed out loud, but his smile faded just as quickly as it had appeared. He was strictly business as he began talking. "I'm going to start you off with a relatively small amount just to see what you can handle. Call it a trial run, if you will. I think 500 will suffice, no?"

"You brought me all the way out here in the middle of nowhere and drag me across the ground just to give me 500 pills?"

"Let me clarify things for you. What I mean is five-hundred-*thousand*!"

"Five-hundred-*thousand*! You can't seriously expect me to sell that many pills!"

"You're right, I don't. I expect you to sell much more than that."

Miko couldn't believe what she was hearing. She felt overwhelmed by Jimmy Chan's proposition. He said something to the driver of the sedan in a foreign language Miko was unfamiliar with. The driver then handed him a briefcase from off of the passenger seat.

Jimmy Chan fumbled with the combination lock between puffs of his cigarette, until a clicking sound was heard. When he opened the briefcase and removed the false bottom, what Miko saw caused her eyes to nearly pop out of her head. Stacked in neat rows inside a specially made tray were thousands and thousands of multi-colored XTC pills in an assortment of sizes. They had varying symbols on them, ranging from dolphins to cartoon characters. Jimmy Chan handed the briefcase to Miko and said, "I believe these are for you."

He briefly told her what he expected to receive in return, and how much time she would have before he came to collect.

Miko nodded in agreement before exiting the car. She clutched the briefcase tightly against her bosom as she was escorted back to her car by Jimmy Chan's bodyguard.

She closed her eyes and drew a cross in the air as she started the engine of her rental car. Seconds later, she was pulling out of the parking lot under the watchful eyes of Jimmy Chan.

Back on the highway, Miko's fingers tapped the car's steering wheel to the beat of Rick Ross' "Hustlin'", as the rapper's deep baritone voice came booming through the speakers. It was a fitting soundtrack for the journey she was about to embark on. Though she wasn't much of a hustler, she would have to become one if she wanted to get out of her dilemma alive. She recalled all the times she rode shotgun with Seven while he went on his "errands", and hoped she could remember what she learned during those experiences. The first thing she had to do was get in contact with a few people that could help her move the pills she had. The only problem was that she didn't have any idea who could.

Part Two

Chapter Nine

Here We Go Again

The evening sky was dark as thick clouds formed overhead, giving way to the upcoming thunderstorm. Smokey stepped out of the doors of the Harris County Jail and exhaled the crisp air deep into his lungs.

It had been over eight hours since he'd heard his name called over the jail's loudspeaker for "ATW". He jumped up from his bunk and headed out the cell, leaving behind all of his commissary and personal belongings. The release process was long and tedious as he and the other releasees were herded from holding tank to holding tank like human cattle. When he reached the final station and was given his property, Smokey s' heart began to flutter inside of his chest. The day he'd been praying for had finally arrived.

Smokey scanned the scene before him as he stood on the bustling sidewalk outside of the jail. He purchased a single Newport cigarette from one of the many enterprising street vendors, and fired it up as he walked past the long line of Yellow Cabs parked along the street. When he reached the corner of San Jacinto, he spotted what he was looking for: a silver 2007 Mercedes-Benz CIS illegally double-parked with its hazards flashing. He flicked his cigarette to the ground and walked hastily towards the vehicle as the raindrops began to come down harder.

Inside the Mercedes Smokey's lawyer, Jerry Goldstein, was asleep behind the wheel with an unlit Cuban cigar hanging from his lips. Seeing that the doors were unlocked, Smokey walked around to the driver's side of the car and swung the door open screaming, "Break yourself, fool!"

Goldstein jumped up in his seat and yelled out, "Jesus fucking Christ! You scared the living shit out of me!"

Smokey laughed so hard his side was hurting. He walked back around to the passenger side and climbed in the car. Once inside, their conversation took a more serious tone.

"Look, I'm going to cut to the chase here," Goldstein started. "I had to pull a lot of strings to get you out of there."

"Shit, just give me a couple of days to come up with the money."

"No problem."

"What about the other stuff I asked you to take care of?"

"I handled everything personally. But, there's just one other thing."

"What's that?" Smokey asked, looking at the lawyer warily.

"What do you want me to tell your wife?"

"Nothing."

"For Christ's sake! She's been calling me so much, my wife is starting to think that I'm screwing her!"

The mention of Jahzay instantly filled Smokey with rage, causing him to bite down hard on his bottom lip, which was a habit of his whenever he got mad.

Noticing the scowl on Smokey's face, Goldstein shut up for the rest of the drive. After making a few turns, he pulled into a parking garage on the outskirts of downtown and parked next to a black Lincoln Town Car with dark tinted windows. "There you go," Goldstein said, pointing towards the rental car. "Everything you need is in the glove compartment."

"Good looking out," Smokey replied. "I'll holla at you in a few days so we can make that transaction." He exited Goldstein's Mercedes and made his way over to the Lincoln. Grabbing the keys from the sun visor, Smokey started the engine and slowly pulled out of the parking garage. His first order of business was to get himself groomed and cleaned up so he could look and feel like a human again.

The Lincoln's windshield wipers struggled to fight back the pouring rain as he traveled to one of his homeboy's barbershops on the south side called Player's Cutz. It was right before closing time when he walked into the establishment. The owner of the shop, Cee, greeted Smokey with a slap on the back and motioned him over to an empty chair.

"Man, I heard what happened to you," Cee started. "I thought you wasn't gon' ever get out that muthafucka."

"Well, you know my money so long, it don't just talk... it sings!" Smokey replied.

The two of them exchanged a little small talk while Smokey got his hair cut into a clean bald fade. When he was finished, he reached into his pocket to pay for the haircut and shave, but Cee stopped him, saying, "This one on me, baby."

"'Preciate it, man," Smokey said before walking outside and entering his car.

His next two stops were at the local weed spot, where he bought an ounce of purple cush, and to Timmy Chan's for a six wings and rice dinner.

On his way to the hotel room Goldstein had gotten for him, the urge to get some pussy suddenly hit him. The first name that came to his mind was Lucy Lu, one of his jump-offs that stayed close to his trap house. When Smokey proposed to Jahzay, he let go of all of his other "pieces of game" except for Lucy Lu, whose skills in the bedroom proved to be much too good for him to give her up so easily. He opened the glove compartment and retrieved the burned-out cell phone that was placed there for him. He dialed her number up, and the familiar sexy voice answered, "Hello."

Smokey skipped the pleasantries and got right to the point. After a few minutes, the arrangement had been made. Smokey made a quick U-turn in the middle of the street, traveling in the direction of Lucy Lu's home. When he pulled into her driveway, she was already sitting on her porch waiting for him. Smokey's dick immediately began to rise in his pants as she got up and walked seductively towards his car, dressed in a skintight blue jean cat suit.

Lucy Lu was mixed with both Philippine and Mexican, and her features bore a striking resemblance to her namesake from the "Charlie's Angels" films. She was twenty-one years old, with a petite 5'6" frame, slanted eyes, and a long mane of jet-black hair that stopped in the middle of her back. But what Smokey liked best about Lucy Lu was her appetite for sex. She was the closest thing to a real life nympho he had ever seen. Plus, she never begged for money or disrespected the game by running her mouth about any of her lovers.

When she climbed inside the car, she was so excited to see Smokey that she screamed at the top of her lungs. After hugging him and kissing him on the cheek, she wasted no time in getting down to business. Before Smokey could even reach the main street that led to Highway 59, she'd already pulled his dick from his pants and began giving him the best head he ever had in his life.

Smokey's hotel room was at the Marriott Inn in downtown Houston. After parking his car in an empty space, he grabbed his change of clothes from the trunk along with the manila envelope that contained his room key and the rest of the items he had requested from his attorney.

The room was modestly furnished, with two twin-sized beds, a big screen color television and a small sitting area. It was nothing like what Smokey was used to staying in, but it served its purpose, which was to give him a temporary place to lay his head while he put his plans in effect.

He threw his things on the bed and tossed the weed and cigars to Lucy Lu, who immediately began rolling up a blunt. In the meantime, he stripped down to his county issue boxers and threw them away as he headed for the bathroom to take a hot shower. Nearly an hour later, he stepped out of the shower feeling like a new man and quickly dried himself off. He walked out of the bathroom, and Lucy Lu was already completely naked just like he knew she would be.

Smokey reached onto the nightstand and fired up a blunt, and watched through the huge wall mounted mirror as Lucy Lu play with herself. Halfway through the blunt, he was high and eager to join her in bed. He put the blunt out and placed it in the hotel ashtray before walking over to the bed.

Lucy Lu raised up on her knees and crawled over to where Smokey stood. Her pussy was shaved bare, allowing Smokey to see the juices glistening between her legs. She reached out and grabbed his already hard penis and hungrily placed it in her mouth. Packing close to eight inches, Smokey was no slouch in the dick department, but by the way Lucy Lu was deep throating him, you couldn't tell. When she felt Smokey's member begin to throb and jump uncontrollably between her jaws, she quickly took him out and let him cum all over her small breasts.

Smokey then quickly slid on a condom and penetrated her from the back. He was surprised at his staying power, and attributed it to his incarceration.

Lucy Lu was loving every minute of it, as Smokey pounded her forcefully with a series of hard thrusts. He nearly went over the edge when she commanded him to put it in her ass. He honored her request, and slipped out of her pussy and into her awaiting asshole. He let out a loud moan as she squeezed her ass and tightened herself around his dick. She screamed for dear life as Smokey bucked wildly and blew his load inside of her.

They took a hot shower together, then Smokey finished smoking the other half of his blunt before falling asleep.

●●●●●●

The following morning, Smokey was up before the crack of dawn, pacing back and forth across the floor of the hotel room. He'd tossed and turned all night, because the anxiety he felt would not allow him to get any sleep. He was fully dressed and smoking on a blunt when he awoke Lucy Lu and told her, "Get ready. It's time to go."

Thirty minutes later, he dropped her off and was driving through his neighborhood behind tint. He had a long day ahead of him, and no time to waste. He mashed the gas pedal of the Lincoln Town Car and sped off towards his sister's home.

Jameisha Renee Roberts was Smokey's only sibling, and although she was one year younger than he was, she was more like an older sister to him. Both their mother and father worked long hours at their respective jobs when they were young, and they would often leave Smokey and Jameisha home alone. She was the one left in charge of the house since the age of eleven, and she would cook her brother's food and wash his clothes.

Smokey loved his sister to death, and coincidentally, he had her to thank for his success in the game, because it was her who introduced him to Seven, who in turn put Smokey down on his team. Jameisha and Seven dated off and on back when they were younger when she still had the figure that earned her the nickname, "Big Booty 'Meisha".

The combination of greasy fast food and two kids caused her "big booty" to get bigger and bigger over time, along with the rest of her body. But even with the increase of her weight, Jameisha's face still possessed its natural beauty. Like Smokey, Jameisha had shiny, coal-black skin, which she wore with pride in honor of her parents' West African roots. She wore her hair in thick dreadlocks that stopped just above her shoulders, and had a big bright smile that was accented by a single gold tooth with the initial "T" inscribed into it.

When Smokey's family found out that he was selling drugs, they all turned their backs on him, except for Jameisha. For that reason, Smokey had vowed that neither her nor his nephews would ever want for anything as long as he was alive and breathing. After her husband was given twenty-seven years in federal prison for armed bank robbery, Smokey picked up the slack and took his sister and her kids in. He eventually bought them a three bedroom brick home in an area of Houston called Scenic Woods. Jameisha's house sat off in a small cul-de-sac.

Smokey pulled his car into his sister's driveway and parked behind her forest green 2006 Toyota 4Runner. Before he could even reach the front door, the youngest of his two nephews, Booby, who was four, was running towards him at full speed. "Hey, Uncle James!" Booby yelled as he grabbed a hold of Smokey's legs.

"What's up, baby boy? Where ya brother at?" Smokey asked him.

"He's gone. But my mommy's home!" Booby said excitedly while leading Smokey into the house by his arm.

Jameisha was laying on the sofa in her living room watching television when Smokey walked in. She had on a long nightgown, and her hair was wrapped inside of a hand-sewn headscarf. When she saw her brother come into the room she said, "I talked to Goldstein. He said you were supposed to be getting out yesterday."

"I did."

"And you just now coming by here to see me?"

"I had something I had to take care of first."

"I bet you did. Probably that nasty ass bitch, Lucy Lu."

Smokey could only laugh. Jameisha knew him better than anybody. He quickly changed the subject by saying, "Jahzay hasn't called you, has she?"

"You know she did."

"You didn't tell her I was getting out, did you?"

"Do I look stupid or something? I told that bitch I haven't heard from you in a couple of weeks."

"Good. I got a cake baked for that bitch!"

"You gon' be back in jail messing with that girl. You should've listened to me when I told you that you can't turn a ho into a housewife."

"One thing I know, and two fa' sho', that bitch gon' get what's coming to her. And before I go back to jail, I'm going to hold court in the streets!"

"Whatever!"

Smokey walked out of the house and into the backyard where he kept his two pitbulls, Kujo and Rocky, chained up. The two dogs ran up to their master as he approached their makeshift doghouse. He pushed the house over a few feet, and the metal combination safe he had stashed underneath it came into view. He knelt down, and with a few turns of the numbered dial, the door to the safe was unlocked.

He opened it up, and the first thing he came across was a throwaway blue steel nine-millimeter Beretta with the serial numbers scratched off. He grabbed the gun along with an extra clip, and stuck it in the waistband of his Red Monkey jeans. Then he proceeded to pull out stack after stack of the money he had stashed inside the safe. When he reached a total of one-hundred thousand dollars, he locked the safe back and replaced the doghouse over it.

After kissing his sister and nephew goodbye, Smokey jumped back in his rental car and left their home, on his way to the 'hood. His right hand gripped the handle of the 9mm handgun in anticipation of what the night had in store.

The Lincoln's glove compartment held the information he would need to complete the first part of his plan. Smokey had worked out every angle right down to the smallest detail, and he promised himself that he would not let anything or anyone stop him from getting his revenge.

Chapter Ten

"The hell if you can't accept my credit card!" Jahzay shouted to the four-eyed woman sitting behind the desk at the Enterprise car rental office. The pudgy office manager responded by saying that Jahzay's card wasn't currently activated. Jahzay cursed the lady out before storming out of the building with a look of embarrassment on her face.

She could not believe her recent string of bad luck. First, she walked out of Sharpstown Mall after buying a new pair of boots, to find that Smokey's Denali was no longer where she'd parked it. She wasn't behind on the car notes, but she still called the dealership to make sure that they hadn't repossessed the truck by mistake. After ruling that out, she called the police department and filed a formal complaint with the auto theft division.

Then, after paying a Yellow Cab driver to take her to the rental car agency, she was turned down because of what appeared to be a problem with her credit card, one that she knew was active after using it just the day before.

She tapped her feet angrily against the curb as she stood outside of the Enterprise office, waiting for another cab to come and pick her up. Her phone started ringing inside of her purse, and she fumbled around inside to answer it. Without looking at the caller I.D. she answered the phone with an agitated, "What?"

"Damn, I take it you didn't get any dick last night!" Miko joked.

"I'm sorry, girl. You just don't know how messed up my day has been going."

"Where you at? I need to see you like yesterday!"

"I'm sitting up here waiting on a cab to come and get me so I can go and pick up my Acura from my mom's house."

"A cab? What happened to the truck?"

"It's a long story. But, anyway, I'm at the Enterprise rental car lot off the Loop."

"Stay right there, I'm on my way."

In no time, Miko's car could be seen pulling into the small parking lot. Jahzay was happy to see that she had finally took the heap of trash, formerly known as a "Bimmer", to the shop, and got a rental car.

When Jahzay got inside the Pontiac, she gave her homegirl a one-armed hug and started telling her about everything that had happened to her that day. When she was through talking, she took a deep breath and said, "So, what was it that you wanted to see me about?"

"I almost forgot in the midst of your tirade," Miko said playfully.

"I'm sorry. I'm just stressed the hell out!" Jahzay said apologetically.

"This is what I wanted to talk to you about," Miko said, tossing a Tylenol pill bottle at Jahzay.

Jahzay caught the bottle and said mockingly, "Let me guess. You got a headache *this big!*"

"Ha, ha. Just look inside it and save the jokes for amateur night at Jus' Joking."

Jahzay looked inside the pill bottle, and her eyes got as big as two half-dollars. She poured the contents out into her hand and said, "You done found Seven's stash or something?"

"Something."

"So what do you need me for? "

"I need you to help me sell 'em."

"That shouldn't be a problem. How many do you have?"

"About 500."

"That's it?"

"Thousand!"

"Oh shit! Are you serious?"

"I wish I wasn't," Miko said.

"I'm not even going to ask where you got 'em from, because if you wanted me to know, you would have told me by now."

You wouldn't believe me if I did tell you, Miko thought to herself as they drove to pick up Alize from school, and drop her off at Jahzay's parents home.

Afterwards, they grabbed a quick bite to eat from the Breakfast Klub, then started on their mission. Miko noticed that Jahzay hadn't said anything about Smokey the entire ride, and he was usually the main topic of conversation for her. She figured that they must have still been having problems and decided not to pry.

Jahzay's cell phone chirped while they were driving down Antoine Drive, and after speaking a few code words into the mouthpiece, she nodded and smiled at Miko. When she hung up, she said, "Here's what we're going to do. I've already been working Smoke's cell phone for him, so we can just go half on the licks until I run out, and I'll re-up from you instead of his connect."

"That sounds fine with me. How much was that for?"

"A thousand a piece. That leaves you with 499 to go!"

Miko followed Jahzay's directions and was led to a newly built apartment complex located off of Homestead Road. They pulled past the empty security booth and went to the rear of the huge complex. Jahzay told Miko to wait in the car and disappeared down one of the dark apartment

After a couple of hours and a few more stops, Miko had sold over five thousand pills, not including the ten thousand she sold to Jahzay at wholesale price. The initial nervousness Miko felt had went away, and was replaced by feelings of excitement as the thrill of hustling began to set in.

During a long period in which Smokey's phone wasn't ringing as much, Jahzay asked Miko to take her to see her "substitute dick", as she called him. Jahzay's brashness always amused Miko, and she secretly admired her love of life.

They traveled the forty-minute drive to the neighborhood of Sunnyside and pulled in front of a small brick home on Jutland Street. The occupants were throwing what appeared to be a party, and it was packed. All kinds of cars were lined up on both sides of the street, and people were standing around, smoking, drinking, and having a good time.

Jahzay hit the two-way chirp on her Nextel phone and said the words, "Come outside."

A minute later, Miko's mouth dropped to the floor as the familiar looking youngster came walking across the lawn towards their parked car. "I know you not fucking with that lil' boy?" Miko asked, though she already knew the answer to the question.

"Girl, he may be only 19, but trust me, he is far from a lil' boy, if you know what I mean," Jahzay said through a sly smile, while holding the index fingers of both her hands up to imitate a ruler.

"Smoke is going to kill you if he finds out," Miko stated matter-of-factly.

"He already knows about my lil' sponsor," Jahzay told her.

"I'm just saying, I don't think it's worth it, that's all," Miko mumbled

"That's what's wrong with these niggas now," Jahzay started. "They expect a bitch to not scratch their itch when they get locked up, knowing damn well if the shoe was on the other foot they will be out here fucking everything that moves. Hell, I'm not stupid. I knew Smoke had other bitches on the side, but I still stuck by his ass, and remained faithful might I add. But what did he do in return?"

"You already know two wrongs don't make a right!"

"I'm not saying that it's right. What I'm saying is that I held that nigga down and did everything that a real bitch is supposed to do while their man is in jail. I stayed up in visitation getting searched and degraded like I'm a criminal. His books stayed fat. And at the end of the day, I respected him to the fullest!"

Miko felt that her friend had a point, but she still couldn't see herself cheating on someone that she was in love with. Their conversation was broken up prematurely by light taps on the passenger window.

Jahzay rolled down her window and quickly reintroduced Miko to the skinny stranger standing outside their car by saying, "Miko, Lil' Rome. Lil' Rome, Miko."

"What's up with it?" Lil' Rome said before adding, "Y'all come inside fo' a minute and eat sumptin'. It's my man's b-day."

Miko refused at first, but was quickly persuaded by Jahzay to stay for "just a second". Besides, she was hungry after all that driving. They walked in behind Lil' Rome, and Miko whispered in Jahzay's ear, "He is cute," which brought giggles from both of them.

Inside the house, the party was crunk. Nearly everyone was jam-packed into the small living room, doing dances like the Two Step and the Pool Place to all the latest songs. Those that weren't dancing were in the kitchen playing dominoes and spades for money.

Lil' Rome introduced Miko and Jahzay to a few of the partygoers before making them both a big plate filled with all kinds of delicious looking finger foods. They were given cold drinks to wash their snacks down, and were seated on an empty couch in the den area of the home.

"Let's go in the back so I can beat that pussy up," Lil' Rome whispered into Jahzay's ear while kissing her neck and rubbing on her thigh.

"I think my friend is ready to go," Jahzay responded while nodding her head towards Miko, who was tapping her foot impatiently.

"I got just the person to keep her company!" Lil' Rome said as he got up from the sofa and ran out to the garage that was connected to the home. He came back shortly accompanied by a tall and handsome gentleman with a seemingly never-ending line of one hundred dollar bills safety pinned to his blue and white Coogi sweater. Lil' Rome formally introduced his companion as, "The birthday boy himself... Koran!"

Just then, Koran and Miko looked into each other's eyes and simultaneously said, "I believe we've already met."

That caused an awkward silence between the four of them, as Jahzay looked at her friend as if she had been holding out on her, and smiled. That's when Lil' Rome broke the silence by saying, "Say, boo, let's leave them alone so they can get acquainted, or should I say, *re*acquainted."

Jahzay and her guy friend left the room chuckling as Miko and Koran stared at each other nervously. That's when Koran said, "Well, aren't you going to wish me a happy birthday?"

Miko thought to herself that he didn't look a day over twenty-five. She said humorously, "I would pin some money on your shirt, but I don't think my dollar would match the rest."

"So how about a kiss instead?" Koran asked as he leaned forward to plant a kiss on Miko's lips. At the last minute she turned her head and his lips landed on her cheek. His frustration was written all over his face as he sighed and said, "Man, what's up with you? What is it you're afraid of?"

"What makes you figure that I'm afraid of something?" Miko replied in a sassy tone, making sure to roll her eyes for added affect.

Before Koran could answer her question, a Latina female with huge breasts approached him from the back and tapped him on the shoulder. Koran said, "Excuse me," before turning his attention to the gorgeous looking female. Their conversation was barely audible over the loud music coming from the home stereo speakers, but the female appeared to be visibly upset. All of the sudden, Miko saw her stick her palm out and read her lips as she mouthed the words, "I need some money."

Koran then reached into the pockets of his Coogi shorts and peeled off five one hundred dollar bills from a large stack of money. The Latina girl gave Miko a smug look before walking away to join her group of friends. The move pissed Miko off. She was never more ready to go than she was at that point.

Koran came back over to where she was standing and asked, "Now, where were we?"

"*We* were just finishing our conversation!" Miko said heatedly while walking off to go find Jahzay so they could leave.

Koran grabbed her arm as she tried to pass him and said, "At least let me explain."

"You're a grown man, and I'm not your woman, so you don't owe me any explanations. Besides, you obviously have your hands full."

"Look, that was just my baby's mother. We're not seeing each other. She needed some money to take our daughter somewhere, so I gave it to her. Simple as that."

"It's never that simple. Koran, you seem like a very nice guy, but I have enough issues already. I don't need to add any baby-mama drama!"

"I feel you. I guess I'll see you around then."

"I guess."

With that said, Miko walked off into the crowd in search of her friend.

Meanwhile, inside the tiny bathroom of the crowded house, the mirrors were fogged up from the heat that was escaping Jahzay and Lil' Rome's bodies. She was seated on the edge of the sink facing him with her legs spread out at a quarter to three. Lil' Rome stood between her thick thighs with his pants around his ankles and his dick deeply thrusted inside of her. Jahzay shrieked loudly as he pounded her soaking wet pussy with all of his nine inches, in between grunts and the routine, "Whose pussy is this?" questions.

Of course, Jahzay lied long enough to reach her second nut, after which Lil' Rome jerked wildly and came himself.

Jahzay quickly fixed her clothes and hair and walked out of the bathroom as if nothing had happened. Just as she was coming out, she bumped into an irritated looking Miko, whose first words to her were, "I'm ready to go!"

The two of them said their goodbyes and thank you's for the food, and quickly left the party. Back inside the car Jahzay said excitedly, "Girl, I got the scoop on that fine ass nigga, Koran!"

"I don't want to hear it," Miko replied curtly.

"Damn! What's wrong with you? Did his breath stink or something?" Jahzay joked.

Silence.

Jahzay continued, "Well, as it turns out, he is the leader of the Get Money Clique, which means he is papered up! I know Lil' Rome is playing with a brick or two, easily, and he gets his supply from Koran. Plus, the nigga only got one child. And, he's not with his baby's mama!"

So he wasn't lying after all, Miko thought to herself. She had to admit that the brother had it going on. And the moistness in her panties could attest to the fact that he was fine as hell. She started toying with the idea of maybe giving him a chance. After all, it had been a while since Seven's murder, and the only boyfriend she'd had since then was her "butterfly" and her "rabbit".

Jahzay was still running off at the mouth when Miko broke in and said, "Okay, I'm sold. Damn! You should have worked at a used car lot!"

Jahzay promised that she would get Koran's number for her the next time that she talked to Lil' Rome. Miko found herself smiling at the thought of finally being able to open up to another man. It was an emotion that she thought she would never be able to feel again.

Chapter Eleven

Koran's birthday house party didn't start to thin out until well past four a.m. And even then there were still guests hanging out in every room of the house, getting high and drinking. Koran had enjoyed himself amongst the company of his close family and friends, but that was just the pre-party compared to the affair he had planned for the weekend.

The next morning, he was scheduled to board a flight headed for Miami with a few of his crewmembers that were in his inner circle. He was having a big birthday bash at Club Vision that would be a ballers-only affair. He decided that he needed to get a few hours of rest before his plane departed, so he prepared to head home. He ran into Lil' Rome on his way out, and they exchanged back pounding hugs before Koran told him to hold it down while he was gone.

Lil' Rome watched as his big homie walked out of the house and burned off in his hoop, which in his case was a fully restored '69 Cutlass Supreme.

Lil' Rome had been sipping promethazine with codeine and sprite all night long, and was tired himself. He chunked the deuce to a few of his partners that were standing around outside in the driveway, then he hopped into his slab and headed out to his southwest side apartment. He crept into the gated complex slowly, after keying in his three digit security code. He was leaning so hard that he didn't even notice the headlights come out of nowhere from behind him. The trailing vehicle slipped through the sliding front gate right before it closed.

Lil' Rome parked his car underneath the cover of his designated parking space and hit his alarm, as he slowly struggled to get out of his car. He stumbled and nearly fell to the ground as he staggered between two parked vehicles. He then pulled down his pants and took a piss right in the middle of the parking lot. After relieving himself of some of the alcohol he'd consumed earlier that night, he managed to make the short walk up to the front door of his first floor apartment. He fumbled with the keys on his key-chain until he finally came across the one he was looking for. He inserted the key into the lock, and as soon as he opened the door, a heavy hand pushed him in the back, sending him flying to the carpeted floor of his apartment. During the fall, the small caliber handgun he had tucked into the waistband of his Evisu jeans came out and slid across the floor and out of his reach.

When he rolled over onto his back, the lights in his apartment came on, and he was staring down the barrel of a big, black handgun held by a masked gunman.

• • • • • •

Smokey's day had been eventful, to say the least. After leaving his sister's house, he headed back to his hotel room where he put the first part of his plan into effect. Once inside his room, he called all of his credit card companies and cancelled each and every one of them. Next, he went down to the nearest branch of his bank,

Wells Fargo, and transferred all monies, with the exception of one dollar, out of the account he shared with Jahzay. He placed the money into a private account that she knew nothing about. Then, using his Yukon Denali's On Star tracking system, he discovered the location of his truck.

On his way to retrieve it, he scooped up a local dopefiend from off of the corner near his 'hood, so he could drive it off for him. When they reached the mall, the dopefiend jumped inside the SUV and quickly burned off, using the extra keys Smokey had given him. After stashing the SUV in a friend's garage, Smokey gave the dopefiend twenty dollars and dropped him back off on the same corner where he'd picked him up. He knew that Jahzay would probably report the truck stolen, and he hoped that would work in his favor after he used it to pull off his next caper.

He spent the remainder of the day reading over the contents of the envelope his lawyer had left for him in the glove compartment.

When Smokey learned the first and last name of the dude Jahzay had cheated on him with, he paid Goldstein a lot of money to gather some information on him. What the lawyer came up with was more than worth the price he'd paid. Smokey had in his possession the address, phone numbers, criminal record, DMV files, and credit report of his intended victim.

When nightfall approached, Smokey decided it was time for plan B. He got dressed in the all black Adidas track suit he'd purchased earlier that day from a nearby outlet store. Then he grabbed his black beanie cap, black Isotoner gloves, and 9mm Beretta off of the nightstand next to the bed. He drove back across town to his homeboy's house where his Denali was parked, and switched vehicles before heading to the southwest side.

It was half past midnight when he arrived at the apartment complex, but the unforeseen obstacle of a code-accessed security gate threw a kink into his plans. He decided that he would have to improvise, so he backed into a narrow driveway directly across from the apartment entrance. He made up his mind that he would wait for Lil' Rome all night if he had to, and he nearly did. He was restless and getting antsy when he heard the sound of trunk rattling music quaking up the street. Smokey knew it had to be Lil' Rome, and indeed it was.

He slumped low in his seat and watched as Lil' Rome made a wide right turn, then a left as he pulled up to the access box. Smokey cranked up his engine and placed his truck in gear while Lil' Rome punched in his three digit code. In an instant, the motorized gate began to slide open, and Lil' Rome quickly went through it with Smokey right on his tail.

Lil' Rome pulled into an empty parking space, and Smokey continued past him before coming to a stop a few spaces down. Smokey then pulled his beanie cap down over his face to reveal the added feature of a ski mask, grabbed his gun, and jumped out of his vehicle. He spied on Lil' Rome as patiently and quietly as a sniper waiting to hit his target, from the moment Lil' Rome exited his car, to the piss he took, all the way up until he placed his key into the keyhole. At that very moment, Smokey jumped from the brick pillar he was hiding behind and shoved Lil' Rome to the floor inside of his apartment.

With blood in his eyes, Smokey peered down at his surprised victim. His outstretched hand tightly gripped the handle of the 15 shot Baretta, as his finger itched to pull the trigger.

Lil' Rome raised his hands in surrender and tried to plead with Smokey. "The work is in the hall closet behind the water heater! Just don't kill me, man! Please! You can take the keys to my slab or --"

"Shut the fuck up!" Smokey screamed before adding, "This ain't about no money, nigga!"

Smokey then took off his ski mask and shouted at Lil' Rome, "Look at me, muthafucka! Don't tell me you don't know who I am!"

Lil' Rome tried to place Smokey's face, but it wouldn't register. Finally, he gave up and said, "Man, you must have me mistaken. I have never seen you before in my life!"

"You sure? I mean my pictures are all over the house!"

"What house? Listen, man, I'm telling you, I don't know you!"

"But I bet you know my bitch, don't you? Oh, yeah, you should know her *real* well. After all, you are fucking her, ain't you?"

Lil' Rome was beginning to get scared. A simple robbery he could deal with, but what he was going through was on some other shit. He looked at Smokey and said coolly, "Say, my nigga, I fuck a lotta bitches, know'm sayin'? So if I messed around with ya chick, it was a mistake, man. I didn't know."

"That's no excuse, bitch ass nigga!" Smokey spat.

Lil' Rome was totally confused. He looked over to the shiny metal that was lying less than ten feet away and decided it was do or die. He tried to buy some time by saying. "If you just tell me her name, I'll let you know if what you heard is true, and we can get to the bottom of this misunderstanding, playa."

"Jahzay! Or did she have you call her Jazzy while you were fucking her?"

All Lil' Rome managed to say was, "Oh shit!"

Jahzay had told him that her dude would kill them both if he found out that they were seeing each other sexually. But what woman didn't say that when she was having an affair? Besides, according to her, her dude was supposed to be locked up in the County facing a possible life sentence for first degree murder. He felt he had no choice but to try and make a move for his gun. He rolled over and grabbed the rubber grip handle of his revolver, but Smokey had the drop on him before he could use it.

Lil' Rome screamed in pain as the first two bullets from Smokey's Beretta ripped through his jeans and tore into the back of his legs. The third shot narrowly missed his upper back, but the fourth and final shot connected with the back of Lil' Rome's skull and silenced his cries forever.

Thinking fast, Smokey went into the hall closet and found Lil' Rome's stash of a brick and a half of powder cocaine wrapped in cellophane. He poked a hole in the plastic using a car key, and sprinkled the white power throughout the small two-bedroom apartment. When he was finished, he replaced his ski mask and ran out of the apartment under the darkness of night. As he sped away from the scene in his truck, he thought to himself, *there's just one thing left to do.*

● ● ● ● ● ●

Jahzay rose early the next morning so she wouldn't be late to her eight o'clock doctor's appointment at the prenatal care clinic. She got dressed in a comfortable sweat suit and a pair of all-white K-Swiss tennis shoes. She combed her hair into a bun and placed her Christian Dior "Stunna Shades" on her face before heading out the door and jumping into her Acura.

She made it to her doctor's office at 7:45 a.m. Her visit went well and ended quickly, with the doctor giving her the usual precautionary advice that he gave to all pregnant women. She was entering her third trimester, yet the only indication that she was pregnant were widened hips, a voracious appetite, and ultra-sensitive nipples. Her belly had grown some, but she soon figured out that it wasn't anything that dark-colored clothing couldn't hide.

Jahzay couldn't wait to have her baby, and part of her nervousness was because she had become insecure about her figure and couldn't wait to return to her brick house form.

During the ride back to her duplex, she pulled the copies of her sonogram out of her purse and stared at them lovingly. She couldn't wait for Smokey to get off the trip he was on, so she could go see him and show him the black-and-white pictures of his son.

When she pulled up in front of her house, she grabbed her purse out of the backseat and strolled up to the front door to let herself in. She thought she'd seen a ghost when she looked up and saw Smokey sitting on their couch smoking a Newport cigarette. Something about his cold stare and icy demeanor didn't feel right, and the negative vibes she was getting made her flesh crawl. She was so startled by Smokey's appearance that she nervously stumbled over her words as she tried to talk.

"Baby, I – I didn't expect to see you here! You could have at least – I mean, why haven't you been... nothing."

Smokey didn't say a word in response. He just continued to smoke his cigarette and stare at Jahzay, almost as if he could see straight through her.

"Aren't you going to at least say something? You been out of jail for God knows how long, and you don't even seem happy to see me. It's like you're a total stranger or something!"

Silence.

Jahzay broke down crying as she continued, "I've been there for you every step of the way, and this is how you treat me? James, talk to me got-damn-it!"

Smokey put his cigarette out in an empty soda can that was sitting on the table and reached into his pocket. He took out a white envelope and tossed it onto the table. He nodded towards it, and leaned back in his seat.

Jahzay slowly walked over to the coffee table and got down on her knees. Using her thumbnail, she broke the seal on the envelope and poured the contents onto the glass top. Three small pictures fell face down on the table. As soon as she turned over the first photograph, her heart broke into a thousand pieces and a lump formed in her throat. She looked up at Smokey, who was crying silent tears, and with trembling lips she said, "Baby, I'm so sorry. I just wanted to hurt you like you hurt me!"

She didn't even bother to turn over the other two photos, partly because she was afraid of what she might see. The picture she held in her hand was very grainy, but there was no denying who it was in the photo. She was positive that Lil' Rome had taken them without her knowledge using a camera phone. The picture showed Jahzay lying in bed, naked.

"Baby, I swear to you," Jahzay continued, "I slipped just *one* time with *one* guy. You have to understand that I was lonely and vulnerable out here without you, and I needed to feel..."

"Go ahead, say it!" Smokey erupted. "Say how much you needed to feel a dick inside of you!"

"It's not just about dick! Look baby, I'm sorry, and I promise that it will never happen again. Please, just let me make it up to you."

"Oh, you're sorry now, huh? You wasn't sorry when you put dat nigga on the phone and disrespected me in my own house!"

"I know. I was trippin', baby. But that nigga don't mean shit to me. He was just a fuck. My heart belongs to you, Smoke."

"Did it feel good to you?"

"I made him wear a rubber, if that's what you're asking."

"Bitch, you let another nigga fuck you with my baby inside of you, and you think it's supposed to make me feel better because he wore a rubber?" Smokey punctuated his last words by exploding to his feet, and turning the coffee table over onto Jahzay. The glass top broke into pieces when it struck her, and the sharp edges left her with several cuts on her arms and face that were bleeding badly.

Smokey walked around the table like he was possessed, and pulled Jahzay up from the floor by her hair. He began to repeatedly punch her in the face with his free hand, while calling her several "bitches" and "ho's." He let her go, and Jahzay's limp body fell to the floor.

She drifted in and out of consciousness as Smokey kicked and stomped her body until she could feel her limbs snap and break under the pressure of his steel-toed Timberland boots. All she could hear was him screaming out, "How did it feel?" over and over gain. He kicked her in the side with all of his might, and Jahzay could feel a sharp pain forming in her stomach, and just like that she blacked out.

Smokey, exhausted from the beating he gave her, spit on Jahzay's bloodied and beaten body. Then he walked out of the house, leaving her for dead.

Chapter Twelve

"Hello!" a man's voice screamed into Miko's ear over the deafening music that was playing in the background.

"I'm sorry, I must have the wrong number." Miko replied.

Before she could hang up the cell phone, the deep voice commanded her to hold. She listened as the background noise was suddenly muted, and the guy with the sexy baritone came back to the line saying, "Now, what were you saying, lil' mama?"

"I was trying to reach a friend of mines, but I think I dialed the wrong number." Miko repeated.

"Who you looking for? Maybe I can help you," the guy replied.

"Koran."

"Why you just didn't say that at first? That's my mans. Hold on."

Miko could hear the stranger on the other end calling out Koran's name, and then the phone went completely quiet. After a much longer wait than Miko could stand, the familiar sound of Koran's voice came booming through the phone saying, "I honestly didn't expect to hear from you after last night."

Miko blushed and said, "How did you know this was me? I didn't give your friend my name when I called."

"When my lil' homie told me you wanted my number, I gave him the one to my business phone to make sure that I received your call. So, you are officially the first-and-only woman to ever get this number."

"I don't know whether that makes me special, or just another one of your business associates."

"Just look at it this way. I'm making it my business to make you feel special!"

"You sure do have a fly mouthpiece."

"And an expensive one, too!"

They talked and laughed non-stop for the next hour, and Miko found Koran to be both charming and humorous, and not to mention brutally honest. When she asked him if he was single, he replied by saying, "Very much so, but I'd be lying if I said I was celibate."

On the other hand, Miko presented Koran with a challenge. Plus, she was still somewhat innocent and hadn't been corrupted by the game, or so he thought.

Towards the end of their conversation, Miko asked him, "Where are you? I would like to spend some time with you if you're not too busy."

"I'm in Miami, celebrating my b-day," Koran answered her.

"Damn! You have a birthday every day!" she teased.

"It seems that way, huh?"

"'Well, that's too bad you're not in town, because I was looking forward to seeing you."

"What do you mean that's too bad? You still can see me!"

"You must plan on sending me a postcard with your picture on it."

"Ha-ha, very funny. But seriously, I plan on sending you a plane ticket, not a postcard."

Silence.

"You still there?" Koran asked.

"Yeah, I just... I don't know what to say."

"Say that you'll be on the next flight."

"Since you're willing to go through all that trouble just to see me, I can't help but to say yes. But I have to check something out first before I give you an answer."

"Well, just call me back when you take care of your business, okay? Bye."

Miko clicked the line over and made sure that both Ms. Nadine and Mrs. Brousard would be okay if she went out of town for the next couple of days. They both said that it would not be a problem. When she called to give Koran the good news, he told her that he had already made the reservations. He told her not to worry about packing any luggage, and gave her the flight information and departure times before hanging up the phone.

Miko was so excited she didn't know what to do. She called Jahzay's cell phone to give her the good news, but was met with a busy signal. With a little less than an hour to spare, she packed a small carry on bag with a few items she felt she would need. Then she headed out the door of her hotel room with a smile on her face.

She made it to Hobby Airport in south Houston a few minutes past six o'clock, and parked her rental before racing down the terminal to her boarding gate. She was just in the nick of time, as her flight was just about to take off. To her surprise, Koran had arranged to fly her in first class, which won him some extra points as far as she was concerned. She sipped on a small bottle of Seagram's Seven and watched a DVD during the short trip. Before she knew it, the pilot was announcing that they were about to land at Miami International Airport.

Miko grabbed her shoulder bag and exited the plane along with the other passengers. She tried calling Koran when she stepped out of the airport, but quickly hung up the phone after seeing that there was no need for that. Standing next to a stretched Navigator limo was a chauffeur holding a sign that read "MIKO" in bold letters. She couldn't help but smile at Koran's thoughtfulness. And she couldn't wait to tell him how much she appreciated him for everything.

She walked over to the curb and introduced herself to the chauffeur, who then escorted her to the rear of the limo. He opened the passenger door for her, and she was kind of disappointed when she saw that Koran wasn't inside. In an English accent, the limo driver said "Mr. Koran wishes for me to drop you at your suite so that you can prepare for the evening's events."

Miko nodded her head and climbed inside the spacious seating area. The Navigator was equipped with plush butter-soft leather seats, a mini bar, two flat panel televisions, a Bose audio system, and a moon roof to gaze at the stars. A bottle of Krug Rosé was already chilling on a bucket of ice, and two glass flutes were sitting next to it. Miko poured herself a glass of the tasty champagne and tried to imagine what kind of night Koran had planned for the two of them. One thing she knew was that she was prepared for the ride.

The driver pulled in front of one of the most lavish hotels in Miami. He walked around the limo and held the door open for her. She crawled out of the back with her bag in tow, and was given a card with the limo's car phone emblazoned on it.

"I assume you will call me when you're ready, Madame," the chauffeur said.

"Of course."

Miko walked inside the sprawling hotel lobby and was amazed at its beauty. She took a quick elevator ride up to her eighth floor suite, and found the room number that matched her key. She slid it into the slot and nearly fainted when she opened the door. Her room was unlike anything she'd seen, except for on television. It had a royal feel to it. She walked over to the bed, and an entire outfit was laid out across the bedspread. Sitting on a tray near the bed were various kinds of fresh fruits and nuts that were setup for her.

She walked over to a door that she thought was a closet, and turned the knob. The door opened to reveal not a closet, but another room that was identical to hers. *Adjoining rooms? Nice touch!* Miko thought to herself.

Miko closed the door back and walked into the bathroom area. Again, she was left almost breathless as she viewed the luxurious bathroom. There were an assortment of soaps, bath oils, lotions and candles positioned around the huge marble tiled Jacuzzi bathtub. She ran her a hot bubble bath and lit one of the scented candles that sat on the counter. She took off all of her clothes and stepped into the bath. It felt so good that she almost lost track of time.

Jumping out of the tub, she checked the time on her phone. It was well after 10 p.m. and she still had yet to get dressed.

Miko dried herself off, combed her hair out and applied a touch of eyeliner and lip gloss to her otherwise naturally beautiful face. Once she'd achieved her desired look, she walked back into the bedroom so she could get dressed. She admired Koran's taste in clothes as she lifted each article of clothing from the bed. She examined them thoroughly, running her fingers across the fabric. She slipped on the Frederick's of Hollywood bra and panty set first. Then she slid into the form-fitting beige Roberto Cavali dress with the open back. It fit her perfectly and felt velvety on her lotioned skin. The open toed four inch Charles Jordan pumps were comfortable, yet stylish, and they matched the designer handbag Koran had bought for her.

Next, Miko looked into a bag marked "Avianne & Co.", and pulled out three small jewelry boxes. The first one she opened contained a pair of sparkling emerald-cut earrings. She thought to herself that they had to be every bit of three carats or more. She was stunned when she pulled the stainless steel black face Movado watch from out of the second box. She could only guess what kind of surprise the last box held. The answer was a small platinum necklace and pendant. When she saw the iced out "K" initial hanging from the necklace, she smiled and said, "I know this nigga didn't!"

Miko was definitely impressed, and the night was still young. She checked herself out in the hotel mirror and nodded in approval. As a finishing touch, she sprayed on some of her "come fuck me" perfume. It had been sitting on her nightstand, untouched since Seven's death. With a sexy look and even sexier attitude, she called her limo driver and made her way downstairs to the hotel lobby.

●●●●●●

Koran was truly the man of the hour, and the night belonged exclusively to him. After making the necessary arrangements for Miko's arrival, he got ready for what he hoped would be one of his most memorable birthdays ever.

He was dressed in a dark beige sport blazer, a Ryan Kenny button up, Antik blue jeans and suede Gucci loafers that matched his coat. His accessories included his top and bottom custom grill, a Breitling Swiss Chrono, and platinum chain with the diamond flooded "G.M.C." piece. He looked like the million dollar man that he was.

Koran arrived at the club around ten o'clock. He was driven by chauffeur in his friend, Steve "Franchise" Francis' personally owned Phantom Rolls Royce. It was only right that he rolled "M-I-Yayo" style while he was in town celebrating.

The club was packed from wall-to-wall. Koran was escorted by the club bouncers past the throngs of club goers. He ended up in the upper level V.I.P. area among several of his peeps.

Indeed, all of the ballers had come out for the party, along with some of the finest women South Beach had to offer. A lot of Koran's celebrity friends and fellow hustlers stopped by his booth to wish him a happy birthday. From Trina and Jackie-O, to Pitbull and Dewayne Wade, everyone showed their love. D.J. Khaled even led the crowd in a hip-hop version of Stevie Wonder's, "Happy Birthday" song.

Koran's baby brother, Tariq was right by his side helping to celebrate the occasion. Tariq was also dressed to the nines. He was fitted in Louis Vuitton from head to toe, and the bling-bling he was wearing was blinding everyone who got close to him.

Also among the well wishers were a dozen half-dressed boppers. They were all competing for Koran's attention and hoping to be the one he woke up with the following morning. But Koran wasn't paying them any mind. He kept glancing at his watch and looking at the club entrance, which prompted his brother to say, "Man, that lil' broad got ya nose open wide enough to stash a ki in!"

Koran ignored Tariq's comment. He was beginning to think that Miko had changed her mind, when he spotted her. She seemed to glide through the doors of the club. He sent one of his mans down to escort her up to where they were. A few minutes later, she was walking towards his booth in the outfit he'd bought her. He thought she looked gorgeous with her hair pinned up, and her scent aroused him as they greeted each other with a warm embrace.

Miko took in every bit of Koran --the look of wanting in his eyes, his smell that seductively teased her nostrils and the bulge in his jeans. Without thinking twice, she stuck her tongue deep down into his mouth. She even surprised herself. She gave him a knowing look then pulled away from him toyingly. She could feel the daggers in her back. Every chick in the V.I.P was looking at her enviously and rolling their eyes, but Miko ignored their obvious jealously. She leaned over and whispered into Korans ear, "I hope you don't think I owe you something just because you bought me a few gifts!"

Koran smiled and replied slyly. "And I hope you don't think that just because I bought you a few gifts, you're going to get into my pants tonight!"

His remark caused Miko to burst out into laughter. She was falling for Koran so hard and so fast that it scared her. The last thing she needed was to relive the pain of losing another lover to the pitfalls of the game.

Koran, for his part, felt that all he needed in his life was a down ass chick behind him in order for him to take his game to the next level. And he felt like Miko was just right for the role. Little did she know, Koran had done his homework on her, and he was more than happy with the report that he'd gotten.

They popped the cork on a gold bottle of Ace of Spades, and the two of them toasted to their newfound friendship.

When the D.J. threw on the latest single by T. Pain, Koran and Miko simultaneously said, "That's my song!" They looked at each other awkwardly, then rushed off to the dance floor. Koran removed his jacket and started getting down. Miko secretly wondered if it was true that men who could dance were good in bed, because he was giving her a run for her money in the rhythm department.

They were both dripping with sweat by the time the D.J. decided to slow things down. Miko and Koran's bodies moved as one to the R&B ballads of K-Ci & JoJo, and Brian McNight. Koran's hands were gently resting on Miko's soft ass. They were doing more bumping and grinding than two-stepping. Their tongues explored each others mouths like they were both searching for a sweet hidden treasure.

Exhausted from all the standing, Koran led the way back to their booth. They hung around the club a couple more hours, drinking and talking. It was almost dawn when their eyelids got heavy and the party began to wind down. They left the club hand-in-hand and were driven back to the hotel in the Rolls Royce.

Miko and Koran walked through the hotel lobby in silence, and took the elevator up to their floor. Their minds were both filled with thoughts of the other, but they were both too afraid to speak out. They stopped at their room doors, which were just a couple feet apart, and stared at each other without moving.

Miko smiled at Koran and said, "You first."

"That's funny, I always thought that ladies were supposed to go first," he quipped.

"Okay. How about we go in together?"

"Together? Are you suggesting a nightcap?"

"No, silly. I didn't mean it like that. As much as I enjoyed myself tonight, and really hate for it to end, I don't think I'm ready for us to sleep together."

"Who said anything about sleeping?"

They both laughed out loud at Koran's humor. Then Miko said, "Boy, you are off da chain, for real! Bye, crazy!"

"Goodnight." Koran waved and entered into his suite, and Miko did the same.

Once inside her room, she turned on the radio and found a smooth jazz station. Then she undressed and ran herself a hot bubble bath. Sitting inside the huge circular hot tub, she recapped the night's events in her mind. She stroked her nipples between her thumb and index finger, imagining what Koran's hands felt like. Like Letoya Lucket, Miko was "torn" between her mind and her body. She didn't want to seem stuck up, nor, did she want to seem too easy. But, she had to admit that she was horny as hell. She stepped out of the tub and walked back into her bedroom more confused than ever.

Koran was lying awake on his king-sized mattress, staring at the ceiling. He had nothing on but a pair of silk boxers and an undershirt. He'd just finished taking a cold shower to relieve himself of the sexual tension he was feeling. Although, it was after 5 a.m., he found it impossible to sleep. Thoughts and images of Miko carrouselled in his mind. He tried to relax by smoking on some purple cush.

Halfway through his joint, he put it out and walked over to the two-inch door that separated him from the woman of his dreams. He leaned his forehead against the door as he contemplated opening it. After several minutes of mental tug-o-war, he said, "Fuck it!" and turned the knob. He was surprised when the door swung open. Miko was standing on the other side completely naked, with a look of desire in her eyes.

Chapter Thirteen

Miko awoke the next morning to a continental breakfast that had been delivered to her suite by room service. She was surprised to find that Koran was gone. *I know this nigga ain't leave me here by myself!* she thought to herself.

She slipped on the hotel issued wool bathrobe and ate a bite of French toast. Next, she got up to get herself together. That's when she saw the note that Koran had left her.

Miko,

I had to make a run. You were looking so beautiful in your sleep that I didn't want to wake you up. (Smile!) I'll be back around noon. Bye.

One love,
K.

Miko was on cloud 9 as she took a soothing bath. While doing her makeup in the bathroom mirror, she noticed the marks of passion that were placed around her bare breasts. They brought back memories of the previous night's lovemaking session. She touched herself as she replayed the scene back in her mind...

When the adjoining door opened and she saw Koran standing there, she was instantly turned on. He looked fine in his silk boxers, and had a wanting look in his eyes.

Miko was completely naked after taking a long hot bath. The beads of water were still glistening on her soft skin. Koran reached out and pulled her in close to him. They were chest to chest as he told her how badly he wanted to make love to her. She responded by saying, "Then show me. I want you to make me feel gooood!"

And that's exactly what he did. Koran carried her over to the edge of his bed, where he sat her down and fell to his knees in front of her. She opened her legs wide, allowing him access to her pearly gates. Miko rubbed his head as he rapidly flicked his tongue against her clit, awakening it from its slumber. The stimulating effect sent waves of electricity up her spine and caused her to emit sensual moans of passion.

Koran alternated between licks, soft bites and light kisses as he traced her pelvic area and moved up her flat stomach before making a pit stop at her navel. While he was doing that, his hands were rubbing and squeezing Miko's breasts. He pinched her erect nipples between his thumb and forefinger. The slight pain caused her to bite down on her bottom lip, but it felt so good that she yearned for more.

Koran laid Miko down on her back and positioned his mouth over her neck and started sucking and nibbling on her until she was squirming underneath him. During a long and passionate kiss, he inserted two fingers between her silky mounds of flesh and into her vagina. A gasp escaped her lips. She'd had all she could take. Her juices began to flow from her and all over his hand. He was turned on by how wet she was and couldn't wait to enter her. He quickly removed his boxers, but before he could mount her, Miko stopped him and said, "Wait! You gotta put on a rubber first!"

Koran respected her wishes, but he was frustrated because he'd forgotten to buy some condoms. But to his surprise, Miko walked into her room and came back with a Magnum in her hand. She smiled at him and joked, "I hope you can fit this!"

"Come here and find out," Koran replied, waving her towards him. He lay on his back, and Miko's eyes widened as she watched all eight inches of Koran's thick manhood stand at attention. She wondered if she could take all that he had to offer, but figured that she would find out soon enough.

Miko wrapped her left hand around the base of Koran's shaft and lowered her warm mouth over the tip, causing Koran's toes to curl. He hissed loudly and ran his hands through her hair as she went down on him. She tore the Magnum wrapper open with her teeth and rolled it down his erection.

Koran was glad that she stopped when she did, because he was about to blow his load prematurely. He wanted to make a good and lasting impression on her.

Miko straddled him, and slowly impaled herself down on top of him. She was so tight that it took her a minute to get all of him inside of her. But once she did, it was on. She started gyrating her hips like a belly dancer while contracting the muscles of her vagina.

It wasn't long before Koran took control by turning her over on her back and placing her legs over his shoulders. He drove into her with deep hard strokes to the tune of her saying, "Yes! Yes! Yes!"

With each thrust, Miko screamed. Her legs began to tremble and Koran knew it was time to go all out. He quickened his pace and increased his force until the headboard started knocking against the wall. The sheets were completely soaked as they came together, and snuggled up in each others arms in blissful silence. And that's exactly how they fell asleep.

●●●●●●

Koran opened his eyes at the crack of dawn and rolled out of bed, making sure he didn't wake Miko, who was still sleeping peacefully. He had some very important business to take care of that he couldn't put off. In the game, timing was everything. One second could be the difference between getting busted or getting away. So, as much as he wanted to stay cuddled up with Miko and sleep in, he just couldn't.

He used Miko's room to take a quick shower and get dressed. He threw on a Pelle Pelle outfit with all white Air Force Ones and a fitted cap. Then he wrote Miko a short note and made a couple of important calls before leaving. He stepped out of the hotel onto the street, where Tariq was waiting with one of G.M.C.'s top lieutenants, named Boohead.

The three of them climbed into a rented Mercedes-Benz G500 after exchanging pounds. Koran sat on the passenger side, with Tariq behind the wheel and Boohead in the back. He fired up the half a blunt that was sitting in the ashtray, and readied himself for what he knew was coming next... his brother's jokes.

Just as he expected, Tariq shot him a funny look and started his ribbing. "Damn, big bro! I ain't think you was gon' make it after lil' shawty drained all your energy last night!"

"You just mad cuz you had to break out your bottle of Jergens last night!" Koran jabbed back, bringing laughter from their homie sitting behind them.

"You know you taught me better than that! I ain't just have one chick last night, I had two!" Tariq boasted with a prideful smirk on his face.

Koran blew the hydro smoke out through his nostrils and said, "Yeah, I bet you did! Your left hand and your right one!"

They all had to laugh at Koran's fly comeback. They lit up another blunt and passed it back and forth between them while they rode through Miami, bumping a mix tape by hometown favorite, D.J. Khaled.

The scenery turned from one of exotic palm trees and beautiful beaches, to one of run down houses and boarded up projects, evidence that they had crossed the bridge and entered into the ghettoes of Dade County.

Their Benz jeep pulled into the parking lot of a small Cuban restaurant near the area of Little Havana. Tariq parked along side a black 600 series Mercedes-Benz, and Koran hopped out with the suitcase he'd brought with him. He climbed into the backseat of the 600 and said, *"Buenos dia,* Papi!"

"Bien. How has life been treating you since I last saw you, *Señor* Koran?" Papi greeted him, with a Cuban cigar hanging from his lips.

Carlos "Papi" Vasquez was an old school Cuban drug lord who looked like he'd just stepped off the set of "Miami Vice". He was an obese man who favored loud colored shirts, and always wore a fedora on his bald head.

He was given the title "El Scorpio", or "The Scorpion" because of the symbol that he always used to distinguish his product from other dealers.

El Scorpio had been Koran's drug connect for the past few years, ever since their chance meeting at a Latin nightclub on South Beach. Over time, they built a trusting business relationship that eventually reached a point where El Scorpio no longer even bothered to count Koran's money during their transactions. He was always trying to give Koran drugs on consignment, but Koran politely refused each time. He didn't want to jeopardize their relationship if something went wrong. El Scorpio both respected and admired Koran's business savvy, and he kept Koran happy by giving him work at the cheap price of just ten a ki'.

When Koran officially retired from the game a year prior, he tried to pass the connect down to his brother, but El Scorpio was adamant about not dealing with anyone but him. So since his retirement, Koran still had to act as a go-between in order for his crew to eat. He never touched anything himself, and he received a nice commission off of every kilo they sold.

"I can't complain," Koran said, answering El Scorpio's question.

"Can I offer you a cigar?" El Scorpio offered.

Koran didn't normally smoke tobacco, but he knew that it would have been perceived as disrespectful if he turned down what El Scorpio called, "The finest cigar in the world!" Especially when the person offering it was Cuban himself. Koran lit the cigar El Scorpio handed him and took a deep puff before they got down to business.

Koran passed his connect the suitcase containing one million dollars in U.S. currency. El Scorpio opened the suitcase and nodded in approval at the neatly stacked large bills. Then he tossed Koran a set of car keys and said, "Be safe, *mi amigo*. I'll see you soon, no?"

"*Si*." Koran said, then exited the Mercedes.

When he got back in the jeep, he gave the car keys to Boohead, who already knew what to do. He jumped out of the jeep and ran over to the Ford Bronco that was parked a couple of spaces over from them. The Bronco had specially made compartments throughout its frame that contained 100 kilos of almost pure powder cocaine. Boohead was responsible for driving the kilos back to Houston, where they would be dispersed between each crew member.

Tariq and Koran rolled out in the direction of the hotel. Tariq wanted to grab a bite to eat, but Koran didn't want to keep Miko waiting any longer than he had to. They made it back shortly, and after a brief elevator ride up to their floor, they parted ways.

●●●●●●

It was noontime when Koran walked through the door of his suite.

Miko had straightened up the bed and was sitting in one of the chairs in her room, polishing her toenails in her bra and panties. She looked up at a smiling Koran and said, "What's so funny?"

"Nothing. I was just thinking of all the faces you were making last night," Koran said, walking over to give her a kiss.

"Whatever! I wasn't the only one making some ugly faces last night!" Miko teased.

"Yeah, right! So, are you ready or what?"

"Ready? Ready for what? I know you don't expect me to go anywhere without any clothes to wear!"

"Oh, I almost forgot. Just throw on something and we can take care of that first."

Miko put on the House of Dereon jeans and blouse she'd worn on the plane ride out to Miami.

Koran had gotten the keys to the jeep from his brother, so after Miko got dressed, they were off to an afternoon of shopping, and an evening of wining and dining.

Their first stop was the mall, where Miko completely lost herself inside all of the specialty shops it had to offer. She left out of the mall with two armfuls of designer bags. Koran had told her to get whatever she wanted and not be bashful, so she did just that. She even picked out a few things for him using the Amex credit card he'd given her.

The two of them were exhausted by the time they were finished shopping --Miko from all the walking she'd done, and Koran from just watching her go. They'd also worked up an appetite. Koran had a lavish dinner planned, with a slice of Miko for dessert.

They drove back to their hotel to change into something more formal.

Koran stepped out of his suite wearing one of the outfits that Miko had picked out for him. He had on a wool Gucci sweater vest, a long sleeved button-up shirt, dress slacks, and winged tip Gucci shoes. His outfit was complimented by a simple stainless steel Hublot timepiece, a tumor sized pinky ring, platinum chain-link bracelet, and five carat studs in both earlobes. Miko was impressed by what she saw, and Koran was equally impressed when he laid his eyes on her.

With so many choices to choose from, it took Miko nearly thirty minutes just to decide what to wear. She eventually opted to go with a violet colored strapless blouse, a designer wrap around skirt that stopped just above her knees, and a pair of Marc Jacobs sandals with the matching purse. She fastened the clasp on the necklace Koran had given her, and put on the rest of her accessories. She made sure to dab her neck with a splash of her "come fuck me" perfume for good measure.

When she finally stepped out of her bathroom, Koran started clapping in mock celebration. She shot him a glance that said, "Fuck you!" and grabbed her purse. He complimented her on how classy she looked. Miko did the same, telling him, "You must've paid a fortune for your stylist!"

The reservations were already made for a table for two at the posh restaurant, Prime One Twelve. They arrived looking like a celebrity couple that had been together for years, walking arm-in-arm up to the maitre d'. After being escorted to their seats, they ordered a bottle of Rosé and toasted to a night they both hoped they would never forget.

They conversed casually over dinner, revealing things about themselves the other didn't know. They found that they had even more in common than they originally thought.

Miko couldn't remember having so much fun, not since the trip to New York she took with Seven before his death. In fact, she was constantly being reminded of Seven during her stay in Miami. She was truly happy that night. For a moment, she completely forgot about all of the problems that were waiting for her back home. She was daydreaming when Koran snapped her out of her trance saying, "How come you haven't asked me about what I do for a living?"

"Because I would rather not know. I'd prefer it if we kept that on a don't ask, don't tell basis," she answered him.

"Is there a reason why you feel that way?" he pried.

"Look, Seven, I--" she bit her tongue in mid-sentence, realizing that she'd just made the worst mistake a person could make while out on a date with a new lover.

Koran looked off and started stirring his drink in silence.

"I'm so sorry, Koran. I didn't mean to say that. It just slipped out. Oh God, I am so embarrassed!" Miko apologized sincerely.

"It's okay. Believe me, I understand. I was once in love too," Koran told her, signaling for the waiter to bring him their check. It was definitely time to go. He paid for the meal and they left the restaurant without saying another word to each other.

Koran drove straight back to their hotel with the jeep's stereo system on full blast. But even the loud music coming from the speakers could not drown out the many thoughts that were going through his mind. When they made it back to where they were staying, he made up an excuse about having to go see his brother on some business. He told her he'd be back to take her to the airport the following morning, then left without even giving her a hug or a kiss on the cheek.

Miko couldn't get to her room fast enough. She let herself in and ran straight to her bed, where she cried herself to sleep.

Bright and early the next morning, she heard a tapping sound coming from her door. When she answered the door, Koran's brother, Tariq, was standing there. He told her that Koran couldn't make it, so he was there to help her pack and make sure she got to the airport on time. She was upset with Koran for not showing up himself, but she understood why, and a part of her even felt like she deserved the treatment she was receiving.

On the way to the airport, Tariq spoke up saying, "You know, my brother is really feeling you."

"I don't know about that anymore, after what happened last night," Miko replied.

"He's funny like that, sometimes. But he'll come around. Trust me."

"How do *you* feel?"

"About what?"

"About me being with your brother."

"You have to understand, my brother sacrificed a lot to make sure that I was happy. Now, I just want to see him happy."

"And you think I make him happy?"

"Yeah, I do."

"Thank you. Will you please just talk to him for me?"

"I got ya. So don't trip."

Miko's chat with Tariq made her feel a whole lot better, and it showed as she boarded her flight back home with a smile on her face. She had no idea that her happiness would only be temporary. Jimmy Chan was waiting to steal it from her when she landed.

Chapter Fourteen

Miko's plane touched down on the runway of Hobby Airport, and she quickly departed in order to beat the rush at baggage claim. Once she retrieved all of her luggage, she found her car parked where she'd left it and took off out of the garage. She wanted to see her son, whom she missed dearly.

She stayed with Elijah Jr. and Ms. Nadine for several hours before leaving to go and check on her brother, Tai.

She arrived at Mrs. Brousard's apartment with gifts for Tai and Timmy from her trip down to Miami. As usual, Mrs. Brousard was cooking, and she demanded that Miko stay until she was finished so she could fix herself a plate of food to go. In the meantime, Miko entertained the two energy-filled boys by playing video games with them on the new PlayStation-3.

It was dark outside when Miko left Buckingham Projects en route to Jahzay's eastside duplex. On her way there, she dialed Jahzay's phone number several times, but each time it just rang and rang until the voicemail picked up. As she got ready to exit off of Interstate 10, she decided to try her phone one more time to make sure she wasn't making a blank trip. On the fifth ring, the line clicked and a voice that wasn't Jahzay's answered by saying, "Miko?"

"Yes. Is Jahzay around?" Miko asked.

"This is Mrs. Merchand, Jahzay's mother," Mrs. Merchand said between sniffles.

"Oh, hey, Mrs. Merchand, I didn't even recognize your voice. Are you sick or something?"

"Miko, it's bad!"

"What's bad, Mrs. Merchand?"

"Jahzay. Somebody... ah, my baby!"

Mrs. Merchand broke into tears over the phone. It would be another ten minutes before she regained her composure long enough for Miko to get the full story. Mrs. Merchand told her everything she knew, which was that Jahzay was found in her apartment unconscious and barely breathing. The EMS crew said that if they had not arrived when they did, she would have died from the excessive blood loss and blunt trauma she suffered. She had a severe concussion, and was in a coma up until the previous night. Even after all that, when the detectives investigating the attack questioned her, she denied knowing the attacker. But they concluded that whoever it was, it was someone that she knew.

Miko was crying by the time Mrs. Merchand finished, and she turned her car around immediately to go see her friend.

Jahzay was hospitalized at Hermann Memorial Hospital, in the medical center near downtown Houston. Miko made it there in no time and rushed inside to the visitor's desk. She got her pass and rode the elevators up to Jahzay's room on the fourth floor. Jahzay was initially admitted into the intensive care unit, but was later moved to a private room after her condition stabilized.

Miko knocked and let herself into the room quietly, thinking that Jahzay was probably asleep. She walked over to her friend's hospital bed and was surprised to see that her eyes were open.

Miko broke down crying at Jahzay's bedside from just looking at the state she was in. White bandages completely covered her face, leaving nothing but her eyes, nose and mouth exposed. She had tubes and cords running from her body, hooked up to different I.V.'s and machines. Several of her ribs and other extremities were broken, and she had nasty looking gashes covering her arms that were being held closed by countless stitches.

Jahzay looked at her friend, and her lips tried to form a weak smile. She said something, but Miko couldn't hear her because she could only emit a faint whisper. Miko leaned in closer so she could hear her, and Jahzay repeated, "I knew you would come."

"Of course, you did! I love you, sis!"

"How do I look?"

"You look like we are going to have to take a trip to the House of Brown when you get well!"

Jahzay tried to laugh, but Miko could tell that it hurt her to. She coughed hard then said, "Every time I ask about my baby, my mama and these doctors never answer me. They just tell me that I need to get some rest and focus on getting better."

"And they're right."

"Fuck that! I need you to be real with me, sis. Is my baby going to be, okay?"

Silence.

Miko was hoping Jahzay wouldn't ask her that question. Mrs. Merchand had already told her the bad news, and Miko promised not to tell Jahzay. Her loyalty to her friend eventually won out, and she grabbed Jahzay's hand and said, "Listen Jazzy, you will have a chance to have a lot more babies in the future."

Jahzay choked up and started crying, which made Miko start to cry too. For the next thirty minutes they both cried together.

A nurse stuck her head in the door and said that the doctors would be coming to run some more tests shortly, and that Miko would have to end her visit soon.

Knowing she would have to leave in the next few minutes, Miko got straight to the point without beating around the bush. She looked Jahzay dead in the eyes and asked sternly, "Who did this to you?"

Silence.

"I --I didn't get a good look at him," she lied unconvincingly.

"Don't give me that bullshit! I'm not leaving until you tell me!"

"You have to promise me that it will not leave this room."

"I can't promise you that. Why in the hell are you protecting this guy?"

"Because it was Smoke, that's why! There! Are you happy now?"

"Smoke? I thought Smoke was in jail!"

Jahzay saw the confused look on Miko's face, so she filled her in on the whole story. She told her that Smokey had been released from the County Jail somehow, and had showed up at their home the other day with a set of pictures of her naked that Lil' Rome had taken without her knowing.

Miko had to pick her jaw up from off the floor when Jahzay was through talking. Just then, the same nurse from before reappeared and told Miko that it was time for her to go. She kissed her friend on the lips, and they exchanged goodbyes. Miko promised to check on her real soon.

Back inside her car, Miko was stressing over the decision she would ultimately have to make. On one hand, she didn't want to betray her friend's trust by telling the police on her man. But, on the other hand, she felt like he should have to pay for what he did to her, one way or another. In fact, she planned to personally make sure that he did.

●●●●●●

Koran and Tariq returned back from their monthly trip to Miami, Florida, and were both happy to be back home. They had stayed down in the M.I.A. an extra day in order to give Boohead enough time to reach Houston before they got there.

The extra day of rest and relaxation proved to be just what Koran needed after what happened between him and Miko. That first night he was a little stressed out, but by the next day he'd regained his usual swagger. He noticed that his brother had been throwing in little hints about how good of a sister-in-law Miko would be. He wondered about that, but never said anything, because he figured that she had probably put him up to it. Either way, he knew that what his brother was saying had a ring of truth to it.

Back in Houston, they met up with Boohead at a predetermined location, which was a Waffle House. They only had a one block ride to go before they reached Tariq's stash house, so he eased out of the parking lot and into the light traffic, with Boohead in front of him.

As soon as they turned onto the street, a blue and white Houston Police cruiser whipped out behind them. The male officer driving the patrol car followed closely behind their truck, and when they made a right turn at the next intersection, he did also. Inside the tricked out Hummer, Koran and Tariq appeared to be unconcerned about the cop that was trailing them, as they smoked on a poorly rolled Swissher Sweet. They bobbed their heads to a screwed and chopped mix CD from D.J. Michael Watts of the Swissha House.

Tariq pulled in behind the Bronco in front of his stash house and hit the brakes as Koran opened the door on the passenger side of the Hummer. The police officer pulled along side their truck and came to a stop, so that his driver's side window was even with Koran's. Koran tossed a rolled up wad of one hundred dollar bills wrapped in a rubber band, into the patrol car and said, "Officer - excuse me - *Lieutenant* Schwartz, how's it going?"

Lt. Schwartz grabbed the large bankroll of money and put it in his pocket before saying, "I'm a lot better now. You boys have a nice day. And give me a holler if you need me."

Lt. Schwartz burned off, and Koran just smiled. He'd been in Koran's pocket for quite some time. A couple of years prior, he approached an associate of Koran's saying that he would offer police escorts and other "services" for the right fee. He was one of the most corrupt cops on the Houston Police force, and nearing the end of his career at 54 years old.

A twice-divorced functioning alcoholic with an expensive gambling habit, Lt. Schwartz was facing the possibility of losing his pension thanks to an ongoing internal affairs investigation. Allegations of police brutality and other violations embroiled his entire squad in a scandal that rocked the department. That, along with high alimony payments, left him in desperate need of some tax free cash, and it didn't matter where it came from.

Tariq parked his Hummer in the driveway of the modest three bedroom brick home he owned, but never stayed in.

Koran gave his brother a hug and told him that he would holler at him and Boohead later. Then he jumped inside of his Cutlass, which he'd parked there before they left for Miami. Before backing out of the driveway, he rolled down his window and said, "And by the way, you win. I'm going to call her!"

While he was still on the south side of town, he decided to holler at his people who lived in Sunnyside, where his party was held. As soon as he hit the corner of Jutland, he knew something was wrong. An eerie feeling suddenly came over him. Parked in front of his aunt's crib were a line of black on black GMC Suburban's with limo tint on the windows. He knew that could only mean one thing --it was time to ride.

The last time they rode out in the Suburban's, they left the home of a rival crew riddled with Ak-47 bullets. And that was over business. It got a lot worse when it was personal beef. Koran didn't know it then, but that's exactly what it was.

Koran found an empty spot to park his car in front of a neighbor's yard, and jumped out, running through his aunt's lawn and up to the front door. Inside the house, several GMC members were loading up handguns and assault rifles, and putting on bulletproof vests. When Koran came running through the front door, one of his crewmembers greeted him with a saddened look on his face.

"What is it, Gino?" Koran demanded impatiently.

"It's Lil' Rome, man!" Gino started. "Somebody robbed and killed him!"

The news of Lil' Rome's murder left Koran frozen in disbelief. Though Lil' Rome wasn't officially a part of the Get Money Clique, he was like an honorary member, because Koran had practically raised him when he was coming up in the game. Koran fell back on the arm of the sofa inside the living room and said, "I just seen that nigga, man! He can't be dead!"

Koran was trying to find a way to blame himself. He had fallen all the way back from the street side of the game, but Lil' Rome's murder would no doubt pull him back in. He had to avenge his man's death. If he didn't, his conscience would not allow him to sleep. He said to himself, *Don't worry, my nigga, I'm not gon' let your death be in vain, baby!*

Gino came up to Koran and told him that they'd already put the word out on the streets that there was a reward for information on whoever killed their partner. And, that they were ready to ride whenever they found out who it was.

Koran thanked him for his loyalty, and walked outside on the porch to get some fresh air. He was still in shock and needed something to take his mind off things. He knew the usual prescription of Hennessy and weed wouldn't be enough to stop him from feeling the way he was feeling, but he knew something that would.

Chapter Fifteen

Miko was having a hard time getting rid of the remaining XTC pills she had. Jahzay was still in the hospital, and her deadline was drawing closer and closer every single day that passed. She tried meeting dealers through some of the people that hung in and around the old projects she used to live in, but the ones she met only dealt in small quantities of a few hundred pills or so. She thought about calling Koran and asking him if he knew some people that might be interested in buying some, but she decided against it at the last minute. She was a little ashamed and did not want to involve him in that part of her life.

On top of her dilemma with Jimmy Chan, she was still faced with the situation concerning Smokey. She didn't know what she was going to do about that. She still had the number to his cell phone programmed into her phone, and on numerous occasions she'd thought about using it to set him up by luring him to some place secluded, where she could kill him. Those kind of thoughts scared Miko, because she was afraid of what she had become. Two years ago she wouldn't have ever even thought about killing someone, let alone actually doing it. But the circumstances in her life had changed her... hardened her. She reasoned that her actions were all justified, and that it wasn't something she wanted to do, but something that she had to do.

Miko was traveling down Cheeves Street in a northeast Houston neighborhood called Northwood Manor, when she received a call from an anonymous number. She pressed the send button and put the phone against her ear, using her shoulder to hold it in place. The caller on the line said, "Where are you? I need to see you!"

She was immediately excited to hear Koran's voice, but his tone really worried her. She told him that they could meet wherever he wanted to. He chose McGregor Park, off of Hwy 288, since he was just five minutes away from there, and it was close to Miko's hotel room at the Double Tree Inn.

Miko agreed and hung up the phone, wondering what was wrong with him that was making him act the way he was acting. The Koran she knew was always reserved, and never seemed to be out of control or rattled... except for when she called him Seven, of course.

When she pulled into the park, his car was already there, backed in a secluded spot. She quickly parked and got out of her car to join him. She opened his passenger side door and slid into the seat beside him. The scent of alcohol hit her nose instantly, and just by looking at Koran, she could tell that something very bad had happened.

He tried to pass her the blunt he was smoking, but Miko politely declined. He'd already heard that she didn't smoke, but he was just trying to see if his sources were correct.

Miko put a soft hand on Koran's cheek and said, "Tell me what's wrong. I can tell that something's bothering you."

A single tear rolled down Koran's cheek, and his outward show of emotion really touched Miko. For a man to openly cry in front of a woman said a lot about how he felt about her. Koran looked Miko directly in the eyes, cleared his throat and said, "I just found out that my homeboy got killed. He was like a lil' brother to me."

"Damn, baby!" Miko consoled him. "I'm so sorry to hear that."

"Me too."

"Is there anything I can do to make you feel better?"

"I'm starting to feel better already."

Koran's comment made Miko feel good inside. She missed Koran a lot, and couldn't wait for the chance to show him just how much. But first, she wanted to know exactly where they stood. She chose her words carefully before placing Koran's hand in hers and saying, "Koran, about the other night, I just want you to know that I'm really sorry."

"On the cool, that lil' incident had me fucked up at first, but I got over it. I just need to know one thing."

"What's that?"

"Do you think you will ever be able to fall in love with another man other than Seven?"

With tears welling up in her eyes, Miko replied," I think I already have!"

Koran leaned over and kissed her on the lips, and she responded by sticking her tongue deep into his mouth. They continued on like that nonstop for over a minute, until they were distracted by the sound of Miko's ringing cell phone. She reluctantly released her lip-lock and answered her phone with an agitated, "Hello!"

The caller on the other end was a guy that she'd met earlier, through a mutual friend. He was interested in buying one thousand XTC pills. After a few "uh-huh's" and "okays", Miko quickly hung up the phone so she would not make Koran suspicious. That's why she was caught off guard when he casually asked her, "So what was that all about?"

"Nothing. Why do you ask?"

"Because you seem to be a little tense all of the sudden."

"That was just my, ah, babysitter. I have to run and check on my son."

Koran looked at her questionably and hunched his shoulders. Miko felt bad after lying to him, and she didn't want their relationship to start off that way. He'd been completely forthcoming and honest with her from the very beginning, and she told herself he deserved the same from her. She decided to come clean so that they could build up their trust in each other. She stared down at the floor in shame and said, "Koran, I can't lie to you. That wasn't my babysitter."

"So, who was it?" Koran asked curiously.

Miko went on to tell him the whole story from the very beginning. How she was forced into selling XTC by Jimmy Chan in order to pay off Seven's debt to him, and protect her loved ones. She made sure she didn't leave out any detail while she explained the circumstances she was facing. She finished her story by saying, "So, that's what the call was about. This guy I know wants to meet up to buy some pills from me."

"That's crazy!" Koran said with a stunned expression on his face. "There has to be another way to get you out of this mess."

"I've thought of everything I could think of. But I don't see another way out."

"Fuck that! I can't have my woman out here selling no got-damn drugs! I promise, I'm not going to let anything bad happen to you!"

"I believe you." And she did. Miko felt comforted and protected in Koran's presence.

Koran, for his part, was not going to sit back and let some so-called gangster extort his woman and not do anything about it. Two million dollars was no small amount of money by far, but he would come up with it if it meant saving Miko from any danger. However, he had a problem with paying it under the circumstances. First of all, Miko didn't have anything to do with Seven's business dealings, nor did she have any knowledge of them. As far as he knew, this guy could be lying just to prey upon a defenseless woman.

And if he did allow Miko to, "work it off", as she'd put it, when would that end? Jimmy Chan could continue to use her up for God knows how long, and there was still no guarantee that he would be satisfied with her efforts. Besides, XTC wasn't Koran's game, so he would even have trouble getting rid of them himself. He would have to figure out what to do, and soon, according to Miko. She'd informed him that her time was running out.

Miko interrupted his thoughts by kissing him passionately around his ear and neck, causing his nature to rise. She palmed his budge in her hand, and in a sexy voice whispered, "You know my hotel room is just five minutes away from here."

Koran got the message, and in the next minute he was following behind her rental car as she led him down South Post Oak Blvd. to her hotel. They made it there in no time.

Once they were inside, Koran was all over Miko, eagerly ripping away at her blouse and pulling off her Miss Sixty jeans. Her fingers fumbled to undo the buttons of his pants. He kicked off his shoes and tossed his shirt to the floor as Miko undid her bra strap with one hand and tore off his boxers with her other one. In less than thirty seconds, they were both naked and engaging in a round of mind blowing foreplay.

Miko quickly grew tired of the teasing and petting, and commanded Koran to make love to her. He catered to her wishes by pushing himself deep inside of her as far as he could go with one long stroke. They had sex for the next two hours, in almost every sexual position imaginable. Koran was panting like a wild man. He went for three rounds, and sent Miko to multiple orgasms. When they were finally spent, all Miko could say was, "You're a beast!"

They cuddled up together underneath the hotel's thick blankets after their tiresome lovemaking session. Koran was caressing Miko's back while she used her index finger to trace the muscles of his six-pack. She enjoyed their intimacy, and she didn't want it to end. For Koran, Miko was even better than he'd imagined in bed and everything he ever wanted in a woman… even if she came with two million dollars worth of baggage.

In the middle of their slumber, Koran's phone startled them awake. It chirped loudly on the belt clip attached to his pants. He lazily eased out from under the bedspread to answer it, just in case it was an important call. When he reached it, he flipped it open and said, "Yeah," after placing it against his ear.

The muffled voice coming from the speaker of the phone must have been saying something very important, because Miko noticed Koran's posture and demeanor totally change. He sat upright and alert as he listened closely to the caller, with a serious expression on his face. Miko eavesdropped on the call as he began to speak.

"I don't care what you have to do, I need you to find that nigga and handle it!"

Pause.

"Holla at me when you do, 'cause I wanna personally be there to see that nigga get what he got coming to him!"

There was another long pause before Koran ended the conversation with, "He fucked with the wrong one this time!"

Koran hung up the phone and stared off into space. The caller was one of his G.M.C. crewmembers, informing him that they'd gotten word back on who killed Lil' Rome. As it turned out, one of Lil' Rome's homeboys was in the County Jail with a guy that they called "Smoke", whose real name was James Roberts. This homeboy of Rome's said that he and Smoke had gotten into a fight after Smoke saw his girlfriend on some pictures that Lil' Rome had sent him. He wasn't sure, but he vaguely recalled that Smoke had mentioned that the chick's name was Jazzy. Smoke had told him that he was going to "kill her and that nigga". It looked like he had made good on his word.

That was all they knew at the moment, but Koran was assured by his man that they were looking for him as they spoke. The name "Jazzy" rang a bell in Koran's mind, but he couldn't place a face with the name. (That was because Lil' Rome had introduced Jazzy to him as "Jahzay".) And besides, Lil' Rome had several boppers that he kicked it with on different occasions.

The fact that his partner had died over some pussy pissed Koran off even more than he already was. He kind of figured that there was more to it than just a simple robbery homicide, mainly because he still had his slab parked outside, a pocket full of cash, and all of his jewelry on him when his body was found.

He sat on the edge of the bed, and Miko crawled up behind him on her knees and started massaging his shoulders. "What was that all about, baby?" she asked him.

"We got an idea who killed my lil' kinfolk. Some nigga name Smoke or Smokey, or something like that, was supposedly plexin' with him over some bopper!"

Miko couldn't believe her ears. That was the last thing she expected to hear Koran say. Up until then, she hadn't even made the connection. She was wondering whether or not she should let Koran know that she knew Smokey, and more importantly, how to find him. If Jahzay were to find out that she played a part in getting her man killed, she would never forgive her. But if Koran found out that she was withholding information that could help him in anyway, he would probably leave her. She was in a lose-lose situation no matter what she did.

"Why are you looking like that?" Koran asked her.

"Oh, it's nothing, I just don't want you to do anything crazy that might come back to haunt you, that's all."

"Trust me, I'm not going to put myself in a position that would lead to something happening to take me away from you."

"Is that a promise?"

"Baby, I'm going to be with you forever!"

There it was again, the word she had come to hate ever since Seven's murder. It was like a jinx to even use it, because after all, nothing really lasted forever. As soon as Koran said it, she began to worry.

He said that he had to leave to meet up with his people, and started to get dressed in a hurry. She wanted to stop him and demand him to stay there with her. With his clothes back on, he blew her a kiss and told her that he would call her later on that night.

As he started out of the door, Miko called out to him. He turned around quickly, but instead of telling him what she really wanted to tell him, all she said was, "Be careful."

"I will," he replied, and walked out of the door, leaving Miko alone and in tears.

Part Three

Chapter Sixteen

Paid In Full

Smokey revved up the engine of his rented Lincoln Town Car and put it in drive as he exited the parking garage connected to his hotel. He'd arranged to meet his lawyer at Houston's restaurant for lunch, so he could discuss the details of his case and pay the money he owed him. Inside the trunk of his car, Smokey had sixty-five grand wrapped in some dirty laundry. Goldstein didn't care where the money came from, as long as it came, and came on time.

Smokey had a lot on his mind as he raced through the afternoon traffic. He felt no remorse for what he'd done to Jahzay, but he did regret not finishing the job like he'd initially planned to. He wondered whether or not she would tell the police who attacked her. The prospect of going back to jail for violating his bond unnerved him.

But he didn't have to worry about that as far as her lover was concerned. Smokey made sure that he was dead, and covered every base he could think of to insure that the murder would not be linked back to him. On top of making the murder look drug-related by leaving behind the cocaine, he tore up the steering wheel column of his truck before dumping it near a bayou and setting it afire.

The pictures he had of Lil' Rome and Jahzay together were also destroyed by fire, so he appeared to have gotten away scot-free.

Another thing that was bothering him was his diminishing stash of cash. In less than a week, he had already run through nearly eighty thousand dollars, counting his lawyer's take, and he had yet to reestablish his connects in the dope game so he could get back on his grind. For the most part, none of his old clientele even knew that he was back on the blacktop, but he was sure that things would quickly return to normal once they all found out. He made up his mind that the first thing he would do after meeting with Goldstein would be to make a few important calls and show his face on the scene.

Smokey's home safe contained what looked to be somewhere in the area of ten thousand XTC pills, plus some cash, which he stashed away inside of his hotel room. He reasoned that that would be enough to start off with before he had to re-up from his supplier.

Last but not least, the thought of how much time he was facing was steadily gnawing at his psyche. He was possibly looking at life without the chance of parole just for the two murders of Bernard "Binky" Holmes and his associate, Corey Fields. Not to mention the fact that they hadn't even brought up charges against him for the third person he'd killed that fateful night. He was sure that if they did, he would be laying on a gurney at the Polunsky Unit in Huntsville, Texas with a needle in his arm in a few years. For Smokey, that last scenario was not an option. Neither was rotting away in a cold prison cell for the rest of his natural life. He told himself that before he allowed that to happen, he would blow trial altogether and do like the Taco Bell commercial says and "Run for the border!"

Goldstein's shiny Mercedes-Benz was already parked outside of Houston's when Smokey arrived there shortly after noon. After entering inside, Smokey spotted his money-hungry attorney chewing on a cigar in a rear corner of the restaurant. He walked over to take a seat.

"Mr. Roberts!" Goldstein exclaimed as Smokey pulled up one of the soft cushion chairs.

"Talk to me quick, not slick, 'cause I ain't got all day," Smokey said matter-of-factly.

"First things first. Did you bring the money?"

"How could I forget? You've left a thousand and one messages on my voice mail. But yeah, it's outside in the car."

"What about the other *issue* I asked you about?"

Smokey reached inside of his pants pockets and pulled out a plastic bag filled with 28 grams of cocaine. He waved the bag in front of Goldstein's face like a hypnotist would wave a watch in front of one of his subjects.

Goldstein snatched the plastic bag from out of Smokey's hand and looked around nervously, hoping that no one inside the eatery had seen the exchange.

Smokey laughed out loud and said, "You should've seen the look on your face! You was scared to death!"

A red-faced Goldstein said, "Ha-ha, very freakin' funny! Anyway, now that that's taken care of, let's get down to business."

"Okay, shoot."

"Look, James --can I call you James?"

"You just did. But don't make it a habit, because you don't know me like dat!"

"Sure. But, as I was saying, they want to prosecute this thing as soon as possible, which usually means that they are confident that they have a pretty strong case."

"So get it reset. I need time to get my money right, so I can have something to fight with."

"In that case, I'm going to need another $25,000 to get you a continuance."

"What?"

"Calm down, calm down! I'm talking about pushing this thing back for another year, at least. Either that, or you can take a plea. And I can't guarantee that you will like what they have to offer."

Silence.

"Let me think about it," Smokey said, pushing away from the table.

"Aren't you going to order something to eat before you leave?" Goldstein asked.

"I'm still trying to digest the bullshit you just got through feeding me!" Smokey replied. "Come get your money before I change my mind about paying you!"

On the way to his room, Smokey was still fuming from the conversation he'd had with his attorney. He tried to block it out of his mind and focus on what he needed to do to get some money, because he was going to need it for what he planned to do. Once he reached his room, he grabbed his business phone that he'd left with Jahzay, and grabbed the large Ziplock bag that contained the XTC pills he'd retrieved from his safe. As soon as he turned on his cell phone it buzzed to life, prompting him to quickly answer it. In less than a minute, he'd arranged to meet the caller at his pager and cell phone shop.

When it was time for him to call his connect, he did so while waiting in the drive thru of an area Jack-N-The-Box fast food joint. He met up with his connect, a nerdy looking white dude named, Tweaker, later on that night. He copped another twenty thousand tabs for a cool sixty grand. Tweaker even threw in an ounce of hydro as an added bonus.

While rolling a Backwood and steering with his knees, Smokey looked out of the corner of his eyes and saw a group of guys he knew from around the way. They were chilling at the detail shop as he passed. He put his car into reverse and backed into an empty car wash stall and got out. He lit up his hydro laced cigar and walked over to the group of guys, who acknowledged him with pounds.

One of the guys named Ron G., from the neighboring 'hood of Fifth Ward, spoke first. "Man, I ain't expect to see ya face around here with all the niggas that are looking for you," he said.

"What the fuck a nigga looking for me, fo'?" Smokey asked.

"You ain't heard? Them G.M.C. boys got twenty stacks on ya head. But only you know what fo'."

"G.M.C.? You talkin' 'bout what's his name's crew, ah... Koran?"

"Yeah. Them niggas been comin' through here in black Suburban's with tinted windows and shit. What's da dillio?"

"Good looking, mane. 'Preciate it."

Smokey passed the Backwood to the group of guys after two more puffs, and mashed out. The idea that somebody as thorough as Koran was looking for him had him shook, and he tried to figure out what it was all about. He wondered if Jahzay had something to do with it, but he quickly dismissed that thought. After going over scenario after scenario, it finally hit him. It had to have something to do with the dude he'd killed.

He took the shortcut back to his sister's house to get his vest and more artillery, because he was almost sure that he would need it.

●●●●●●

Smokey snorted another line of cocaine from off of the small mirror that he held in his hand. He had never tried cocaine before the previous night, when Lucy Lu persuaded him to try it with her. She suggested that it would help ease his worries and make him last longer in bed, so he thought, *What the hell, one time won't hurt.*

But what Smokey didn't know was that the feeling he would feel would prove to be too good for him to try just once. And Lucy Lu was right, it not only helped to ease his worries, it completely erased them. In fact, it made him feel as invincible as Tony Montana standing at the top of his balcony with a submachine gun in his hands.

It had been three days since Smokey had learned about the plot Koran had to take his life. He immediately went into hiding. He hadn't sold not one pill since meeting up with his connect. He quickly got bored being holed up inside of his hotel room, and decided to send a cab to pick up Lucy Lu on the second day of his self-imposed exile. She jumped at the chance to spend some time with Smokey, and showed him just how excited she was to see him by dropping to her knees as soon as the door was closed behind her.

For the next day and a half, all they did was fuck, get high, eat pizza, and fuck some more. Unfortunately for Smokey, the sex got old quick, and when the powder was gone, he had to have some more. He looked over at Lucy Lu with contempt and asked, "Why didn't you bring more than this lil' shit?"

"Because I didn't expect you to snort up all my shit, that's why!" she shot back.

Whack!

Smokey slapped her across the cheek so hard that the entire left side of her face turned bright red and stung like hell. She started crying as he yelled out, "Bitch, don't you ever get out of line with me, again!"

Reaching for his cell phone, he called his mans who he'd scored the ounce of powder from for Goldstein, but was unable to get him. "Shit!" he said before asking Lucy Lu, "Where can we get some powder from this late?"

She told him she knew a spot on the south side, and asked to use his phone. For some strange reason, she walked away, turning her back to him while mumbling something into the phone, but, Smokey thought nothing of it. She turned around and said to him, "It's all set."

It didn't take long for them to make it to the spot Lucy Lu directed him to. He pulled the Lincoln into the driveway of a home in Hiram Clarke, and using Smokey's phone, Lucy Lu dialed a number and said, "We're here."

Smokey couldn't wait to feel the rush of the cocaine. He was snapped out of his thoughts by the sound of screeching tires as a black GMC Suburban came to an abrupt stop right behind him, blocking his car in the driveway.

"You bitch!" Smokey screamed, placing the barrel of his 9mm up to the side of Lucy Lu's head and squeezing the trigger. She was shot while trying to exit through the passenger side door. Blood splattered all over the car's exterior as her body fell out of the seat and onto the pavement below.

At the same time, two masked men were jumping out of the Suburban's side doors, firing assault rifles at Smokey's vehicle. Glass and sparks were flying everywhere as the AK-47 bullets tore into the frame of the Lincoln Town Car.

Smokey ducked down deep into his seat, threw the car in reverse, and backed up blindly into the black Suburban. He ran over one of the gunmen in the process. The force from the collision nearly knocked the entire rear bumper off of the Lincoln Town Car, and caused Smokey to bump his head into the steering wheel, opening a deep gash across his forehead.

The other gunman quickly got back to his feet after jumping to the ground in order to avoid being hit. He lifted his AK-47 up in a firing position, but Smokey beat him to the draw. Pointing his pistol out of the open passenger side door, he emptied his clip into his target's body. Smokey had been shot once before, and he refused to go through that experience again, so when the driver of the Suburban pointed his handgun out of the driver's side window, Smokey quickly threw his car into gear and sped off.

The Suburban gave chase behind him. Smokey hoped that he wouldn't turn down a dead end, being that he was unfamiliar with the streets in that neighborhood. The back fender of his car was rubbing against his rear tires, but he refused to slow down, because that could mean his death. His heart was pumping fast as the adrenaline rushed through his veins.

The driver of the Suburban continued to fire wild shots at Smokey's vehicle in an attempt to shoot out one of the back tires, but luckily for Smokey, he could not get a good aim and steer the large SUV at the same time.

Smokey knew that the game of cat and mouse would eventually have to end. He had to make his move, and make it fast. He hit the next block going fifty miles per hour, with the Suburban right on his heels. When he rounded the corner, he cracked his driver's side door and threw on the Lincoln's emergency brake, while simultaneously jumping from the car. He hit the ground hard and rolled over fifteen feet as the Suburban rounded the corner and slammed into his car, creating a fiery mushroom cloud that lit up the night sky.

Smokey was badly bruised from his fall, but he was happy to be alive, unlike the driver of the Suburban and his two partners.

After taking countless pain-filled steps, Smokey reached the corner of Fuqua and Almeda. He spotted a young white woman getting out of her car at a Chevron Gas Station. He ran up on the unsuspecting girl and flashed the empty 9mm while placing a finger to his lips to signal for her to remain quiet. She followed his instructions, and smartly handed over the keys to her red Dodge Neon.

Smokey hit Highway 288 as fast as he could, knowing that the lady would run right into the gas station and report what happened. He mashed the gas and headed straight back to his hotel room to regroup. The game had suddenly changed, and he had to start playing for keeps.

Chapter Seventeen

"Damnit!" Koran screamed into the phone before tossing it into a corner and collapsing into one of his plush office chairs. The call he received was from his brother, Tariq, informing him that they'd just lost three of their best soldiers the night before. And on top of that, Smokey still managed to get away. Just when Koran thought nothing else could go wrong, it did.

He felt responsible for the lives that were lost, and their blood would forever be on his conscience. But just like his homeboy Lil' Rome, he vowed that their deaths would not be in vain. But his revenge would have to wait. His first order of business was to take care of the Jimmy Chan issue.

Koran had picked up the remainder of the pills from Miko the day before. He planned to give them back to Jimmy Chan in hopes that an agreement could be reached between the two of them. His fingers traced the business card he held in his hand with Jimmy Chan's phone number on it. Miko had given it to him reluctantly after he told her about his plan to solve their problems. She knew it was easier said than done.

Koran picked up his black cordless office phone and dialed the seven digit number attached to the New York area code. A recorded message began playing after two rings, and Koran left a message after the beep. He explained that he was a friend of Miko's who had something that belonged to him. He left his name and number on the answering machine, and hung up the phone.

Not even a minute had passed before Koran's phone began to ring. "Hello," Koran spoke into the receiver after pressing the call button.

"Yes, I believe you have something of importance you would like to discuss with me," Jimmy Chan said in a businesslike manner.

"That's correct. But I don't like to discuss business over the phone. Give me a time and a place where we can meet up and talk."

Jimmy Chan complied by giving Koran the location of a Japanese eatery near midtown. They set the meeting time for five o'clock that evening, and they both assured each other that they would not be even a minute late.

Koran's next call was to his brother, Tariq, and his head of security, D-Bo. He put them both up on game as to what was going on, and told them to meet him there. Everything was set, and Koran hoped the meeting would go smoothly. If not, he planned to be more than prepared for anything that was thrown his way.

Koran's platinum Range Rover HSE pulled into the parking lot of Miyako's, off of Kirby Drive, at fifteen minutes to five. Seconds later, Tariq pulled in behind him in his Hummer, with D-Bo riding shotgun. Koran exited his SUV carrying a suitcase in his hands. He was dressed in all black Sean John coveralls and a pair of Timbs.

Tariq and D-Bo jumped out of their ride and followed Koran through the stained glass doors of the restaurant. Their oversized LRG hoodies concealed their bulging waistlines.

Once inside, the three of them were ushered into an enclosed seating area that was sectioned off by a thick curtain. The small establishment was completely deserted, which struck Koran as being odd since it was approaching happy hour. Their beautiful Japanese escort bowed gracefully then excused herself from the gentlemen's presence.

Koran pulled back the curtain to find a middle-aged Asian man seated Indian style at what appeared to be a table with no legs. He was flanked by two stiff-looking bodyguards who stood with their arms folded. They were all dressed like they were on their way to a funeral. Koran thought, *At least they won't have to change clothes if it goes down!*

"Mr. Koran, I presume?" Jimmy Chan said after swallowing a bite of food.

"Your presumption is correct. And you must be Jimmy Chan," Koran responded.

"That would be me. Please, have a seat. The sushi here is the best in the city."

"No disrespect, but the only thing I eat raw is pussy!"

"Very well then. What is it that you have of mine?"

Koran threw the suitcase to one of Jimmy Chan's bodyguards, who anxiously opened it expecting to see stacks of money. Instead, all he saw were thousands of XTC pills sealed in Ziploc bags. He said something to Jimmy Chan in Vietnamese, which caused him to give Koran a chilling stare.

"Is this some sort of joke?" Jimmy Chan asked with a confused expression.

"You don't see me smiling, do you?" Koran stated coldly.

"There must be a misunderstanding. You see, these no longer belong to me. They are the property of Mrs. Harris."

"That's where you're wrong, potna! You're gonna have to find somebody else to sell ya drugs for you."

The entire room got quiet. All of the sudden, Jimmy Chan reached inside of his jacket pocket and nearly set off a shootout. In the blink of an eye, Tariq and D-Bo had their guns drawn and aimed at Jimmy Chan's two henchmen, who also had drawn their own weapons and taken aim.

The tension from the standoff was eased when Jimmy Chan slowly pulled his hand out of his pocket and produced a 14kt gold case. He waved the case like a white flag before opening it and pulling out one of the Marlboro 100's it contained. He lit the cigarette, took a puff, then said, "You are making a grave mistake, Mr. Koran."

"Anything she owed you is now *my* responsibility, and I plan to pay you in full. And in cash, ya feel me?"

Silence.

"I'm going to start by paying you a down payment of $250,000," Koran added, pulling up his shirt to reveal two leather money belts crisscrossing his torso.

Tariq looked at his brother like he was crazy. He had never had any pussy that he felt was worth that much in his entire life. But if it was what Koran wanted, then so be it. He was going to ride with him all the way.

Jimmy Chan took another long drag from his cigarette and exhaled a cloud of smoke. He then said, "I'm afraid it's not that simple. I want all of it or nothing. You have twenty-four hours!"

"There's no way I can come up with that kind of money overnight! It's not like I have two million dollars stashed in my mattress!"

"Then there's no deal, and no further need for discussion. I believe this meeting is over!"

Koran just nodded and turned to leave. Tariq and D-Bo backed out slowly with their weapons still pointed at the Asian gangsters. Once out of sight, they all bailed from the restaurant and hopped into their rides. Tires squealed as they mashed out of the parking lot and headed home.

Koran knew that wasn't the last time he would be hearing from Jimmy Chan, and he expected an all out war. But he wasn't going to break his promise to Miko, even if it meant risking his own life to save hers.

●●●●●●

Miko eased inside of the freezing cold hospital room with a bagful of cosmetics, including her friend's favorite Mac lip gloss. Jahzay was sitting in a foldout chair watching television, and she didn't even notice Miko creeping up from behind. Miko covered Jahzay's eyes with her hands, and in a masculine voice said, "Guess who?"

"Whoever it is, I hope you have a dick, because my fingers have been cramping up like crazy!" Jahzay joked.

"You are off the chain!" Miko replied. They both burst out in laughter, which Miko thought was a welcomed sound coming from Jahzay.

She looked a lot better since the last time she and Miko had seen each other, and she was almost fully recovered from her surgery... at least, physically she was. However, it was going to take much longer for her to recover from the psychological trauma that she'd endured. Jahzay's emotional scars were still fresh, and the healing process had yet to begin. It would never begin until she completely let go of her feelings for Smokey, something she was not quite ready to do.

Miko kissed her on the cheek, lifted up the bag and said, "I brought something for you."

For the next hour and a half, they played dress-up in front of the mirror in Jahzay's hospital room, just like they did when they were little. They both laughed and reminisced about old times. They were talking about their days at Fleming Middle School, when Jahzay's smile faded and she began to cry. She looked at her best friend and with tears in her eyes asked, "Why, Miko? *Why?*"

Miko didn't have an answer for her. The old saying that, "Everything happens for a reason" just wasn't good enough. After all, why would God give her a baby just to turn right back around and take it away? That's the question that Miko posed in her mind as she hugged her play sister tightly against her bosom.

Moments later, a sweet little lady nurse came into the room and gave Jahzay a sedative that quickly put her to sleep. Miko eased out of the room and left the hospital feeling sad and depressed.

During the short walk back to her parked car, she broke down in tears and buried her face in her palms. All of the sudden, a black sedan came from out of nowhere and slid to a stop less than two feet from where she stood.

She froze in her tracks as the foreign automobile nearly knocked her off of her feet.

Instinctively, she reached for the small .32 pistol Koran had given her. She had her right hand gripped around the handle ready to pull it out of her purse when her fears were eased. The driver's side window of the vehicle rolled down, and an old-looking white guy stuck his balding head out and shouted. "Hey, lady! Watch where you're going, why don't cha! Jeez!"

Miko let out a sigh of relief as she released the handle of her gun and waved the car along. She drove away from the hospital a nervous wreck, and in desperate need of a drink.

Koran had called her earlier saying that he would be at the clothing store later in the day if she wanted to see him. She couldn't wait to ask him about what happened at the meeting with Jimmy Chan.

She exited the beltway and drove down the feeder road until she came to a red light. She looked to her right, and to her surprise, Smokey's sister, Jameisha, was gassing up her vehicle at a Shell gas station. Miko made a quick right turn into the station entrance and pulled up to the pump next to Jameisha's Toyota 4Runner.

Miko and Jameisha had never gotten along. They were close to exchanging blows too many times to count. That was mainly because Jameisha secretly envied Miko's relationship with Seven. Jameisha never got over her love for Seven, and it pained her to see him with another woman, especially someone as beautiful as Miko. Those feelings of envy and jealousy instantly turned into hate when Miko had Seven's child, something Jameisha was never able to do. As for Miko, she didn't hate Jameisha, but she could feel the negative vibes whenever they were around one another.

Miko jumped out of her car and walked right up to Jameisha, pointing a finger in her face while shouting, "You need to tell yo' ho ass brother the next time he put his hands on Jazzy, I'ma put them laws in his muthafuckin' life!"

"Bitch, I don't *need* to do shit! And furthermore, you and that gold diggin' ass slut can kiss my black ass!" Jameisha shot back.

Before Jameisha could even react, Miko grabbed her by her cheap weave and punched her in the face. Jameisha was swinging wildly trying to get out of Miko's clutches, but it was useless. Miko never loosened her grip as she continued to rain blows on Jameisha until her face was badly bruised and her mouth was bloodied.

A crowd of onlookers gathered around to watch the beat-down, and Miko put on a show. When somebody yelled out that the gas station attendant was on the phone with the police, everyone jumped back into their rides and burned off.

Miko let go of Jameisha's hair and she fell to the ground as her legs gave out. Miko raced back to her car after spitting on Jameisha and saying, "Now who's da' bitch?!"

Miko looked into her rearview mirror nervously, expecting to see a police car behind her. She wondered if anyone had gotten her license plate number as she sped away from the scene. After saying a quick prayer to herself, she drove towards Koran's place of business. Her hair was disheveled and she looked like she'd been through hell, so she pulled over to the side of the road and grabbed her compact and lip-gloss. After applying her makeup and getting herself together, she smiled at the reflection she saw in the mirror and continued on her way. She was not about to let Koran see her looking the way she was looking. When she made it to his shop, she threw her car in park and ran inside with one thing on her mind.

Chapter Eighteen

Srewston's Hip Hop Shop boasted the title of being the city's "number one urban retailer". Koran owned two stores of it's kind: one on the north side of Houston, and one on the south side. The walls of both outlets were lined with every style of designer urban wear you could name. They also sold sneakers and some of the hottest mix tapes and street DVD's out.

Miko could barely contain her anger when she walked through the doors of the south side store and saw Koran's baby mama. Pocahontas was standing near the back with her hands on her hips. Their eyes immediately connected with one another, and they gave each other resentful looks that said exactly how they both felt about each other.

Miko had to admit that Pocahontas was not a bad looking female. In fact, she was gorgeous. She stood bowlegged at 5'5" tall, and her hip-hugging denim jeans couldn't have been more than a size 4 at the most. Her skin and face were blemish free, and her Mexican background gave her an exotic look.

Miko walked over to where she was standing, and with a hint of jealousy in her voice she asked, "What the hell are you doing here?"

"That's funny, I was just about to ask you the same thing!" Pocahontas fired back.

"I don't know if you've heard or not, but Koran is *my* man now!"

"And he is, and will always be *my* baby daddy! So you might as well get used to seeing my face, bitch!" She stood face to face with Miko.

They were seconds away from coming to blows when Koran came out of his office saying, "Ladies, ladies! Can we all just get along?"

"You still fuckin' this bitch, or something?" Miko asked him with an attitude.

"If I wanted the dick, I could get it! You can believe dat, bitch!" Pocahontas scoffed, putting Koran on blast.

Both women shot piercing stares at Koran. Just by looking at them, he knew he was in for a lifetime of headaches. Sensing that Miko was in her feelings, he tried to clean up the situation. He stepped towards her and hugged her tightly while saying, "Baby, I told you that you're the only woman for me!"

Miko looked over Koran's shoulder and smiled at Pocahontas, who was turning red in the face. She couldn't stand to see another woman wrapped up in the arms of the man she still loved. She crossed her arms in front of her and pouted. "Give me my money so I can go!"

Koran broke his embrace with Miko and reached into the pockets of his PePe jeans. But before he could retrieve his wad of cash, he was distracted by the sound of his ringing cell phone. He stopped what he was doing and answered it, putting off his baby mama's request.

That angered Pocahontas even more. It was then when she vowed to make Koran pay for the way he was treating her. An idea popped into her head when she overheard Koran mention something about a shipment of T-shirts he was having delivered to him. She remembered that Koran often used the word "T-shirt" as a code word for kilos. Her ears served as miniature satellites, picking up on Koran's every word as he went over the details of the shipment.

Koran hung up his cell phone and asked, "Now, where were we?"

"You was about to give me the $2,000 I asked you for so I can leave!" Pocahontas reminded him.

"Riiight! How could I forget? After all, that's the only reason you ever come by here anyway," Koran commented.

"Whatever, nigga!"

"Your middle name should be 'IRS' the way you be taxing a nigga! And don't think I don't know that all this money ain't for Karma. So get off the gas!"

Pocahontas was speechless. After all, what could she say? Their daughter wasn't even in school yet, so it didn't take a lot of money to take care of her... at least not as much as Pocahontas led him to believe. Most of it went towards her high maintenance fees and uncontrollable shopping addiction.

Koran knew what the deal was, but he figured that he would rather play her game than have the Attorney General all up in his business. He dug into his pocket and peeled off 20 crisp Ben Franklin's from his bankroll.

Pocahontas didn't even say "thank you" when he handed her the money. Instead, she turned her nose up at Miko and stormed out of the exit. Pocahontas could have sworn that she heard Miko laughing behind her as she walked out of the door, but she just kept walking while thinking to herself, *Go ahead. Have your fun while you can, bitch. 'Cause when it's all said and done, I will be the one getting the last laugh!*

Back inside the store, Miko and Koran entered into his plush office and got comfortable. They were relaxing on his leather couch, laughing and talking.

"I swear, you better check that ho next time she come around me, or I'ma have to strangle her po' ass!" Miko half-joked.

"Please, be my guest. You'd be doing us both a favor!" Koran said playfully.

They both laughed out loud and hugged each other close. Their eyes locked as they simultaneously said, "I have something to tell you."

Again they laughed out loud, amused at how they were always thinking the same thing, and saying things at the same time. It happened again as they both blurted out, "You first!"

"In the words of Ms. Queen Latifah, *"Ooh, ooh, ladies first, ladies first!"* Koran sang.

"Boy, you are so crazy!" Miko started. "But just remember you said that the next time I'm trying to get a nut!"

"Ha-ha. You got dat!"

"Okay. I just wanted to talk to you about the guy who killed your friend. You said his name was Smokey, right?"

"Yeah, what about him?"

"Well, I know who he is. Actually, I know him very well. The girl who it was supposedly behind, is my best friend, Jazzy. She's the girl I was riding with the night I met you at your birthday party."

"That *was* her name!" Koran shouted. Everything was starting to make sense to him. He knew that he'd heard that name before, but he couldn't place a face with it, until then. He wanted to know what else Miko had been keeping from him, so he put on a poker face and asked, "Is there anything else you think I should know? I mean, since you're cleaning out ya closet and all."

"Baby, I know you're upset, but I wanted to be absolutely sure before I told you. Plus, I didn't want to betray my friend. She would never forgive me if she knew I was responsible for something bad happening to him. And I would not be able to forgive myself if something bad happened to you in the process."

"So, why are you telling me all this now?"

"Because he nearly killed my friend the other day, and even though she doesn't want him to be held responsible for his actions, I do. And to add to that, my loyalty is with you. That's why I want to give you this."

Miko handed Koran a piece of paper with a name and other information scribbled on it. Koran stared at the paper then said, "That's one of the things I wanted to talk to you about."

"What is it?" Miko asked out of concern.

"Last night, one of my dudes got a call from a chick he knew, saying that she was with the nigga. Anyway, my mans had her trick the nigga into taking her to one of our trap houses, where they would be waiting."

"So, what happened?"

"To make a long story short, he... he..." Koran was getting pissed off just by thinking about what happened.

He was so upset that he could barely talk about it without breaking down. He took a deep breath and regained his composure before continuing. "He got away somehow. But not before he killed three of my niggas and the chick he was with."

Miko didn't know what to say. She never would've imagined that Smokey would flip out the way he did. After hearing the pain in Koran's voice and seeing the hurt in his eyes, Miko was glad that she told him what she knew. Jahzay would just have to get over it.

There was one more thing that had been bothering Miko, and she hoped that Koran would help clear it up for her. She came right out and said what was on her mind. "So, how did the meeting with Jimmy Chan go?"

Koran paused to think about his answer before saying, "Not like I wanted it to."

"What is that suppose to mean?"

"It means that he didn't wanna take the pills back. And when I offered to make a deal with him, he refused."

"So, where does that leave us?"

"Look, boo, let me worry about Jimmy Chan. Try to focus on something else."

That was easier said than done. In fact, all Miko could think about was Jimmy Chan, because she was sure of one thing, and that was that he would not go away that easy.

●●●●●●

Later that night, Miko and Koran were lying in bed after making love for the second time. They got up to take a shower, then decided to order room service. Koran threw on a pair of loose fitting basketball shorts and a wife beater, and Miko slipped into a pair of spandex pants and a sports bra.

In the middle of yet another round of foreplay, they were interrupted by a knock at the room door. A voice on the other side of the door announced, "Room service."

"I got it, boo," Koran said, leaping up from the bed to answer the door. He opened the door and smiled politely at the hotel employee standing next to the food cart. When Koran reached out to hand him a tip, the employee quickly removed the towel that was draped across his forearm, revealing a handgun equipped with a silencer. The Asian-looking man pointed the gun in Koran's face, but before he could pull the trigger, Koran slammed the room door against his hand. The pistol fell to the floor and Koran took advantage of the opportunity.

He didn't know karate like the heroes in the movies, but if there was anything growing up in the 'hood had taught him, it was how to fight. He showed his survival skills by kicking his would-be killer in the center of his chest, sending him flying back into the wall on the opposite side of the hallway. Koran didn't give him a chance to recover. He was all over him, delivering powerful left and right combinations, until the Asian gunman was knocked out and bleeding on the floor.

"Let's get outta here!" Koran screamed at Miko, who was gathering up a few items. Koran picked up the handgun his attacker had dropped and grabbed Miko by her arm, leading her towards the elevators down the hall. When they reached the elevators, a bell sounded and one of them opened up. Two more Asian men dressed in dark suits stepped out of the elevator.

"Shit! Run, baby!" Koran yelled out, pushing Miko through a door marked "Stairs." They descended the flight of stairs two at a time as the two men pursued them.

Pow! Pow! one of the Asian's semi-automatic handguns sounded.

One of the bullets ricocheted off of the metal railing right next to Miko's head.

They kept running as fast as they could until they reached the ground level. They busted through a door that they thought led into the lobby of the hotel, but instead they were standing inside a dimly lit parking garage. They ran and ducked behind a Ford Excursion that was parked twenty feet away from the door, and both of them crouched down in firing positions. Koran pulled out the Glock 40 with the silencer, and Miko pulled out her .32.

As soon as the first guy came running through the door, they both let off a barrage of shots, sending him stumbling backwards in a storm of bullets. He fell to the ground as his partner busted through the door behind him, firing a fully automatic submachine gun.

Koran and Miko had no choice but to take cover and run. With their heads ducked down, they ran away from the shooter and hid amongst the maze of cars and trucks. When the gunfire finally stopped, there was complete silence. They listened for footsteps, but all they could hear were their hearts pounding in their chests.

All of the sudden, they heard something hit the ground a few feet away from them. They both knew what had caused it. The gunman was putting in another clip.

Koran looked over at Miko and said, "No matter what happens, I want you to know that I love you, and I will die for you if I have to!"

His statement caught Miko totally off guard. The only response she could think of was to kiss him softly on his lips. That's what she was doing when they heard a car engine cranking up in the distance. They jumped to their feet, and Koran said, "We have to split up if we wanna make it outta here alive. I want you to go back the way we came and get some help while I distract him."

She didn't agree with his plan to split up, but she reluctantly nodded her head and ran off in the direction of the hotel.

The car's headlights bounced off of the concrete walls as it rounded the corner and eased up the aisle where Koran was hiding. *Here goes nothin'!* he thought to himself as he jumped out into the path of the oncoming vehicle, and right into the gunman's line of fire.

Miko heard the sound of squealing brake shoes, then what sounded like a marching band of gunshots, playing a tune of death. She screamed out Koran's name and fell to her knees in tears. *It can not end like this! Not again!* she thought to herself as she cried for yet another lover. She forced herself back to her feet and continued running towards the stairwell. When she reached the last aisle, a single headlight hit her. A car was quickly approaching her from the left. She turned to face it, raising her gun up to shoulder level and squeezing the trigger two times.

Click! Click!

"Shit!" she shouted, realizing that she was out of bullets. Before she could react, the car came to a stop just two feet in front of her. She was suddenly glad that she'd run out of bullets, because had she not, she would have shot and probably killed the man she loved.

Koran was sitting in the driver's seat of the bullet hole riddled black Audi. Miko burst into tears at the sight of all the blood that was covering the windshield. She silently prayed that Koran was not hurt badly. She ran up to the car and peered through the shattered glass as she asked him, "Baby, are you okay?"

Koran smiled and jokingly replied, "The blood came with the car!"

Miko sighed in relief. She ran around to the passenger side and hopped in. Koran mashed the gas and took off out of the garage in a hurry. Miko was happy that they'd escaped the trap Jimmy Chan had set for them, but she wasn't sure that they would be so lucky the next time.

Chapter Nineteen

Jimmy Chan slammed his fist down on top of the cherry wood tabletop inside of his leased mid-town penthouse. One of his workers had just given him the disappointing news of Miko and Koran's escape from what he thought was a foolproof trap. Speaking in his native tongue, he instructed the head of security of his Red Dragon organization to summon the hitman who survived the failed assassination attempt. Jimmy Chan hoped to get the answers he was looking for.

The head of security was a menacing looking Asian, who resembled, Bolo, the actor who was famous for making his chest muscles jump in all of the old karate flicks. He did as he was told and quickly disappeared from the room. He reappeared minutes later, leading the surviving gunman by his arm into the living room of the penthouse. "Bolo" bowed before his ruthless leader, and the other man excused himself from the room, leaving Jimmy Chan alone with the obviously frightened assassin.

"Chin Wong," Jimmy Chan called out, breaking the uncomfortable silence. "I am very disappointed in you. You have failed me miserably."

In his native Vietnamese dialect, Chin Wong pleaded, "Sir, there were two men there with weapons protecting the girl. We did not surprise them. They seemed to be expecting us."

Jimmy Chan smiled. Chin Wong felt relieved that his master was fooled by the lie that he'd just told him. But when Chin Wong bowed his head to show his respect, he realized that the joke was on him. He nearly fainted when he looked down and saw that he was standing on a wide sheet of plastic that had been rolled out over the plush carpeting of the living room. When he raised his head, he had a look of pure terror etched upon his face. His eyes fastened upon the shiny metal blade that his master held in his fist.

"Mr. Chan, I --"

"Silence!" Jimmy Chan commanded. "I don't want to hear any more of your lies and worthless excuses. I have no room in my organization for failures."

With lightning speed, Jimmy Chan grabbed Wong's collar. He stuck the razor sharp blade of the butterfly knife into the belly of his failed soldier. The blade slid in deeply, and with a savage twist of his right hand, Jimmy Chan sliced upward, cutting through muscle and organs. When the blade slid free of Chin Wong's sternum, he was already dead on his feet.

Jimmy Chan released his corpse, which fell forward onto the plastic floor covering. He called out for his henchmen, who promptly entered the room and started rolling Chin Wong's lifeless body up in the thick plastic sheeting. Before long, Chin Wong was rolled up like a pig in a blanket.

After giving his workers instructions on how and where to dispose of the evidence, Jimmy Chan telephoned his next-in-command and said, "John Woo, gather up the vehicles and a few of our best soldiers. I feel like going for a little ride. "

John Woo knew exactly what that meant, and he'd been expecting the call. He had been Jimmy Chan's right hand man since the beginning of the Red Dragon Organization, which he was the co-founder of. Over time, he had grown to know his leader like a book, and he used that to his advantage, because he knew that the day would come when he would have to cross out his friend and boss. As Jimmy Chan would say, "It's nothing personal -- just business!"

Sitting in the back of a black BMW 7 series with tinted windows, Jimmy Chan contemplated his next move like a master chess player. He was chain smoking cigarette after cigarette and twirling a pair of Chinese concentration balls in his palm. That was a habit of his when he was in deep thought. His resources stretched far beyond that of the average street-level hustler, so with just a couple of brief phone calls, he learned everything he needed to know about the man who called himself Koran.

He figured that what he needed to do was set an example of just how powerful and dangerous he could be. After tossing ideas around back and forth in his head, he devised a plan that he felt would get his point across, and get Koran's full attention. But he would only give one warning. After that, he would not stop until Koran and the girl's heads were ground up like raw sushi.

The two identical black sedans cruised up Martin Luther King Boulevard shortly after midnight, and pulled into the parking lot of a small strip mall. No stores were open at that time of night, and there were no other vehicles in sight on either side of the two-lane boulevard. The car Jimmy Chan was riding in came to a stop behind the car carrying four of his soldiers. Three of the four henchmen exited the car and got prepared to carry out their mission.

On the other side of town, two more black sedans were sitting in the parking lot of another shopping center. Inside one of the cars, John Woo was awaiting orders from his boss. He was accompanied by three Red Dragon soldiers, and they were all eager to kill anyone within their reach if given the word.

Back on the south side of town, Jimmy Chan was giving his henchmen commands as they hurriedly carried out his instructions. Minutes later, one of the workers in the first car signaled that they were ready for him to give them the word. After calling John Woo on his cell and giving him the go ahead, Jimmy Chan motioned for the men in the first car to proceed.

In an instant, two separate buildings on different sides of town and miles apart from each other were simultaneously blown to pieces.

Jimmy Chan rode away from the scene with a fiery blaze burning behind him, and a very rare smile plastered on his face. He was going to sleep well that night knowing that his latest message would be heard loud and clear.

●●●●●●

Koran's face held a stunned expression as he surveyed the charred and blackened area where his clothing store once stood. The only thing worse than him losing one of his shops to an apparent bombing, was losing both stores to bombings. To say that he was devastated would have been an understatement. And to add insult to injury, it was going to take a while for the insurance to cover his losses due to the fact that the fire department concluded that it needed to be investigated as arson.

was no doubt in Koran's mind as to who was responsible for the act. A playing card with a red dragon design on it was found on the sidewalk in front of both store fronts. The investigators had yet to realize the significance, but Koran knew exactly what it meant as soon as he saw it. Jimmy Chan had obviously left his calling card as some sort of warning or scare tactic. But instead of scaring Koran, it just made him more furious.

What had Koran confused was how Jimmy Chan had found out that he owned those particular businesses, especially since they were technically owned by a corporation. He started to feel like no aspect of his life was safe from Jimmy Chan and his Red Dragon organization. After all, if they knew about the businesses he owned, they had to know where he lived. And there was no telling what else.

He had to warn Miko, who was probably still asleep at his place. He'd told her she would be safe there after the incident at the hotel, but now he wasn't so sure about that. She needed to get out of that house as fast as she could.

Miko got Koran's frantic call telling her to get dressed and be outside in five minutes. He said he was sending a car over to pick her up. He hung up the phone before she could ask him what was going on, but she knew that whatever it was it wasn't good. In less than ten minutes, she was dressed in a blue jean jumpsuit and standing in front of Koran's mini-mansion, awaiting her ride.

In the distance, she heard the rumbling of bass approaching the residence, and knew that it couldn't be anybody but one person... her new brother-in-law. Seconds later, she was proven right when Tariq's H-2 Hummer came into view and pulled up to the front gate of the estate. He buzzed himself in and the mechanized gate opened slowly. The man Miko had playfully dubbed "bruh-n-law" eased his tank of a truck around the circular driveway and came to a stop directly in front of her.

"Wassup, lil' sis?" Tariq shouted as Miko climbed into the passenger seat with her bags.

"What the hell is going on, bruh-n-law? I'm worried about Koran," Miko responded.

"Yo guess is as good as mines, baby girl. My bro just called me out the blue and told me to come scoop you up, so here I am."

"He didn't say what for? I mean, there has to be a reason for all this."

"He just said that it wasn't safe for you to be here no more. That's it."

Obviously annoyed from all of the questions, Tariq turned up the volume of his Alpine stereo system, and Fat Pat's "Ghetto Dreams" album quaked through the subwoofers.

Miko got the message and folded her arms across her chest as they drove off. Her mind was working overtime as she wondered what Koran had meant when he said that she was not safe. She had a feeling that it had something to do with Jimmy Chan, but she hoped that she was wrong. She desperately needed to talk to Koran, because he was the only one that could answer her questions.

Tariq had said something about taking her someplace safe where Koran would be waiting for her. When they reached the four-way stop sign at the corner of

Koran's street, a black sedan pulled out in front of them. Looking into his rearview mirror, Tariq noticed that another black sedan had pulled up behind him.

"What the fuck? Hold on tight, sis!" he yelled out while mashing the gas pedal of his Hummer to the floor. The midsize sedan was no match for the thousands of pounds of steel as it smashed into the side of the stalled vehicle. The two figures behind the dark tint were turned into sardines as Tariq continued past them with the other car still in pursuit.

The other car maneuvered to the passenger side of the Hummer, and one of the assassins popped out of the open sunroof, firing a Mac-10.

Miko just knew she was dead as the bullets hit her window, but was surprised when they just ricocheted off. She looked over in shock and saw Tariq laughing at her.

"I forgot to tell you, they're bullet-proof!" he said between chuckles, referring to the windows on his H-2.

The two vehicles raced through the residential neighborhood at speeds of up to 55 mph. During the car chase, Miko pulled out her small .32, which again brought laughter from Tariq, who seemed to be enjoying himself. He looked at Miko and asked her, "What'cha gon' do with that lil' shit?"

"More than you can do with what you've got, which is nothing!"

"I'm just saying, dat look like da lil' gun ole boy was shootin' in 'Harlem Knights'!"

"Ha-ha, very funny! Now pay attention to the road, Chris Tucker!"

"Here, grab the wheel so we can switch spots."

Miko took control of the steering wheel and placed her left foot on the gas pedal as Tariq crossed over her and made his way to the back of the truck. Miko positioned herself in the driver's seat and immediately noticed that she was quickly approaching a dead-end. She screamed out over her shoulder, "Tariq, we're headed towards a dead-end!"

"Don't trip! Just slow down and keep driving!"

Tariq pulled a lever on the side of his custom made speaker box and it opened up to reveal a small arsenal of firearms and a bulletproof vest. He grabbed a fully automatic SKS with an extended banana clip and cocked it back. When he felt Miko slowing down, he opened the back door to his SUV and started firing. He didn't stop shooting until the barrel of the assault rifle was smoking, the clip was empty, and the car that was following them looked like Swiss cheese. Both the driver and the passenger died in the hailstorm of bullets, and their car slowly veered to the side of the road, where it came to a stop against the curb.

●●●●●●

After a long and quiet drive, they ended up in a Missouri City suburb. Tariq pulled his SUV into the driveway of a modest one-story brick home and parked next to Koran's Batman inspired Dodge Viper. They both exited the truck, and Miko followed his lead into the sparsely furnished home that once served as a G.M.C. stash house.

Koran was pacing the floor nervously when they walked in. He looked up and smiled when he laid eyes on

Miko. They ran towards each other and embraced as Tariq yelled out sarcastically, "Yeah, I'm happy to see you, too!"

"It sounds like somebody is a little jealous, baby," Miko teased.

"Jealous of what? I ain't with all dat lovey-dovey shit!" Tariq stated defensively.

Koran broke in, "What took y'all so long? I was about to call you when y'all walked in."

"We ran into a little road block in the form of two Jackie Chan lookin' mu'fuckas with machine guns!" Tariq replied.

"I knew they would try to hit my house next!"

"What do you mean, *next*?" Miko asked.

Koran looked at her through his heavy eyelids and said, "I just found out this morning that both of my clothing stores were firebombed last night!"

"How do you know it was Jimmy Chan's work?" Tariq asked, while trying to digest what he'd just heard.

Koran pulled out the playing card that was left at the scene and showed it to Miko and his brother. When they fixed their eyes on the red dragon, there was no doubt as to whom was behind the bombings.

Tariq snatched the card from his brother's hand and yelled out, "Man, I knew we should've blazed dem mu'fuckas when we had da chance!"

"You gon' get yo' chance, baby bro, don't trip," Koran replied. "But I need you to keep ya cool for now, because we still gotta take care of that business involving that nigga, Smokey!"

"You're right, bro. I'm just trippin' off this shit, man."

"Baby, I'm starting to get scared," Miko blurted out. "I think we should try to figure out another way to handle the Jimmy Chan situation."

"What'chu mean? We're in too deep to get cold feet now. And besides, I'm doing this for you."

"Let's just give him what he wants before anyone else gets hurt. Because Lord knows, I don't need anymore blood on my hands!" When Miko finished speaking she was in tears, and both men were speechless.

Koran thought long and hard about what she'd said. Deep inside, he knew she was probably right, but his pride wouldn't let him openly admit that. He was obviously out of his league, and his clique, no matter how thorough he thought they were, would undoubtedly be outmatched if they went to war with an international syndicate like the Red Dragons.

On the other hand, the only way he could produce two million dollars in such a short amount of time would be to put his hands on some work, but that was an option he wasn't ready to consider. As he pondered over his dilemma, the video for Mike Jones', "Still Tippin'" came on, on the wall-mounted flat screen in front of him. That's when an idea suddenly hit him. He snapped his fingers and said, "I got it!"

"Got what?" Tariq and Miko asked in unison.

"I have a plan that I think will get us out of this jam with Jimmy Chan and his crew."

"I hope your *plan* includes bustin' his mu'fuckin' head for what he did to my paint job! " Tariq said.

Miko looked on in bewilderment as Koran dialed a number on his cell phone. He jumped up and began pacing the floor. When the call was answered, Koran asked for "Dr. Teeth." Dr. Teeth was a well-known video director for many popular hip-hop and R&B artists from around the city of Houston.

After a few minutes of back and forth dialogue, an agreement was reached, and just like that, their money problems were solved. Hanging up the phone, he called out to his brother, "Say, baby bro, I need you to take care of that shipment I got coming in this week."

"Anything you need, bruh."

"For right now, I want you to get with the clique and take care of that bitch ass nigga, Smokey!"

"A'ight, I'll hit you up later," Tariq told his brother, giving him a half hug. He looked over at Miko and said, "You better take care of my brother, baby sis."

"Don't worry, I got this," she replied with confidence.

When Tariq was gone, Koran used his cell phone to call in a few more favors that were owed to him. He was sure that he would need them for what he was planning to do.

He turned around to find Miko staring at him with a smirk on her face. She put her hands on her hips and said, "I'm afraid to even ask what you got going on in that big head of yours."

"Then don't. Come here and see what's going on with my other big head!"

"I've been so worried about this bullshit that I've been neglecting my *mini-you*, haven't I?" Miko said.

"The only thing that you need to be worrying about from now on is where you want to spend our honeymoon at."

Silence.

"What are you trying to say, baby?"

"I'm not *trying* to say anything. I'm saying it. When all of this is over, I want you to be my wife!"

"Are you serious?"

"Is Oprah rich?"

Miko didn't even have to say "yes", because her reaction said it for her. She leaped into Koran's outstretched arms and kissed her man's soft lips, causing him to instantly harden. That kiss led to intense foreplay, and before they knew it, they were both naked, lying in the missionary position on the carpeted living room floor.

Koran wasted no time pushing his love inside of her, and Miko welcomed every inch of him deep within her being. They moaned and groaned in pure ecstasy, and for the next forty-five minutes, neither one of them had a care in the world.

Chapter Twenty

DEA Agent Matt Everhart couldn't believe his luck as he traveled down Interstate 45 in his black Ford Expedition. He was on his way to meet one of his newest confidential informants, or as they were better known in the 'hood, snitches. Just the day before, he was called into his supervisor's office and told that he was being reassigned to a case that he'd previously been removed from for misconduct.

Apparently, someone had come forward with some new information that prompted the reopening of the investigation. That came as a surprise to Everhart, because for the past two years he'd tried unsuccessfully to get people to cooperate with the DEA. He even went so far as to offer informants large sums of money, luxury automobiles, and even sentence reductions. But the fact was that no matter how great the reward, nobody was crazy enough to cross out anyone in the Get Money Clique.

To Agent Everhart, the Get Money Clique, or G.M.C. as he'd come to know them, were the equivalent of a modern day Gambino crime family. And their elusive leader, Koran Yusuf, played the role of a Black John Gotti. Of course, Agent Everhart's perception of them was greatly exaggerateed. But to him, everything he'd heard was true.

He estimated that they alone were responsible for thousands and thousands of the kilos that were sold on the streets of Houston going back five years. Not to mention countless drug-related murders. But he couldn't pin anything on them that was solid, and that drove him crazy. His obsession with bringing down the G.M.C. organization was ultimately his own downfall.

Matt Everhart was born and raised in the Cajun country area of Louisiana, and his accent was a dead giveaway. At just 34 years old, he was still young, but the scruffy beard and unkempt hair on his head made him look a lot older. He stood an even six feet, and maintained a solid physique thanks in part to his sports background.

When he was in his early twenties, he became one of the youngest agents to achieve his position in the history of the DEA. Throughout his adolescent and college years, he was pushed by his father, a FBI agent himself, to uphold the family tradition by joining the ranks of law enforcement. It didn't take much urging, though. Matt Everhart was born to be an agent.

After breezing through four years of college at Tulane University in New Orleans, he earned degrees in both Criminal Justice and Psychology while maintaining a near perfect G.P.A. After his schooling, he went straight into the academy, where he excelled at the rigorous and grueling physical and mental exercises. During his training, he also racked up several accolades for excellent marksmanship on the gun range. Once he graduated from the academy, his dad pulled a few strings to get him in at the DEA, where he'd been ever since.

His first couple of years in the DEA were uneventful and outright boring. His job mostly consisted of sitting around the office all day pulling desk duty. The most excitement he got was when one of the field agents would tell him about the latest investigation they were working on. He imagined himself out there in the trenches alongside his fellow officers, and he couldn't wait for the opportunity to prove himself.

He would finally get his chance when the agency needed extra agents for a major undercover sting operation that was going down at the Port of Houston. A government snitch had managed to infiltrate a Colombian drug cartel, and it was time to make the arrests. However, during the controlled "buy and bust", things went completely haywire, and a gunfight ensued between the two sides.

The agents' shotguns and semi-automatic pistols were no match for the smugglers' fully automatic submachine guns. Two agents ultimately found themselves trapped in the line of gunfire.

Fortunately for them, Agent Everhart appeared out of nowhere and saved both of their lives. He shot and killed two armed gunmen.

After the smoke cleared, Agent Everhart was rewarded for his bravery in the line of duty, and given a promotion to senior field officer.

From that point on, Matt Everhart's entire life revolved around his work. That left no room for a love interest or social functions. He soon became disliked by his fellow agents, who resented his arrogance and considered him a showoff. However, that only made him work harder.

He wanted to be better than his peers. Over the years leading up to 2004, he oversaw several high profile busts and seized millions of dollars worth of drugs, money and property for the agency.

It was around that time that he was given the assignment of his dreams --to take down the G.M.C. That proved to be a lot harder than he expected. For the next year he focused on nothing but the G.M.C. case. He would eventually amass a dossier that was over two inches thick. It contained the names and other information on suspected crewmembers. After running into numerous dead-ends, his frustration grew to a point where he became known as a "loose cannon". He resorted to tactics that were both unethical and unconstitutional --all in the name of justice.

Koran and other members of the G.M.C. eventually grew tired of Agent Everhart's threats and constant harassment at their places of business. That led to them filing a harassment suit against the DEA, which ruffled some feathers at the agency. When a famed congresswoman from the city stepped in, that was all she wrote. She found out that Agent Matt Everhart had, among other things, tried to coerce witness statements, and the investigation into the G.M.C. was officially closed. Afterwards, Agent Everhart was quietly demoted and returned to desk duty.

All that's about to change now, he thought to himself as he mused over his meteoric rise and fall within the agency. He was seated in the lounge area of a Magic Johnson owned Starbuck's Coffee Shop. He had his head down, blowing into his hot cup of coffee, when someone behind him cleared their throat. He looked back to see a pretty female standing behind him.

She was dressed in a conservative pant suit and high heeled pumps. Her eyes were hidden behind a pair of oversized Christian Dior shades, and her hair was pulled back into a neat ponytail. Agent Everhart started to feel underdressed for their meeting, with his blue jeans and faded Houston Astros baseball jersey. He took in her wonderful perfumed fragrance as she extended a meticulously manicured hand and asked, "Agent Everhart?"

"That's me. What can I do for you?"

"I'm your... what do you call it? Oh, yes. I'm your C.I., Yessenia. Yessenia Ramirez."

Yessenia, better known as Pocahontas, went on to explain her relationship to Koran. Of course, Agent Everhart already knew everything she was telling him, but he decided to entertain her anyway. He then made her sign some papers and pulled out a tape recorder before she began talking.

Agent Everhart literally had a hard-on, but not from looking at the shapely young woman seated across the table from him. No, he was aroused by what she was telling him about the shipment of kilos that Koran was scheduled to receive later on that week.

According to Pocahontas, the deal was going down on the upcoming Friday at a warehouse Koran leased on the city's southwest side. The only drawback was that she didn't know the exact time of the drop, but that was something she was sure the agent could easily find out.

Agent Everhart agreed that he would have more than enough time to gain that piece of information, get the necessary search and seizure warrants, and set up a sting.

His mind was turning rapidly when Pocahontas broke into his thoughts saying, "Of course, you do realize that my name cannot come up under any circumstances. If someone found out that I was doing this..."

"Ms. Ramirez, I assure you that the fact that you have provided us with this information will remain strictly confidential. Your name will not be disclosed in any way."

Agent Everhart flat out lied to her to ease her fears about cooperating. He knew as well as anyone that she would be forced to take the stand and testify in court if any one of the defendants decided to test the Fed's ninety-eight percent conviction rate by going to trial. But as long as he got what he wanted, which was to send Koran and his gang of thugs to prison, he didn't care about what would happen to Pocahontas as a result.

"I have one other thing to ask you," Pocahontas started. "I was told that I would receive a percentage of whatever proceeds y'all seized from the bust. Is that true?"

"Yes, that sounds about right. For instance, if we get, let's say, one million dollars in the raid, that means you will receive something in the neighborhood of $300,000."

Agent Everhart paused briefly to let the numbers sink into Pocahontas' brain. Her eyes were the size of half-dollars as she started calculating all the ways she could spend a small fortune of over a quarter million dollars. At that moment, she became even more eager to go through with the deal. She had thought about backing out, but she wanted Koran to pay for the way he'd been treating her since meeting his new fling. The prospect of getting $300,000 just made her revenge that much more sweet.

Agent Everhart never asked what her motives were for setting up the father of her child. He could tell she was scorned and probably acting out of anger. Whatever the reason was, he was about to get his wish once and for all. Koran was going to pay for the embarrassment that he'd caused him. He tied up a few more loose ends with his newly acquired C.I. and ended their meeting with a firm handshake and a command for her to call him if she heard anything else.

Pocahontas' high heels clicked against the tile floor as she exited the coffee shop. She had a devious smile on her face, like a child with a dirty little secret. She threw on her sunglasses and hopped in the champagne-colored Porsche Boxster that Koran had bought her for her birthday just a year earlier. She grew to hate that car, because it served as a reminder of a time when she was number one in Koran's life --a time that would never come again after he found out the secret she'd been keeping from him. It was a day that she would never forget.

●●●●●●

It was a cold and dreary winter day and Karma had gotten so sick that she needed to be taken to the emergency room at Texas Children's Hospital. Koran was unable to reach Pocahontas on her cell phone, and was worried to the point of heart failure. After the doctors ran tests and diagnosed Karma's illness as nothing more than a fever, Koran was both relieved and thankful.

He was going over his daughter's medical records while signing a stack of forms he'd been given, when he saw something that grabbed his attention. While looking over a form, he noticed a box marked "Blood Type" and noted that Karma's was "Type O". He found that odd, because he was type AB positive. Up until then, he'd never paid any attention to that fact, or even questioned whether or not Karma was his child. He didn't even read the birth certificate before he signed it, because there was no doubt in his mind that Karma was his daughter. Plus, at the time he really wanted a child to call his own.

The fact that Karma didn't share any of his facial features was something he had intentionally overlooked since her birth. Maybe it was denial, but whenever his family brought it up, he would always say that she would "grow into it". His brother was the main person urging him to get a blood test, but Koran refused because he felt like Tariq was just hating. It was common knowledge that Tariq never trusted Pocahontas, and neither of them liked the other, so Koran paid it no mind and focused on being the best father he could be.

That day after the hospital visit, Koran couldn't handle being unsure any longer. He scheduled an appointment at a DNA lab, and for a $500 fee he had tests run on himself and his daughter. When the results came back, his worst fears were confirmed. Karma was not his child. Koran was so enraged he actually contemplated killing Pocahontas for her deceitfulness.

She came home one day from grocery shopping at a local Kroger supermarket. When she entered the front door of their home carrying Karma, she found Koran sitting in the dark with his head down. She flipped on the light switch and jumped back startled. "Damn, *papi!* You scared the hell out of me! Why are you sitting in here in the dark?"

"You knew!" was Koran's reply.

"Knew what? Koran, I don't have time to play these guessing games with you."

Pocahontas sat Karma down along with the bag she was carrying. She smelled the strong scent of alcohol in the room and decided that it wouldn't be a good idea to provoke Koran in any way.

He took a swig of his bottle of Crown Royal and slammed it down onto the glass coffee table. The coffee table shattered on impact and caused Pocahontas to jump back. He got up from the love seat and shoved the test results in her face while barking, "All this fucking time, you had me thinking that I was Karma's father! Bitch, I ought'a kill you!"

Koran pulled out his .357 and cocked the hammer back. He pointed the gun at Pocahontas as she pleaded, "*Papi*, I --I didn't know! I promise! There must be some mistake!"

"The mistake was made when I started fucking with yo' trifling ass!"

"*Papi*, I swear to you! Please believe me!"

Koran wasn't trying to hear it. He aimed the barrel of his gun at Pocahontas' tear soaked face. Just as he was about to squeeze the trigger, Karma started crying and wailing on the floor beside them. Koran looked down at the little girl he'd grown to love as his own, and he couldn't help but to start crying himself. He dropped the gun onto the floor then scooped Karma up into his arms and hugged her tightly.

Pocahontas overcame her fear and joined them. They hugged each other and cried together in silence. Things were never the same for their family. From that day on, the news of Karma's true paternity would stay between them. Pocahontas never told anyone, and neither did Koran - except for one person - his little brother, Tariq.

●●●●●●

"Hey! I'm glad I caught you," Agent Everhart said, snapping Pocahontas back to the present. "I almost forgot to give you my card."

"Oh. Okay. I was a little caught out there for a minute."

"That's normal. I'm sure you have a lot on your mind right now. "

"Yeah, that's true. But I'll be sure to give you a call if I hear anything else."

"You make sure you do just that."

They both said their good-byes.

Pocahontas turned the ignition on her Porsche and the engine purred to life. Agent Everhart watched closely as the sports car jerked then sped out into traffic. He then climbed back into his Ford Expedition and headed towards the DEA's downtown headquarters. He still had to put all the pieces into place to ensure that absolutely nothing went wrong. If it did, he knew he would probably end up writing parking tickets in Alaska for the rest of his career. He promised himself that he would make sure that every member of the G.M.C got the punishment that they deserved... even if he had to give it to them himself.

Chapter Twenty-One

Smokey sat in a cocaine-induced daze inside of his hotel room. Ever since the failed attempt on his life by Koran's crew, that's where he'd been hiding out. His money stash was getting smaller and smaller due to the fact that he was afraid to show his face on the scene. Hustling was out of the question, because he didn't know who he could trust. He was sure that Koran would be even more aggressive in his search after he found out that his homies had been killed during the attack. Another reason his money was dwindling was because of his ever increasing drug addiction. His ounce a day coke habit was steadily eating into both his pockets and his nose, but he had no intentions on quitting or even slowing down, for that matter.

He was trying hard to figure out how he'd gotten himself into the position he was in. He went from being a respected and wealthy hustler that was worth well into the six figures, to being a destitute dopefiend in denial. His drastic transformation came within a matter of weeks after being introduced to cocaine. At one time he had everything a man could want; a nice home, a couple of fly automobiles, and a loving fiancée who was expecting his baby. "That's it!" he shouted to the walls of the empty room. An image of Jahzay popped into his head. "It's all that bitch's fault!"

He was beginning to blame Jahzay for everything that had gone wrong in his life. Every time he got high, he would contemplate killing her for ruining his life. He reasoned that if Jahzay wouldn't have cheated on him in the first place, he wouldn't have had to kill her lover, and therefore, would not be in the predicament he was in. "Yeah," he said to himself. "I should have finished that bitch off when I had the chance!"

He snorted another line of cocaine, and a voice inside of his head said, *It's still not too late!*

●●●●●●

Jahzay sighed loudly as she flipped through the channels of the small television set inside her hospital room. She was dying from boredom, and each day she stayed in that lonely room it began to feel more and more like a prison. She couldn't wait until the doctors cleared her to leave. She was eager to get out of there and back to living a normal life again. She missed all of the little things she often took for granted, like taking long walks in the park and being able to get up and go to the fridge when she wanted to.

But most of all, she missed her daughter. Although her parents brought Alize to visit her frequently, it just wasn't the same as being at home with her. Tears began to well up in her eyes just thinking about her baby. She needed a shoulder to cry on, but no one was around to lend her one, not even her best friend and play-sister, Miko.

She hadn't received so much as a phone call from her friend in days, and that hurt her. Deep down inside of her, the seed of contempt was growing towards Miko because of her untimely absence. It wasn't like Miko to abandon her like that, especially considering everything that she was going through. She never once thought that maybe Miko was going through something herself. When it did hit her that that was probably the case, she began to feel guilty for thinking the worst of her friend.

All the time she spent by herself in that room gave her a chance to really think long and hard about the situation she was in. She had no idea how she would overcome her latest obstacle, or where her life would go from there. But, even after everything she'd been through, from losing her baby to fighting for her life, she still could not bring herself to hate Smokey. And please believe, she tried. It was a classic example of how victims blamed themselves for the abuse inflicted upon them by their lovers.

Jahzay protected Smokey to the end. She found every way possible to take responsibility for what happened to her. She even went so far as to say that she actually might have deserved the near-fatal beating he gave her. She convinced herself that it was her actions that caused it to happen. She laid down in her bed and the floodgates of her eyes were opened.

The tranquilizer she'd taken earlier that night was starting to kick in. Within the next five minutes she was drifting off into a dream state...

"Smokey?" Jahzay called out in a soft whisper. She saw a vision of her former lover standing at her bedside, smiling down at her. She whispered his name again, but he couldn't hear her. He looked so real --so much so that she could even see what he was wearing, right down to his G-Unit T-shirt and faded blue jeans. She wanted to reach out to him so badly, to tell him how sorry she was for betraying him, and how bad she wanted to make things right between them. If only he would just talk to her.

As she was thinking that, she noticed that the figure standing over her was no longer smiling. A sinister scowl had replaced it, and his eyes had a look in them that she'd seen only one other time in her life, the time that her former pimp, Pretty Boy, had tried to kill her. Yes, it was undeniable. She was staring at the look of death, and her dream was quickly turning into a nightmare...

All of the sudden, Smokey slapped her across the face. He hit her so hard that her entire head turned upon impact. It was at that moment when she realized that she wasn't dreaming at all. Smokey was in the room, and he was going to kill her!

●●●●●●

Miko was feeling imprisoned herself as she spent yet another long and dull day trapped inside of the house she and Koran were temporarily staying in. If it wasn't for the incredible sex that they were constantly engaging in, she would have tried to saw her way through the burglar bars that covered the windows and doors. Inside the bedroom, empty pizza boxes and half-drank beer bottles littered the floor.

She and Koran had just finished another round of passionate lovemaking and he was taking a shower. That's when her phone rang. At Koran's request, she'd been letting all of her calls go through to her voicemail, but something inside of her said that she should answer that one. And she was glad that she did. "Hello," she answered, yawning into the phone.

"Hello, Miko. This is Mrs. Merchand, Jahzay's mom."

"Oh, heeey! How are you doing Mrs. M?"

"Not so good, I'm afraid. Something has happened to Jahzay!"

Not again! Miko thought as she braced herself for what Mrs. Merchand was about to say.

Mrs. Merchand went on to tell Miko that the hospital had just called her saying that there was a disturbance in Jahzay's room. She said that she didn't want to go into details over the phone, but that she would explain everything in person. She suggested that Miko meet her at the hospital as soon as she could. Miko replied that she was leaving out the door immediately.

Miko's hands were trembling when she hung up the line. She threw on a pair of knickerbockers, a wrinkled up T-shirt, and house shoes. Her appearance was the least of her concerns. She grabbed the keys to Koran's Dodge Viper and was heading out of the door before she realized that she was locked in.

She was searching for the burglar bar key when Koran stepped out of the bathroom with a towel wrapped around his waist. The first words out of his mouth were, "Were do you think you're going?"

"I have to go check on Jazzy at the hospital!" she said sternly.

"I thought we'd already discussed that. You are not to leave this house for --"

"You don't understand! Something bad has happened in Jazzy's room at the hospital. She may be dead for all I know!"

Koran could see that it was useless to try to argue the point. Whatever went down really had to be serious, because Miko was a nervous wreck. He decided to bend his rules a little and give in. "Okay, you can go, but only under one condition. I'm going with you."

"Whatever you say, but I'm driving!"

Ten minutes later, Miko and Koran were flying up the highway in the super-fast sports car. She was passing the other commuters like a driver in the Daytona 500. She was thankful that they didn't get pulled over, as she found an empty parking space at the hospital.

Miko was running on auto pilot, and Koran was struggling to keep up with her. She ran through the sliding doors in the front of the hospital and bolted towards the elevators, where she caught the first one going up.

When they reached Jahzay's floor, the entire hallway was filled with uniformed police officers. One of the elevators was taped off with yellow crime scene tape, and two guys in cheap suits were taking pictures. A Black woman who appeared to be an employee of the hospital was crying and sobbing while being questioned by detectives. Miko and Koran stepped past them unnoticed and bobbed and weaved their way through the dozen or so staff members that were running around in a frenzy.

Miko began to imagine herself walking into Jahzay's room and seeing her friend lying on the floor dead. She blinked her eyes hard in an attempt to block out those gruesome images. She felt sorry that she hadn't been back to check on Jahzay like she'd promised to. Glancing down the bustling corridor, her eyes met with Mrs. Merchand's, who was motioning for them to come and join her in the waiting area. Miko started her way with Koran by her side. The two women exchanged a long hug, each supporting the other.

Miko was the first to speak. "How is she?"

"I'll let her tell you herself. She's heavily sedated, but I think she will be happy to see you."

Opening the door, Miko was relieved to see her friend sitting up in bed. She didn't look so well, but at least she was alive. Her room looked like it had been through the second coming of Hurricane Rita, and her face was reddened and puffy. A patrolman was standing guard at her bedside. A short Italian looking detective in a trench coat had just finished getting Jahzay's statement and could be overheard saying, "Don't worry, we're going to find Mr. Roberts and make sure that he doesn't have a chance to do this to you again."

Miko and Mrs. Merchand nodded at the officers as they passed them on their way out of the room. Mrs. Merchand said to her daughter, "You have a visitor, sweetheart."

Jahzay's face lit up. She was so happy to see Miko all she could do was smile. Mrs. Merchand leaned into Miko's ear and said, "I'm going to leave you two girls alone. If you need me, I'll be right outside the door talking to that handsome young man of yours!"

Miko blushed as Mrs. Merchand winked her eye and departed the room.

Miko took Jahzay's cold hands in hers and said, "Now, tell me what the hell happened to you."

Jahzay was obviously a little drowsy due to the painkillers she'd been given, but she still managed to fill Miko in on most of what she could remember. As it went, Smokey had somehow gotten past the security desk and appeared at her bedside. At first, she thought she was dreaming until she felt the sting of his palm across her face. The second blow was from Smokey's fist and caused her to tumble out of the bed and onto the floor. She scrambled to get to her feet, but Smokey was too quick and too strong. He hopped over the bed and pinned her to the floor with a knee to her chest.

Smokey then proceeded to sling her around like a ragdoll. Jahzay ended up with her back against one of the walls, and his large hands around her throat. All the while he was beating her, he cursed at her furiously. Jahzay tried to kick and claw at him in an attempt to somehow free herself from his grip, but to no avail.

She felt herself weakening and blacking out as her eyes rolled into the back of her head. However, her will to live had overcome her lack of oxygen, and she'd summoned up strength she didn't know she possessed. Using her thumbnails to gouge his eyes while biting his wrist gave her a chance to escape, as Smokey's grip around her throat momentarily loosened.

Her first impulse was to lunge towards the call button hooked to her bed. She found the switch and pressed it repeatedly. When Smokey saw the flashing red light and heard the crackling of the intercom, he knew what time it was. He panicked, realizing that Jahzay would escape her fate once again. He screamed out in frustration, "You bitch! You sneaky bitch!"

The door swung open and a nurse's aide came in to check the call button. Smokey ran over the small man like he was back in his glory days as a high school defensive lineman. That was the last Jahzay had seen of him, and she was glad of it. She was still a little scared though, because Smokey still had yet to be caught. The last thing she remembered was waking up with a roomful of nurses staring down at her.

"Did you tell them it was Smokey who attacked you the first time?" Miko asked softly.

Jahzay nodded, then said, "He was going to kill me, Miko. I just know it!"

Jahzay burst into tears as Miko sat on the edge of the metal framed bed and consoled her. They embraced each other for nearly ten minutes until Jahzay was all cried out and yawning. Then there was a weird silence between them as Jahzay stared deeply into Miko's eyes. Miko felt kind of awkward at that moment and was about to say something to lighten the mood when Jahzay said, "I love you, Mi-Mi."

Without warning Jahzay leaned over and kissed Miko softly on the lips. At first, Miko was stunned motionless. She didn't know how to respond to Jahzay's advances, but then she caught herself and jerked her head back. Miko knew that her friend was doped up and a little out of it, but that was just a little too much. Seeing the embarrassed look on Jahzay's face made Miko feel a little sorry for her.

Jahzay was hurt by her friend's reaction but tried to save face. She forced an apology and broke down crying again until she fell asleep in Miko's arms. Miko laid Jahzay down so she could get some much-needed rest, and then quietly crept out of the room.

She entered the small chair-lined waiting area and found Koran and Mrs. Merchand drinking coffee and talking like they were old friends who hadn't seen each other in years. Miko walked over to them and said, "You two seem to be having fun."

Koran and Mrs. Merchand looked at each other mischievously and started laughing, which prompted Miko to ask, "What's so funny? And don't say 'nothing'!"

Mrs. Merchand looked at Koran, then back at Miko and said, "Oh, nothing!" Then all three of them laughed.

Miko offered to stay with Jahzay until Mr. Merchand got off work, but Mrs. Merchand assured her that that wouldn't be necessary. She told Miko that Jahzay would probably be released soon, anyway. In the meantime, the hospital would be beefing up their security and screening all visitors thoroughly.

"Okay, if you insist," Miko stated.

"I do."

"Just tell her that I'll be a phone call away if she needs me for anything."

"I'll make sure I do just that. Now get on outta here. You should know that it's not polite to keep a man waiting. Especially one as fine as this!"

"Bye, Mrs. M. You are so crazy!" Miko said, giving her a hug and kiss on the cheek.

Mrs. Merchand told her good-bye, and said to Koran, "Remember what we talked about, and do like the Nike commercial says!"

"Just do it!" they both said in unison.

Back inside the car Miko, was feeling left out and couldn't wait to ask Koran what he and Mrs. Merchand were being so secretive about. While driving back to their temporary home, she turned down the music and asked, "So, what was all that about?"

"All that what?" Koran replied as if he didn't know what she was asking about.

"Don't play stupid with me, Koran!"

"Oh, now I know what you're talkin' 'bout! It was nuthin', really."

"Then how come I get the feeling that you're lying to me?"

"Me, lie? Never!"

Him not lying was a lie in itself, and the bulge in the pocket of his pants proved it. He wasn't quite ready to reveal the truth to Miko. For the time being, he was going to hold his tongue and keep his secret to himself.

Miko looked at him out of the corner of her eye and said, "Well, don't expect to get none of *this* pussy tonight!"

Chapter Twenty-Two

The day of the shipment had arrived, and Tariq couldn't wait to get it over with. He needed to focus on more important things... things like getting into the panties of the new honey he'd recently met.

After finishing his morning workout, he showered and picked out something to wear. He decided on a pair of baggy Red Monkey jeans and a 4X white tee. The S. Dots on his feet, coupled with the fitted Houston Astros cap over his do-rag, made his cipher complete.

Tariq exited his crib and jumped into his customized silver AMG 55 on chrome twenty inch Giovannis. He burned rubber out of his driveway with his Pirelli's smoking. The top was down, and the sun was shining bright while his sound system bumped Jay-Z's "Kingdom Come" CD. He still had a lot of time to kill before the drop, so he decided to run a few errands.

His first stop was at the nearby liquor store where he bought a six-pack of Coronas for the ride. He also made sure to cop a box of Optimo cigars so he could twist up a couple of blunts. He made a quick call to one of his workers as he headed towards the 'hood to check his traps.

The next few hours were spent picking up money from some of the street hustlers he fronted work to. With all that driving back and forth, along with the two blunts he'd smoked, Tariq was starving.

Looking at the iced-out Avianne Co. watch on his wrist, he figured that he could squeeze in a quick bite to eat before he had to be at the warehouse to meet Koran's supplier. He dialed the phone number of the newest addition to his stable of dime pieces and set up a late lunch date for the two of them that he hoped would lead to a quickie in the parking lot.

Tariq and his new lust interest, Ki-Ki, met up in the parking lot of P.F. Chang's Chinese restaurant on Westheimer Road. He pulled his Benz into an empty parking space next to Ki-Ki's new Porsche Cayenne SUV. He noted that she was pushing a Lexus Sports Coupe when they first met. *This broad's definitely doin' her thang!* he thought to himself as he entered the restaurant.

Tariq hated to admit it, but Ki-Ki had him open. She was fine as hell, had her own money, and the hard-to-get cat and mouse games she played made her a challenge, something he'd never had before. They talked and flirted over drinks and fed each other bites of food. After a lunch that seemed to go by too quickly, they parted with a kiss and went their separate ways.

It was time to take care of the business at hand, and Tariq knew that he wouldn't hear the end of it if something went wrong. He raced up Westheimer until he reached the tollway that took him straight to the warehouse. Fifteen minutes later, he was driving past all of the wholesale outlets lining Harwin Drive on the city's southwest side. Unfortunately, he didn't notice the DEA agents following closely behind him in the gray Ford Taurus.

● ● ● ● ● ●

The day of the drug bust couldn't have come any sooner for Agent Everhart. It was the moment he'd been waiting on for years, and he crossed his fingers in hopes that everything would go according to plan. He knew that the bust had the potential to be one of the biggest of his career. All it took was one member of the Get Money Clique to roll over for a lesser sentence, and their whole organization would crumble in federal court.

In the days leading up to the sting operation he'd dubbed "Operation White Tee", Agent Everhart had secured warrants for phone and wiretaps. He also set up mobile surveillance teams to stake out known G.M.C hangouts and follow their members around. The conspiracy laws would easily net all of Koran's associates, and the "Relevant Conduct" statute would tie in all of the related crimes they'd committed, without the burden of proving them to a jury. In short, Agent Everhart planned to mount a case so strong against Koran and his crew, that even the new Supreme Court rulings wouldn't be able to save them from all getting life sentences.

However, to the dismay of the agent, none of his efforts had yet to produce any more evidence than they already had --which was absolutely nothing! The members of G.M.C were smart enough to know not to talk business on their cell phones, and it seemed as if Koran had fallen completely off the face of the Earth. The C.I. could no longer reach him, and that caused Everhart to worry. All they had managed to gather was evidence that Koran's younger brother, Tariq Yusuf, was some sort of wannabe male gigolo, and that someone close to the organization had recently been murdered.

Agent Everhart was starting to question his C.I.'s credibility, and at one point, he even considered calling off the bust. But, he'd come too far to turn back. The wheels were already in motion, and his superiors were breathing down his neck. His thoughts were interrupted by the chirping of his Nextel two-way. He talked into the speakerphone, "Agent Everhart here."

A voice came booming through the speakers informing him that the target had just turned onto Harwin and was heading in the direction of the warehouse. The anxiety agent Everhart was feeling caused him to break into a sweat and gnaw on his cuticles. He got on his two-way radio and started barking orders at the team of DEA agents he was in charge of. They all got into position and prepared for Koran's arrival. The plan was to wait until Koran and his supplier were together so that the agents could arrest them right in the middle of their transaction.

Agent Everhart was a little disappointed wen he looked through his binoculars and saw that it was actually Tariq arriving, and not Koran. But he reasoned that Tariq would be a more than worthy consolation prize, especially since he was the number two man in the G.M.C chain of command. Plus, he was known to carry firearms everywhere he went, and a handgun found in the commission of a felony was sure to add another five years to his sentence, at least.

Tariq got out of his car, oblivious to the many eyes that were beamed on him. He was pissed off because the delivery truck was thirty minutes late, and he had plans to meet back up with Ki-Ki. He was just about to call Koran and tell him that the driver was a no-show when he scoped out a white truck driving into the warehouse lot.

"'Bout muthafuckin' time!" Tariq fumed, checking his watch for the umpteenth time. He got out of his car and proceeded to unlock and raise the warehouse door manually. He entered into the warehouse and turned on the lights as the truck eased in slowly behind him. The inside of the warehouse was filled with boxes that contained inventory for both of Koran's clothing stores and his online resale/auction businesses.

The driver killed the engine and hopped down from the cab. He was a dirty looking white guy who smelled like a mixture of motor oil and chewing tobacco. With a mouthful of the latter, he extended a hand out towards Tariq, who just frowned at his attempt at friendliness.

"Let's get this shit over with before the pussy I got waitin' on me gets cold!" Tariq told him.

"No problem, sir," the visibly peeved truck driver responded. "I just need you to sign these--"

The word "papers" never left his lips. He and Tariq were blinded by the high beam headlights of an oncoming Ford Taurus. The words "Get on the ground!" could be heard booming through a bullhorn.

Tariq quickly complied with the commands. It wasn't his first time going through something like that, so he already knew the drill. As he began to lay down on the pavement, he saw several agents running towards him wearing bulletproof vests, with their weapons drawn. He smelled a foul odor nearby and noticed a puddle forming beneath the truck driver who was lying next to him.

As funny as that sight was, Tariq was in no mood to laugh. After having a heavy knee placed in his back, he was quickly handcuffed and thrown into the back of a paddy wagon. Looking through the van's windshield, he could see the DEA agents clearly. They were roughing up the frightened truck driver, and pointing a finger in his face threateningly.

Tariq said the *Al-Fatihah* in Arabic to calm his nerves. He wondered what the ordeal could possibly be about. Luckily for him, he'd left his gun at home, which was a rare occurrence. He breathed in deeply and said to himself, "Well, at least I don't have to worry about a pistol case!"

Outside the van, Agent Everhart was still questioning the urine-soaked truck driver. "Look you son-of-a-bitch! I'm going to give you one last chance to save your trailer park trash ass. Now, tell me what you know about this shipment!"

When he didn't get the response he was looking for, Agent Everhart had the driver cuffed and placed under arrest for suspicion.

He walked over to the cargo area of the delivery truck and placed a call on his cell phone. A few minutes later, a FOX 26 news van rolled up on the scene. With an ego as big as his, Agent Everhart couldn't pass up an opportunity to have his face on primetime news, especially for a bust of that size. When the broadcast crew was ready and the cameras were rolling, the agent announced, "Ladies and gentlemen, feast your eyes on this!"

He turned the latch and raised the sliding door of the truck to reveal a mountain of cardboard boxes stacked up in rows. He climbed into the back of the truck and sliced open the top of one of the boxes with his pocket knife. After thoroughly inspecting the box, he concluded that it contained nothing but T-shirts. He smiled nervously as the light from the T.V. camera shined on him.

Agent Everhart continued his search with even more vigor. He *knew* that there were kilos of cocaine hidden inside one of those boxes, and he was determined to find them. Over forty boxes and two hours later, he was drenched in sweat and breathing heavily. T-shirts were strewn all across the cargo area of the truck, but there were no drugs to be found.

Feeling defeated, Agent Everhart sat down on top of one of the empty boxes and covered his face with his hands. Then, without warning, he charged the camera crew, screaming, "Turn that got-damn thing off!"

By that time, all the other agents had already accepted the fact that their major bust was just that --a bust. All they managed to come up with was a misdemeanor bag of weed they'd found in the console of Tariq's Mercedes-Benz.

Heads were definitely going to roll as a result of the mishap, and Agent Everhart would be the first one on the chopping block.

Tariq sat and watched the whole thing unfold. He wondered what in the world the overzealous agents expected to find in the boxes, but he was sure that they weren't just trying to add to their wardrobes. When the agent that appeared to be in charge stormed the camera crew, Tariq couldn't help but laugh in amazement.

All of the sudden, the back door of the van swung open, and Tariq instantly recognized his old nemesis, Agent Matthew Everhart. "Matt, long time no see!" Tariq jeered. "Shouldn't you be somewhere having a staple fight in the office or something?"

Agent Everhart had the look of death in his eyes. His reddened nostrils flared and he charged Tariq like a wild bull. He had a vise grip around Tariq's neck, trying to strangle the life out of him. Agent Everhart's supervisor, who showed up on the scene for damage control, had to pull him off of Tariq and restrain him.

"You'll be hearing from my lawyer, mu'fucka!" Tariq croaked, rubbing a hand across his throat.

"I'm going to get all of you motherfuckers!" the crazed agent screamed. "And that wetback, nigger-loving bitch, Yessenia is going to pay for this!"

Tariq couldn't believe what he'd just heard. He thought his ears were playing tricks on him. Either that, or the agent had just stated that Koran's baby mama had tried to set him up. If so, then Agent Everhart was right about one thing – that bitch was going to pay!

Chapter Twenty-Three

Smokey pressed the gas pedal of his car down to the floor as the hemi engine roared down Highway 59. He was racing towards his sister's house so he could gather up what little money he had left in his stash and say his final goodbyes. After he left there, he planned to head straight for the Mexican border, because he was sure the police would be after him soon. But first he had to stop by the hotel room he was staying in to grab his things.

He pulled into the parking garage and was in and out in a matter of minutes. He threw his camouflage duffel bags into the backseat and peeled off in the direction of his sister's home. During the drive, he fired up a cocaine-laced blunt. As he relaxed into his high, he reflected on the scene he had narrowly escaped only hours earlier...

Smokey was a little surprised at how easy it was to get into the hospital and inside Jahzay's room. It was getting out alive that proved to be the hardest part. He walked up to the ghetto-looking receptionist that was sitting behind the horseshoe-shaped desk and cleared his throat to get her attention. She shot a nasty look his way and continued talking on the phone. Smokey snatched the phone from her hand. She stopped popping her gum long enough to snap, "Can't you read? Visiting hours are over! O-V-E-R!"

A little charm and a crisp Ben Franklin was all it took for him to convince the 'hoodrat that visiting hours could be extended for certain visitors. She quickly gave him Jahzay's room number and turned a blind eye when he walked past her towards the elevators.

Smokey intended to kill Jahzay when he entered the room. He thought she was still bedridden and wouldn't be able to put up much of a fight, but of course, he was wrong. After she hit the call button he panicked and ran out of the room.

As Smokey was making his escape, an elderly looking man in hospital scrubs was coming in. Smokey ran right through the small man and left him lying flat on his back in the middle of the hallway. He continued running until he reached the elevators. He repeatedly pressed the call button as the elevator slowly crawled upward. He impatiently watched the numbers above his head as they lit up one after the other.

The elevator's arrival was signaled with a loud bell sound, and the doors slid open to reveal an armed security guard. He and Smokey stood face-to face for several seconds before the toy cop reached for his nickel-plated .38 Special. Luckily for Smokey, the security guard was out of shape and his reflexes were ridiculously slow. Smokey kneed the overweight white man in the crotch and followed through with a powerful uppercut to the midsection that dropped him to his knees. Smokey reached for the guard's gun, but he refused to give it up so easy. The security guard had a death grip on the gun as Smokey fought to get his hands firmly around the handle and wrestle it away from him.

The elevator door closed and it began to move downward, which cause both men to lose their balance.

When their bodies tumbled to the floor, the gun went off with a loud pop. Neither man moved. Suddenly, the security guard's body shuddered and a fountain of blood poured from his mouth, covering Smokey with blood.

Smokey shoved the guard off of him as he struggled to breathe. He'd had the wind knocked out of him when the security guard's enormous frame landed on top of him. He was thankful that the puddle of blood he was laying in was not his own. He looked over at the dead man's corpse and thought to himself, *Better him than me!*

When the elevator reached the first floor, Smokey stumbled to his feet and ran. He flew past the receptionist and out the front exit of the hospital.

The receptionist dropped the phone and watched in shock as Smokey fled the hospital in his blood soaked shirt and jeans. Her eyes followed the blood trail back the way Smokey had come, and she caught a glimpse of the body of the security guard before the elevator doors slid closed. Picking up the phone she yelled, "Girl, I'll call you back!"

Just then, Smokey's car sped past the front entrance, burning rubber out of the parking lot. She made a mental note of the make, model, and color of the vehicle and quickly dialed 9-1-1.

● ● ● ● ● ●

Smokey turned into his sister's driveway and threw his car in park. He jumped out and ran into the backyard, causing his dogs to bark and growl until they picked up the scent of their master. He was cleaning out his safe with his back to the house when he felt the cold steel of a gun barrel against the back of his neck. Before he could react, a voice said, "You picked the wrong house tonight, muthafucka!"

"It's me, 'Meisha!" Smokey yelled out, recognizing his sister's voice.

Jameisha removed the shotgun barrel from Smokey's neck and said, "Boy, you damn near got yo' ass killed creepin' up in this muthafucka!"

"I thought you'd be sleep this late at night."

"Shit! I was until them damn dogs started barking like they'd lost their fuckin' minds! Hell, if nobody was back here, I was gon' shoot they asses!"

"I just came by to get the rest of my shit so I can hit the highway."

"Hit the highway?" Jameisha repeated. Something about that statement didn't sound right to her. She gave her brother a knowing look and said "What the hell you done got into now, James? Damnit, you just got out on bond!"

"Everything's gon' be a'ight. I just need to lay low for a while until my trial," Smokey lied, handing her a stack of money. He retrieved a German Luger from his safe and said, "Tell my lil' niggas they uncle gon' always love 'em".

Jameisha didn't even respond. She hugged her brother tightly and silently prayed that she would see him again. A single tear fell from her eyes as the realization hit her that she probably wouldn't.

Smokey felt terrible as he drove away from his sister's home. He made a left onto Homestead Road.

As he was speeding away, a fleet of black Suburbans were turning onto his sister's street, heading directly towards her house.

Chapter Twenty-Four

Tariq stormed into his brother's spot with his fists balled up and a scowl on his face.

Koran looked up from his T-Mobile Sidekick and said, "Where da hell you been? I've been calling you for the past hour to see if everything went straight!"

"Where have I been?" Tariq snapped. "I'll tell you where da fuck I've been! For the past few hours, I've been in da back of a fucking police van!"

"A police van? What for?"

"For some bullshit, that's what! Ya boy, Matt Everhart tore da fucking warehouse up like a nigga had some bricks or somethin' in dat muthafucka!"

"Whoa! Wait a minute! What was Everhart doing there?"

"Do you understand da words dat are coming outta my mouth? I was set up, K! Dat bitch tried to get us hit, dawg!"

"I'm tryin' to soak all this in, man. What bitch are you talking about?"

"Pocahontas, man!"

"*Pocahontas?* You trippin', lil' bruh! Why would she... I mean, she didn't even know about the shipment. How can you be so sure it was her?"

"Because Everhart slipped up and said her fuckin' name, that's how! You think I'd make an accusation like that without knowing fa' sho?"

"I just can't believe it, that's all! I don't get it. What did she have to gain by doing something like dat? It was just a shipment of fucking T-shirts!"

"But what if it wasn't? Ya feel me? What if it was a shipment of kilos? Shit, I was lucky I forgot my fuckin' gun at home! We wouldn't even be having this conversation right now!"

"I gotta talk to her to see what she has to say. There has to be another explanation for this."

"*Talk to her?* Have you heard anything that I've been sayin' for the past ten minutes? That bitch is workin' with them people! And you know what our policy is for snitching!"

"This is different! This is the mother of my child we're talking about!"

"*Mother of your child?* Are you fuckin' serious? Look, I'm not even going to go there wit'cha. But rules are rules, and it won't look good if you start bending them now."

Koran knew that his brother was right. He just wasn't willing to admit it... at least not yet. He recalled Pocahontas being at his shop when he was talking to his supplier about the shipment, so she could have easily overheard his conversation and thought he was talking about drugs instead of actual T-shirts.

He planned to confront Pocahontas about what he knew, to see how she would react. He'd been with her long enough to know when she was lying to him. If what his brother was saying turned out to be true, he was going to give her a chance to leave town, but only under one condition. She had to leave Karma in his custody.

"So, what you gon' do, man?" Tariq asked impatiently.

"I'll take care of it. Just give me some time to think. That's all I ask."

Tariq stared at Koran long and hard, shaking his head in disbelief. For the first time that he could remember, he felt betrayed by his brother, and things would never be the same between them. Tariq never thought he'd see the day when Koran put a bitch before his own flesh and blood. If it were anyone else, there wouldn't have been a second thought as to what course of action to take. It was simple. In their world, if you snitched, you paid the consequences with your life. It was those same principles that had enabled them to stay in the game as long as they did without anyone snitching on them. If word got out that they'd gotten soft, there was no telling how it would effect their reputation.

Tariq was really the one running the show after Koran's early "retirement", and he was ready to start calling his own shots, whether his brother liked it or not. He turned on his heels and quickly stormed out of the room. He didn't even bother to say another word. It would have just been a waste of breath. Koran's mind was made up... and so was his.

●●●●●●

Ki-Ki bounced up and down on Tariq's dick while he sat upright in her queen-sized bed. "Ah, ah, ah!" she panted as she found her rhythm.

It was just starting to get good to her when Tariq's dick went soft for the second time that night, frustrating her in the process. He slipped out of her wetness and said, "I ain't feelin' it."

"Damn, baby!" Ki-Ki whined. "What's wrong with you tonight? I'm usually the one who gets tired."

Before Tariq could even respond, Ki-Ki had already positioned her mouth on his limp penis in an attempt to give it CPR. "Slurp, slurp, mmh, slurp!" were the sounds coming from underneath the satin sheets as she bobbed her head up and down on his member.

Tariq was trying to get into the mood and focus, but it just wasn't working for him that night. He had too much on his mind.

When Ki-Ki finally came up for air she said with an attitude, "What? My head game ain't good to you no more or something?"

"Naw, boo, it ain't that," he reassured her. "It's just so much shit going on with me and my brother, I... I don't know."

"I understand, baby. But you know you can always talk to me, right? About anything."

"Yeah, I know. But I think I may just need me a drink."

"Well, I don't have anything but water and tea. Sorry."

"It's cool. I'ma go for a drive and maybe stop by Mr. A's."

"I'll be waiting right here when you get back."

"You better be ready, too, cuz I'ma tear dat ass up!"

Tariq lit up a Black-n-Mild as he pushed his drop top Mercedes-Benz around Loop 610. He made it to the small nightclub in no time, and parked his whip at the front entrance. After paying his admission, he went straight to the bar and ordered a double shot of Seagram's Seven. He downed his glass in one gulp and chased it with an ice cold Budweiser. With his elbows resting on the bar, he observed the large crowd of men and women as they danced and talked the night away.

It was hot and stuffy inside the smoke-filled club. The dance floor was packed with fine women, bouncing their asses to the grooves coming out of the sound system. Tariq was about to order one more drink and bounce until he spotted a group of sexy ladies walk through the front entrance.

The chick in the middle of the group caught his eye immediately, causing the adrenaline to rush throughout his body. He thought the alcohol he'd drank had him tripping, but when she turned in his direction and he got a better look at her, he knew it wasn't the Seagram's. Yes, it was her alright! He was staring directly at Pocahontas.

Pocahontas had been trying her best to stay off the scene since she put the Feds in Koran's life, and for the most part she'd done a good job. But partying and club hopping was what she lived for, and she couldn't stay away for long without dying of boredom. Her friends convinced her to go out for a few drinks since it was ladies night at Mr. A's Nightclub. She was reluctant at first, but when they promised to pay for everything, it was an offer that she just couldn't refuse.

Pocahontas hadn't been answering any of Koran's repeated phone calls and was continuing to dodge him. She couldn't bring herself to face him after what happened. But that wasn't due to guilt, it was because of the fear she felt. Truthfully, she wasn't remorseful about her actions at all. The only thing she regretted was that it didn't go as planned.

When she and her friends were seated, a bottle of champagne was sent to their table by an anonymous admirer. Being the greedy bitches they were, the bottle was emptied in no time. Several more bottles followed, one after the other. After a couple of hours, all three of them were sloppy drunk.

Tariq saw that it was the perfect time to let his presence be known.

One of the chicks that was with Pocahontas got up from the table and staggered towards the restroom area. The other one had her face down on the table and appeared to be asleep. Pocahontas was singing along to an old Keith Sweat song when Tariq pulled up a chair next to her and said, "Well, if it ain't my favorite sister-in-law! What a surprise!"

Pocahontas was so drunk that it took her a minute to realize who it was that was talking to her. When her eyes came into focus, she instinctively jumped backwards. She tried to get up out of her seat, but her legs would not cooperate.

"Where you going, ma? I just sat down," Tariq said. He didn't want to give her any indication that he knew about what she'd done, so he played it cool. "You a'ight? You look a little pale."

"I --I'm just fine. Thank you." Pocahontas slurred.

"Are you sure? I think I should drive you home," Tariq insisted.

"No! I mean...ah...I c-came with my friends," she stammered.

"I know you're not talking about her!" Tariq asked, pointing at the chick snoring beside them. "C'mon, I'm not taking 'no' for an answer!"

Tariq practically pulled Pocahontas out of the club by her arm. When a bouncer started looking at them suspiciously, Tariq said, "This is my cousin. She's had a little too much to drink, so I'ma take her home."

Tariq tossed Pocahontas into the passenger side of his ride and slammed the door shut. Next, he climbed in himself and peeled out of the parking lot. He knew Ki-Ki was expecting him, but she would have to wait. He had more important things to attend to.

●●●●●●

The morning sun crept through the glass of the bedroom window, awakening Koran from his slumber. He reached over to the other side of the bed and was surprised to find that Miko was not there. The alarm clock on the dresser read 7:45 a.m.

He took his morning piss and walked towards the kitchen in nothing but his boxers. *Where da hell is she?* he thought to himself as his anxiety started to kick in. The growling of his stomach sent him to the cabinet in search of something to eat. He grabbed a box of Frosted Flakes cereal and shut the door. He was just about to grab a bowl when he heard two shots being fired in the distance. Koran dropped the box of cereal onto the floor and sprinted back to the bedroom to get his gun. He noticed that his 9mm Sig Sauer was not in the dresser drawer where he'd put it, and he immediately feared the worst. In his mind he saw a picture of Jimmy Chan squeezing the hairpin trigger of his handgun and killing his beloved Miko. Two more shots rang out, snapping him out of his daydream.

Pop! Pop!

Koran ran in the direction the shots were coming from. The sounds seemed to be coming from the backyard. Without breaking his stride, he grabbed a metal fire poker from the fireplace as he passed through the living room. He busted through the open sliding glass door that led out onto the patio. He was ready to take a swing at whoever was out there, but he was stopped dead in his tracks by a single gunshot and the shattering of glass.

"What the hell?" Koran said to himself when he saw Miko standing there with the Sig Sauer in her hands. She'd made a makeshift gun range out of some empty beer bottles she found in the trash.

"I didn't know you had such a good aim!" Koran said to her in amazement.

"And I didn't know you had a pretty little thing like this laying around!" Miko replied, referring to the four pounds of steel she was holding in her hand. "I was looking for a pair of your boxers to put on when I came across it. I hope you don't mind."

"Naw, it's okay. You just scared the shit outta me, that's all. I didn't know what the hell was going on. By the way, where'd you learn how to shoot like that, anyway?"

"My father was in the military. When I was a little girl he used to take me out in back of our house to shoot cans before he..."

Koran could tell that the memory of her father bothered her, so he quickly changed the subject. "You hungry?"

"Sure! What do you have in mind?"

"I'm making my specialty. A big bowl of Frosted Flakes!"

Koran's silliness brought a smile to Miko's face. They went back inside and ate breakfast before taking a steamy shower together.

Koran was drying himself off when his cell phone started ringing. He answered the line and briefly listened to the caller speaking on the other end. *Whoever it was must have been screaming,* Miko thought, because she could hear a female's voice saying something in Spanish.

Koran threw the phone across the room and started cursing and swinging wildly.

Miko became more and more frightened by the second, as Koran screamed and tossed furniture around. It almost felt like déjà vu. A picture of Seven throwing a tantrum after receiving the call about his mother popped into Miko's mind. She got Koran's attention and asked him, "What's wrong, baby?"

Koran had forgotten that she was even there for a minute. He was nearly in a state of shock. All of the sudden, he fell to his knees and began sobbing. "She's gone! She's gone!"

"Who's gone, baby?" Miko demanded to know.

"Karma's mother! They killed her!"

"Who would want to kill your baby's mother?"

"I can only think of one person... Jimmy Chan!"

Chapter Twenty-Five

Goldstein was chewing on a cigar while browsing internet porn sites when the doorbell sounded inside of his home. He got up from his seat and proceeded out of his study and into the foyer. When he looked through the peephole, he couldn't see anything but the front of a Papa John's hat. He rolled his eyes and swung the door open saying, "Say, you schmuck, we didn't order any --"

"Special delivery, muthafucka!" Smokey said as he rushed through the door and shoved the empty pizza box he was carrying into Goldstein's chest, knocking his frightened lawyer back on his heels and causing him to nearly swallow his cigar, whole.

"What the hell is all this?" Goldstein asked in surprise. The hard-on in his tiger-striped Speedo shrank back down to size as fear started to set in. He nervously tied the front of his bathrobe and said, "Damnit, Roberts! You scared the living shit out of me!"

"I need ya help" was all Smokey said as he walked past Goldstein and into his study.

Goldstein followed in behind him. He was unsure about what Smokey was going to ask him to do, but he was sure that he wasn't going to like it. Besides, helping a wanted fugitive was out of the question. He'd seen the news reports and knew all about the serious charges

Smokey was facing. There was no way he was getting involved with that, no matter how much money Smokey offered to pay him.

Goldstein poured up two cups of coffee then said, "What in God's name were you thinking, James? Or were you even thinking at all?"

"I guess not," Smokey replied sullenly, sipping the hot coffee from his mug. "But what's done is done. I need you to fix it."

"*Fix it?* Now you really have lost your mind! If Johnny Cochran was to come back from the dead and walk through that door right now, he wouldn't even be able to 'fix' this shit!"

"Why not? If O.J. Simpson could kill two people and get away with it, why can't I? You said it yourself, 'money talks'!"

"First of all, you don't have O.J. Simpson's money! You're a street-level fucking drug dealer that just happens to have a citywide manhunt out for him."

"There has to be something you can do."

"Hell, I can probably lose my fucking license just by having you here!"

"But you're my fucking lawyer!"

"That's right, and as your lawyer, I have to advise you of the facts. And the fact is, you're screwed! The best I can do for you is try to work out a plea agreement for life without parole. But that's only if you do the right thing and turn yourself in."

"I ain't going back to jail! You have to help me get out of the country. I was thinking either Mexico or Canada."

"You've obviously been watching too many movies. What you're planning to do is not as easy as it sounds. Especially after 9-11."

"Are you saying you're not going to help me, muthafucka!" he snapped, grabbing Goldstein around his neck and lifting him off of his feet. The much smaller man squirmed and gagged under the pressure of Smokey's powerful hands.

"Now, tell me you're going to help me! Say it!" Smokey barked, tightening his grip for emphasis.

Unable to answer, Goldstein tried his best to nod in agreement. At that point, he was willing to do anything Smokey wanted him to in order to save his life.

"You promise, muthafucka!" Smokey asked again.

Goldstein made an indiscernible noise and his eyes rolled back into his head. When Smokey finally released him, he fell straight to the floor with a loud thud. Smokey stood over his attorney's coiled up body and said, "Now this is what I need you do." When Goldstein didn't respond, Smokey said heatedly, "Are you listening to me?"

Silence.

Smokey knew something was wrong. He knelt down and placed a finger on Goldstein's neck to check his pulse. When he didn't feel anything, he turned him over onto his back. Goldstein's face had turned pale and he wasn't breathing.

"Nooo! You can't die on me, muthafucka!" Smokey screamed while using both of his hands to press down on Goldstein's chest like he'd seen on TV. There still was no response from Goldstein. He was so frustrated that he started beating on Goldstein's chest and crying.

The realization that he'd accidentally killed the only person that could help him was too much for Smokey to bear. He got up from his knees and scrambled out of the study, leaving Goldstein's body lying on the floor. He made his way out to his car and fled away from his lawyer's home. But he knew there was nowhere for him to go.

Hiding in the closet of her bedroom, a terrified Mrs. Goldstein breathed a sigh of relief as she heard the front door of her home slam shut. She'd just hung up her cordless telephone after frantically calling 9-1-1 to report what she perceived to be a home invasion. She eased out of the closet and down the staircase that led to her foyer. She became even more frightened when she didn't receive an answer after repeatedly calling out her husband's name. When she reached the door to his study, her screams could be heard all the way at the neighbor's house next door.

Smokey was leaving out of the affluent subdivision where Goldstein's home was located when he saw flashing lights approaching him. Seconds later, four police cars and an ambulance were passing him by at high speeds with their sirens wailing. He had an idea where they were headed. He just didn't think that they would have arrived so quickly. He reasoned that their prompt response was the norm in the white folks' neighborhood. In the ghetto where he was from, bodies were usually already decomposed by the time an ambulance arrived.

Smokey hit the highway and turned his music up as loud as it would go. He hoped the sounds coming from his speakers could drown out the thoughts in his head... thoughts that were filled with Jahzay's screams. He planned to drive nonstop until he reached the border town of Laredo, Texas. From there, he would cross over into

Mexico. He had enough money on him to survive once he got there, but what he didn't have enough of was gas. He exited the highway to fill up his tank at the first gas station he saw.

Driving along the feeder road, Smokey rapped along to T.I.'s "Top Back Remix". In the middle of the song, he just happened to glance in his rearview. What he saw made him do a double take. Two blue and white patrol cars were on his tail, and they were gaining ground on him fast. Smokey pressed his gas pedal down to the floor in an attempt to outrun the officers that were pursuing him. The last thing he planned to do was pull over and give up without a chase.

There was a small chance that he could've gotten away from the two squad cars, but when he saw the bright high beam lights flash through his windshield, he knew it was over. The helicopter hovering above him circled his vehicle. No matter how many corners he hit, he would not be able to shake the "ghetto bird", not unless he ditched his car and fled on foot. So that's exactly what he did.

Smokey threw his duffel bag over his shoulder and grabbed the handle of his Luger. When he reached the next intersection, he made a quick right and slammed down on the brakes. The car skidded to a stop and Smokey bailed out, running between two houses. He jumped a fence and came out on the next street, only to find that he'd run right into a roadblock. There were police cars everywhere.

When the officers noticed him come out from between the houses, they flashed their beams in his face and commanded him to "Freeze!"

But Smokey did the exact opposite. He pointed his gun at the policemen and started shooting as he ran to his right. With nowhere else to go, he ran inside of a 24-hour convenient store a half a block up the road.

●●●●●●

Jahzay couldn't wait to get out of that boring and depressing hospital room. With just one more day to go before she was cleared to go home, she was ready to put what had happened to her behind her and move on with her life. Physically, she felt fine, but it was going to take a little time for her psychological and emotional wounds to heal. Smokey had left her with scars that couldn't be seen with the natural eye, but if you looked deep enough, the constant pain that she felt was evident. More than anything else, losing her baby had taken a huge toll on her, and she didn't know if she would ever truly be able to get over it.

After a forty-five minute yoga session, Jahzay took a hot shower and prepared for bed. She'd taken up yoga after her doctor recommended it to her, and she found that it helped her a lot throughout her recovery process.

Unable to sleep, she turned on the small television set in the corner of her room and surfed through the channels with her remote. There seemed to be live news broadcasts on every local station she turned to. She wondered what could be so important that all the major news shows were covering it. When she stopped on Channel 13's Eyewitness News program, she found out, and the realization left her shocked. A black female reporter was reporting:

"...Thanks, Melanie. This is Sharee Dennis, reporting live from the north Houston area of Bammelwood. Holed up inside of this family-owned all night convenience store is a man authorities believe is the wanted fugitive, James Terrell Roberts. The suspect has two hostages inside of the store with him, and as you can see, the SWAT team has been called out to the scene. James Roberts is wanted on murder charges, along with other crimes, and is believed to be armed and dangerous..."

Jahzay sat there with a stunned look on her face as the reporter continued to explain the facts. A commercial for Calgon then interrupted the broadcast. Jahzay found that ironic, because at that moment she wished there was something that could "take her away!" As much as she wanted to hate Smokey, she just couldn't. And even though he'd tried to kill her --not once, but twice --she still didn't want to see things turn out the way they had for him.

She was in tears by the time the broadcast came back from the short commercial break. The words "Breaking News" flashed across the bottom of the screen, and Jahzay turned the volume up on the television as loud as it would go so she could hear the latest update:

"...And it has just been confirmed by local authorities on the scene that there was only one gunshot fired inside of the store. H.P.D. hostage negotiator, Nick Harper, has indicated that the suspect fatally shot himself in the head after an hour long standoff. I repeat, James Terrell Roberts has just committed suicide..."

The reporter's last words kept repeating over and over in Jahzay's head; *"James Terrell Roberts has just committed suicide... James Terrell Roberts has just committed suicide..."* She'd heard it with her own ears and she still couldn't believe it, probably because she didn't want to believe it. But, whether she wanted to accept it or not, the truth was the truth. Smokey was gone.

Chapter Twenty-Six

Miko and Koran arrived at Pocahontas' upscale Fourth Ward area condo to find that Tariq was already there waiting for them. Koran had called and told him to meet them there.

Koran ran towards his younger brother and hugged him tightly, while Tariq feigned grief for his brother's sake. He didn't expect for Koran to take Pocahontas' death as hard as he had. He felt sorry for him, but he wasn't sorry for his actions. He knew that he did what had to be done, and thanks to some last minute thinking on his part, his involvement in Pocahontas' murder would go undetected forever.

Koran's eyes were puffy and reddened from crying. The investigators still had the crime scene taped off, but they let him through since he was the father of the deceased woman's child. Koran thanked Allah that Karma was with her grandmother, Rosa Lee, and wasn't there to have to witness her mother's death, or even worse, get killed herself.

Koran stepped into the living room and instantly covered his nose from the stench coming from his baby mother's dead body. Nothing looked out of place, and there was no sign of forced entry. When he stepped in the doorway leading into her bedroom, several men in suits were snapping photographs and jotting down notes. He finally got a good look at the woman he'd once planned to marry.

Pocahontas' half-naked body was lying awkwardly in the center of her queen-sized waterbed. The medical examiner on the scene said that she appeared to have been strangled to death. That much was obvious by the wire that was still wrapped tightly around her small neck. But the thing that confused the detectives the most was the playing card that was left lying on her chest. When Koran saw the picture of the red dragon, it immediately confirmed his suspicions.

Miko was talking to Tariq about Koran's unusual outburst back at his home. Tariq was grilling her about the details when Koran walked back out of the condo. He wasn't crying anymore, but Miko noticed that there was something very different about him. He had a look in his eyes that she'd never seen before. When he made it to where they were standing he said, "I want Jimmy Chan, and everything he loves, *dead!*"

●●●●●●

"I got ya money, muthafucka!" Miko barked into Jimmy Chan's ear when he answered his page. "Every last dime of it!"

"You *what?*" Jimmy Chan asked, not believing what he'd heard. "I mean, I didn't expect you to come up with it so soon."

"We had a deal! I've kept my end of the bargain, now it's time for you to keep yours!"

There was complete silence while Jimmy Chan thought over his decision. Miko's payment had come as a total surprise, and was causing him to have to rethink his plans for expansion. Of course, he could have done it without her, but it would have proved to be a lot more difficult. *That's it!* he thought to himself. *If Mrs. Harris thinks she's going to make it out of this alive, she is in for the shock of her life!*

Unbeknownst to Miko, Jimmy Chan planned to take the money, then send one of his hitmen to seal the deal, which meant killing her in cold blood. Yes, it would be a win-win situation for him. He had to smile at the pure genius of his plot. He agreed to meet up with her, and they set up a time and place. He warned her not to bring anyone along with her, or else... not even Koran.

"Baby, I'm scurred! What if this is some kinda trick?" Miko whined to Koran as he went over his plan one more time.

"Here, take this, and remember that everything's going to be just fine," Koran assured her, handing her the Sig Sauer that she loved so much.

Miko tucked the gun in the waistband of her Miss Sixty blue jeans and concealed it with her oversized T-shirt. Then she grabbed the duffel bag that contained the money and climbed behind he wheel of Koran's Dodge Charger. Koran gave her a kiss and watched her drive off, while silently praying for her safety.

Next, he hopped into the passenger seat of his black GMC Suburban, where Tariq and D-Bo were waiting for him. D-Bo started the engine, and the three of them took off in the direction Miko had gone. They were strapped with a small arsenal of automatic weapons, and ready to go to war if they had to.

Jimmy Chan was riding in the backseat of his BMW, smoking on a cigarette while his driver raced through the late night traffic. Following behind him was John Woo and two of his henchmen, one of which had the orders to kill Miko after the exchange was made. John Woo was just ready to get it over with so their organization could focus on more important things. Not that two million dollars was chump change, it was just that he no longer shared the same trivial interests as his leader, which was the main reason he was preparing to stage a hit on Jimmy Chan, and take over the leadership responsibilities of their organization himself.

The two sedans backed in one behind the other along a dark stretch of road on the outskirts of Houston. They killed their lights and waited in silence for Miko to arrive with the money.

Jimmy Chan lit up another cigarette and inhaled deeply. He still planned to pursue his ambition to take over the City of Houston. It would just have to be done using a different means. He reasoned that Miko was expendable. There were probably hundreds of prospective hustlers that could fill Seven's shoes, and he was determined to find one.

A pair of headlights turned onto the long dirt road and started slowly moving in their direction. The driver of Jimmy Chan's car clicked his hazard lights on and off to let her know they were there.

When Miko reached them, she pulled to the side of the dirt road and turned off her headlights. The Charger came to a stop right in front of Jimmy Chan's Bimmer. She checked the chamber of her gun and stepped out of her vehicle with the duffel bag in her hands. She was sweating bullets by the time Jimmy Chan and his driver exited their ride. He walked up to her and said, "So nice to see you again, Mrs. Harris."

"Hopefully this will be the last time I have to see your face!" Miko shot back.

"I trust that the money is all there," he said, reaching out to grab the duffel bag from Miko's hand. Miko gave him the bag, which he then tossed to his driver while ordering him to check it. He looked at Miko and said, "You never can be too sure, now can you?"

Miko noticed the men in the other vehicle making sudden movements and withdrew the pistol from the small of her back. Jimmy Chan's driver was about to reach for his weapon, but Jimmy Chan stopped him. He held his hands up in surrender and told Miko, "Its okay, Mrs. Harris. There's no need for this. You can go now."

Miko kept her gun aimed at his forehead as she backed up to her car. She wanted to just put a bullet in his dome and end it all right there. At least then she wouldn't have to worry about him coming back to try to cause her or her family any harm. She didn't trust him at all, and it showed. She was almost in a rage as she shouted, "If you ever try to hurt anyone I love again, I swear on my mama, I will kill ya ass myself!" She let off a shot in the air, causing both Jimmy Chan and his driver to take cover. Then she quickly jumped in her ride and threw it in reverse. When she reached the corner, she whipped the hemi-powered Dodge around and mashed out of there.

The car John Woo was riding in pulled up next to Jimmy Chan. When the rear window rolled down, John Woo asked him, "What do you want us to do, boss?"

"I want you to catch up with her and make her regret that she ever pulled a gun on me without using it. And after you kill her, make sure you bring me back a little souvenir to remember her by!" Jimmy Chan commanded, referring to their practice of cutting out their victims' organs.

The BMW sped off in pursuit of Miko's fleeing car. Jimmy Chan and his driver got into their car and left for his penthouse. He thumbed through a few stacks of the money Miko had given him with a rare smile on his face.

Then something hit him. He turned on the car's interior light and examined the money closely. "What the…! This is all counterfeit!" he yelled out after noticing that he'd been fooled. The two million dollars was actually just "video" money Koran had borrowed from his director friend, Dr. Teeth.

Jimmy Chan was pouring the fake money out of the bag when the blue and red lights started flashing behind them. His driver said something in Vietnamese, and Jimmy Chan replied, "Shit! I told you earlier to stop driving so fucking fast!" Jimmy Chan tried to put the money back into the bag without being seen by the trailing policeman.

When they came to a stop, the H.P.D. patrolman walked up to the driver's side window and peered into the vehicle suspiciously. He asked the driver for his license and registration, but Jimmy Chan spoke up saying, "He doesn't speak very good English, sir. So you can deal with me if you'd like to."

"Was I talkin' to you, Bruce Lee? But, I tell you what. Since you wanna do my job for me, why don't both of you's two little eggrolls step outta the fuckin' car!" the officer snapped.

They did as they were told and took a seat on the curb. The police officer then proceeded to search the vehicle. He wasn't inside the car 30 seconds before he came out holding the duffel bag. He placed them both under arrest.

"May I ask what we're being detained for, officer?" Jimmy Chan asked out of fear. The thought of going back to prison in Texas scared him. He would have preferred to die before he allowed that to happen.

"Well, son, it looks like you two's into somethin' illegal. I mean, with this fancy car and all o' dis drug money you got here, ole boy!"

"I can account for every last dime of that money, sir. I own a shrimping company, and I am in town on business."

"Sure you are! And I'm fucking Nick Nolte!"

"Huh?"

"Listen. You can explain it to the judge. But for now, I'm taking you two's down to the station."

They were both thrown in the back of the squad car in handcuffs.

Thirty minutes into the ride, a strange feeling overcame Jimmy Chan. Something was bugging him about the officer and the not-so-routine traffic stop. First of all, what was a city cop doing patrolling a suburb outside of Houston? Secondly, why were they traveling in the *opposite* direction of the downtown police station? Jimmy Chan openly voiced his concerns to the policeman. "Excuse me, sir. I'm not from around here, so correct me if I'm wrong, but, isn't the county jail back that way?"

"You know, what? I think you're right, ole boy!"

"Then why are we still going this way?"

Lt. Schwartz turned around with a wicked grin on his face and said, "Because you two son's of bitches got a special judge you's gotta face! And his name is Koran!"

Right then and there, Jimmy Chan realized that he'd been set up, and that he would not make it out alive.

●●●●●●

After exiting the highway, Miko looked into her rearview mirror and spotted a black sedan gaining on her fast. She remained calm and didn't panic as she continued onward towards her destination.

John Woo and his two hitmen were right on Miko's tail and were getting ready to make their move.

Miko hooked a hard left at the corner, then made another quick turn to her right. The sedan did the same and kept on following her, oblivious to what was behind them. All of the sudden, Miko mashed down hard on her brakes and slid to a stop right in front of them. The sedan's tires screeched as the driver hit his emergency brake and turned his steering wheel to avoid colliding into Miko's rear bumper.

They tried to get out of their ride, but before they could exit, the three men who'd been following them jumped out the Suburban and ran up to their car.

All you could hear were screams and the sound of shattering glass as the BMW was riddled with bullets. The fully automatic choppers the three men were carrying let off burst after burst, ripping huge holes into the vehicle. When the gunfire finally stopped, over a hundred shell casings littered the street. Koran and his crew fled the scene quickly. They figured that no one could've survived that kind of attack. But that remained to be seen.

Inside the car it was like a swimming pool of blood. Flesh and bone fragments were all over the interior and windows. But, miraculously, John Woo was still clinging on to his life as he sat slumped over in the backseat. He was losing a lot of blood from the gunshot wounds he'd received. He wasn't sure, but he could have sworn he heard sirens approaching in the distance. That gave him hope. If only he could find the strength to stay conscious until an ambulance got there. His eyes opened and closed as he fought what appeared to be a losing battle against death itself. Unable to hold off the inevitable any longer, he closed his eyes just as the paramedics arrived on the scene. His last thought was that he was going to kill everyone who was involved... if he managed to survive.

EPILOGUE

(The Aftermath)

Jahzay was singing one of her favorite gospel hymns as she descended the steps of First Morning Light Baptist Church. When she returned home from the hospital, the first place she went after visiting her family was church. It was there where she reconnected with God and found out who she really was as a person. Since her affair with Li1' Rome, she'd been celibate and hadn't so much as smoked a cigarette or took a drink of wine.

Jahzay was well off financially, and she wasn't stupid by far. During her short stint as a hustler, she made sure to put some money up into an account that Smokey didn't know about. It was supposed to have been for rainy days, but she couldn't have imagined the storm that would eventually blow into her world. She sold everything that she owned that reminded her of Smokey, including their cars and the home they shared. But even still, she would never be able to forget the trauma that he'd caused her.

She now stayed in a two bedroom townhome with Alize, and she drove a new model Honda Accord. Gone was the club-going Jahzay. The new Jahzay chose to spend quiet evenings alone at home, watching movies with her daughter. She found her a good paying job as a loan officer at a local credit union, and she even starting writing a novel, which she planned to publish with Street Knowledge Publishing.

As far as men were concerned, she no longer was interested in the thugged out baller types, because in her opinion, they weren't worth the trouble. She'd learned that the hard way. It took her having to go through several bad relationships for her to come to her senses. As a result, she'd promised herself that she would use her two fingers faithfully before she allowed another trifling man to take her through the same bullshit.

While sitting at the intersection waiting for the light to change, a candy painted Cadillac EXT pulled up alongside of her car. When the chromed out Caddy came to a stop, the 24-inch Davins sitting underneath it kept spinning. Jahzay was momentarily hypnotized as she looked on in admiration. The driver of the fly ride looked so good, she grabbed her Bible and said a short prayer to control her temptations. He smiled a diamond-grilled smile, and he had "hustler" written all over him.

When the light turned green, they both eased off slowly. The driver of the Caddy was motioning for Jahzay to follow him so he could holler at her, but she kept her eyes on the road and tried to ignore him. *Girl, he is not what you need in your life right now,* she thought to herself. And she was right. She'd come too far to let herself be turned around by some street nigga. What she needed was a good Christian man that could compliment the new Jahzay. But the Mehki Phifer looking stranger wasn't making it easy for her.

He stuck his hand out of his window and pointed towards a small bar and grille. Then he sped up and pulled into the parking lot of the strip center.

Jahzay was wrestling with the decision of whether or not she should pull over. When she reached the entrance to the parking lot, she braked slowly and turned her wheel while thinking, *I guess one drink isn't going to hurt.*

●●●●●●

Agent Everhart sat slouched down in the driver's seat of an unmarked Crown Victoria, with a mouthful of chewing tobacco. The tinted windows on the car concealed him as he watched the activity at a house a half a block up the road. He focused his binoculars on the many luxury automobiles that were pulling into the circular driveway of the lavish two-story home. In his eyes, all of the young Black men getting out of the expensive vehicles were either drug dealers or gangster rappers, and he couldn't stand either one.

He took a swig from his whisky-filled flask and grimaced as the strong liquid burned the insides of his chest. He didn't care about getting caught drinking on the job. In fact, he no longer cared about anything, except for the mission he was on. Alcohol had become his savior since he took the fall behind the "T-Shirt" fiasco. He'd become the laughing stock of the agency and the butt of all the jokes that were told at the office water cooler.

Since then, things had been all downhill. He was forced to read a letter of apology to Tariq on the evening news, and also to serve a lengthy suspension without pay. After returning from his suspension, he was demoted and assigned to permanent desk duty pending his transfer to another region. Of course, he wasn't going to let his superior's orders stop him from finishing what he'd started. Nothing was going to stand in his way.

Agent Everhart was not supposed to be doing any fieldwork at all, let alone an undercover stakeout. But he had a debt to settle. That's what brought him to the party he was watching.

The adrenaline started pumping in his veins when he saw his target answer the front door for an arriving house guest. Agent Everhart raised up in his seat to get a better look at him. He focused in on a smiling Koran and said out loud to himself, "You're gonna slip up, motherfucker! And

●●●●●●

Everyone showed up for the party Koran was throwing in celebration of Miko's graduation. Tai, Alize, Karma, and Elijah Jr. were all upstairs with the rest of the kids, playing inside of the game room. All of the grown-ups were chilling around the backyard swimming pool, drinking and playing dominoes and spades. Koran was manning the barbeque pit, wearing an apron that read, "I paid the costs, but *SHE's* the boss!"

Tariq was the only person that had yet to arrive. He'd called earlier saying that he was on his way, and that he was bringing his new "fiancée". Koran still couldn't believe that his brother had fallen in love. That was a first for the self proclaimed pimp. But his views on relationships weren't the only thing that had changed about Tariq. Koran felt like there was a distance between him and his brother since the ordeal with Jimmy Chan.

When Koran brought it to Tariq's attention, he blamed it on his added responsibilities within the organization. Koran had fallen back to focus more on his family, leaving Tariq as the sole leader of the G.M.C., so he didn't have time to kick it with his brother like he used to. But that was just the half of it.

The other reason for the strain on their relationship had to do with Pocahontas. The guilt Tariq felt for killing her would not allow him to look his brother in the face.

Koran sensed it, too. He couldn't be sure, but something in his gut told him that there was more to Pocahontas' death than he first expected. First of all, he was almost positive that he'd given Tariq one of the two red dragon playing cards that were left at his shops. But when he asked Tariq about the missing one, he denied ever seeing them. Then there was his brother's belief that Pocahontas had tried to set them up. Koran didn't want to say it, but if he ever found out that Tariq had anything to do with the murder of his baby mama, he would have to answer to him.

● ● ● ● ● ●

Miko was upstairs in her bedroom changing clothes after Elijah Jr. spilled grape juice all over her outfit. She slipped into a pair of shorts and a T-shirt and headed back downstairs. On her way out the door, she stopped to glance at her "wall of memories". She called it that because it was covered with hundreds of pictures she'd taken of all the important people and events of her past. Included in the mural was a faded picture of her standing with her mother and father as a little girl. There was a framed portrait of Seven, who she knew would be proud of her for finally graduating from college. A blown-up photo of her and Jahzay brought a smile to her face. She thought they looked like a ghetto Salt & Pepa with their old school hair do's and played-out outfits.

Miko's eyes moved to the left and landed on a group of pictures that were taken at her and Koran's wedding and subsequent honeymoon on the island of Anguilla, two events that she would never forget. It was the wedding of her dreams. All of their family and friends were in attendance as they tied the knot inside of Miko's old church.

Koran proved to be a great husband, and an even greater father figure to her young son. She couldn't wait until they had a child of their own. And they were definitely working on it. She also looked forward to putting her newly acquired degree to good use in the criminal justice field. But in the meantime, she planned to just kick back and enjoy life.

The situation with Jimmy Chan made her appreciate the time she got to spend with her family more than ever. Every night she fell to her knees and thanked God that it was all over, and that nothing bad had happened to the people she loved. Now she could finally move on.

Miko was snapped out of her daze by Koran's voice as he screamed out, "Hey, babeee! Come downstairs, Tariq's here. He wants you to meet your future sister-in-law."

"Okay, I'll be down in a sec, baby!" Miko yelled back to him. She was excited to finally meet the woman who had succeeded in doing the impossible, which was taming a beast like Tariq. Miko didn't know much about her, only that her name was Ki-Ki, and she was supposedly well to do.

Miko closed her bedroom door and started down the stairs. When she reached the living room where the three of them were standing, she stopped dead in her tracks. Koran and Tariq looked in each other's direction when they saw the reactions on both of their girl's faces. The tension in the air was thick as they stared each other down.

Miko never would have figured that the "Ki-Ki" Tariq spoke so highly of was Kierra Washington, King Tut's daughter!

About The Author

Willie Dutch is quickly making a name for himself as one of the rising stars in the world of Urban Books. Since penning the critically acclaimed first installment to the "A Day After Forever" trilogy, his unique writing style has been featured in magazines such as Street Literature Review, Street Elements and he has even started his own blog. The 28-year old Houston native has also written and recorded music professionally.

The multi-talented father of one continues to take his experiences in "The Game" and bring them to life in the pages of his novels. Proving that nothing, not even the Feds, can knock the hustle. He has put it down once again in this, his second novel, "A Day After Forever 2: The Payback".

To Contact write To:

Willie Dutch
c/o Fan Mail
4542 Firnat Street
Houston, TX 77016
        or
williedutchbooks@yahoo.com

Street Knowledge Publishing LLC
P.O. Box 345
Wilmington, DE 19899
TOLL FREE:1.888.401.1114
www.skbookstore.com

Date: _____

Purchaser _____

Mailing Address _____

City_____**State**_____**Zip Code**_____

Qty.	Title of Book		Price Each	Total
	978-0-9822515-6-0	Bloody Money	$15.00	
	978-0-9822515-9-1	Bloody Money 2	$15.00	
	978-0-9799556-4-8	Bloody Money 3	$15.00	
	978-0-9799556-0-0	Tommy Good Story	$15.00	
	978-0-9822515-0-8	Tommy Good Story II	$15.00	
	978-0-9746199-1-0	Me & My Girls	$15.00	
	978-0-9746199-0-3	Cash Ave	$15.00	
	978-0-9822515-1-5	Merry F$$kin' Xmas	$15.00	
	978-0-9799556-1-7	A Day After Forever	$15.00	
	978-0-9822515-3-9	A Day After Forever 2	$15.00	
	978-0-9799556-2-4	Court & the Streets	$15.00	
	978-0-9822515-5-3	Court In The Street 2	$15.00	
	978-0-9746199-6-5	Don't Mix the Bitter with the Sweet	$15.00	
	978-0-9799556-9-3	Playing For Keeps	$15.00	
	978-0-9799556-3-1	Pain Freak	$15.00	
	978-0-9799556-5-5	Dipped Up	$15.00	
	978-0-9799556-6-2	No Love No Pain	$15.00	
	978-0-9746199-4-1	Dopesick	$15.00	
	978-0-9799556-7-9	Lust, Love & Lies	$15.00	
	978-0-9799556-8-6	Money and Murder	$15.00	
	978-0-9746199-7-2	The Queen Of New York	$15.00	
	978-0-9799556-5-5	Dipped Up	$15.00	
	978-0-9746199-8-9	Sin 4 Life	$15.00	
	978-0-9822515-4-6	A Little More Sin	$15.00	
	978-0-9746199-5-8	The Hunger	$15.00	
	978-09746199-3-4	Money Grip	$15.00	
	978-0-9822515-7-7	Young Rich & Dangerous	$15.00	
		Total Books Ordered	Quantity	
			Subtotal	
SHIPPING/HANDLING (Via U.S. Priority Mail) $5.25 for 1st book, $2.00 for each additional book			Shipping Total	
Institutional Check & Money Order (No Personal Check Accepted)		**Total**	$